W9-COG-777

A PLACE
IN MIND

Sydney Lea

STORY LINE PRESS

1997

© 1997 by Sydney Lea
First Paperback Printing

All rights reserved. No part of this book may be reproduced in any
form or by any electronic or mechanical means including information
storage and retrieval systems without permission in writing from the
publisher, except by a reviewer.

Published by Story Line Press, Inc.
Three Oaks Farm, Brownsville, OR 97327

This publication was made possible thanks in part to the generous
support of the Andrew W. Mellon Foundation and our individual
contributors.

Cover illustration and book design by Chiquita Babb

Library of Congress Cataloging-in-Publication Data
Lea, Sydney, 1942—
    A place in mind / Sydney Lea.
        p.   cm.
    ISBN 1-885266-39-1
    1. Outdoor life—Maine—Fiction. 2. Friendship—Maine—
    Fiction.
    1. Title.
    [PS3562.E16P55 1997]   97-921
    813'.54—dc21   CIP

The author would like to acknowledge the generous support of the John Simon Guggenheim Memorial Foundation and of Bernard and Mary Loughlin of the Tyrone Guthrie Centre for the Arts.

For Annie Fitch and Earl Bonness,
and in memory of the MacArthur boys

We spend our years as a tale that is told.

—Psalms

A Place in Mind

Prologue

THERE'S a boy in the river.

The river connects McLean Lake to the ocean, twenty-five miles distant. Down where it enters the sea, it spreads into a great brackish bay. When the tide is high, and the onshore wind stiff, the river flows back on itself. But up here, where the boy stands, bare feet fighting for purchase on one rock, then the next, farther and farther out till at last he can reach the deep cut under the opposite bank with his crude cane fly rod—here the flow seems all one way.

Only a trained student of water's movements could properly speculate on the river's prehistory. No such person will come to McLean for a long time, and the boy himself is too young even to ponder what has washed to the salt since houses first appeared on these shores. The remote and tiny town was incorporated a scant century ago, but—given the child's age—this is ancient history. He knows that, before he was born, his mother's favorite uncle drowned not far from where he now casts. His mother predicted the drowning, though the prediction struck no one as remarkable. On the Fourth of July, Uncle Charles tried to take an open canoe over the eleven-foot drop of Big Falls. His mother's distinction lay in having announced, "Uncle will die this afternoon." Charles was a vanilla drinker and a notorious daredevil; so others probably thought the same without saying so. In the village a kind of stoic reserve has always been a greater value than urgent speech. The boy's mother still tells her story, a little angry that no one has ever wondered at her moment of second sight.

The boy considers none of this. He's thinking about catching the biggest salmon he can.

He is watched by Edward, who owns the store above the pool. His neighbors don't like Edward much, are jealous. By the town's standards, he is prosperous. No better educated than anyone else here, still he managed long ago to get hold of the store, and has been at the heart of the place's slight commerce ever since. He writes insurance policies; he sells the Indian boat seats that the summer people seem to collect; he is caretaker of the property owned by a hideous but moneyed widow from Massachusetts. He'll get that property, they say.

Edward appears, in the cruel parlance of his neighbors, to have "shot blanks." There were no children by either of his two wives, both long buried. The women had not complained at their childlessness, at the rigid conventionalism of their lives—they were comparatively well-off, they knew, and knew also that self-pity (especially female) was a vice that invited instant and frigid local censure.

Edward probably feels sad at having no wife, no heirs, as he studies the bold little boy drifting his fly on McLean Stream. The boy's last name is also McLean, though it rouses no wonder in him, the fact that he and the river and the town and the lake are all called after the same forgotten trapper.

How much, Edward muses, has drifted here, out of McLean Lake, down the stream, into the ocean. Infinite logs that got by the boom, were waterlogged, sank, and over the years slid past eddy and rock. Scores of log drivers who misjudged the floating mass of wood's next moves. Edward himself was once a driver, and once lucky to have come off the water with only the long scar on his cheek. He's been a cunning fisherman as well, so that just now he thinks of the billions of may- and stone-fly nymphs that perished in salt before they had had their ephemeral airborne day. Of those that did hatch, many were rushed at by fish, swooped at by nighthawks, picked—in their delicate transformation from pupa to spinner—off alder leaves by songbirds. The rest, for brief hours, performed their dances of copulation and oviposition and, male and female alike, at length dropped spent to the moving film, from which fish pecked at their numbers again, while precise bats and swallows skimmed them. The host remaining broke up in the rapids and joined the far ocean, their minuscule parts now parts of its waters.

Many artificial flies went that way, too, working from wounds in old salmons' mouths, from stones and sunken timbers that fishermen had sworn at. Edward can imagine them all going down together, the visionary parade of tinsel, light steel, and feather turning Big Falls to a shower of astonishing color.

He comes back, wondering how a man's mind flouts chronology, even though body and soul seem ever to fare forward. Ducks have flopped over Big Falls as well: tiny goldeneye chicks or merganser, weakened by the snap of a turtle's jaw on foot or leg, or by trying to follow their mothers across a wet June's spate. And the mothers themselves: old hens enfeebled by a lifetime's effort. Beaver kits and beavers; small and grown mink; water snakes; minnows; newts. Even land animals, like the aged hare, stiffened with fever, who seeks to drink at the river's edge: the flow proves too much, and in he tumbles, too tired to thrash. Coon. Deer. Fox. Dog. Down.

There is a certain look on the old man's face as he stares at the child. Edward suddenly feels he has suffered, wishes that somebody knew. His only close friends are a few summer "sports," and the friendships flower in the short warm months alone.

The boy is up to his armpits now, below the bridge. The high chimney of the defunct Tannery, all that remains since fire took the place before he was born, makes a shadow, long and slender but wide enough to cover him in darkness. Someone enters the store; Edward turns to attend him. He will not come back to the window. If the boy loses his footing, then, he will wash away unseen. A small number of the village's population will come to the small funeral. There will be rites of mourning, neighborly gestures. Coarse loaves of bread will be left, steaming, on the McLeans' doorstep. More intimate women friends will bring cooked meals into the kitchen every few days, and male friends wait to catch the boy's father in his work shed to share "a little tap" there. Having sipped in near silence, at length the father and his benefactor, in a way uncanny to a stranger, will stand simultaneously, one stepping out onto the road, the other onto the worn path up to the house.

Should the boy wash down, he'll be forgotten within a generation. Among his young peers he is remarkable for physical strength and agility, for elegance and daring, for his comic flair; yet even in the context of so small a town's short history, he is tiny.

But the river won't bear him away. He knows as much, and the knowledge gives him an even headier self-assurance than usual. It has led him out to his stand in the current.

His parents, seeing him there, would be more angry than frightened. This would be silly, he thinks: he knows he is safe.

How?

If there's a remarkable thing about him, it's that he believes in familiar spirits—or perhaps a familiar spirit. He doesn't really consider whether there are many or one. He likely assumes that everyone has such spirits, that such ghosts account for people's changeable moods. Doesn't everyone know, on rising, that a given day will be good, bad, or indifferent? Not the specifics, of course. The boy himself couldn't have said, for example, what kind of misfortune had been in store for him a month back. An older person like Edward might have felt a little shiver, surmising an omen of his own death. The child understood merely that something bad was to happen. As it turned out, he trod on a small nail in his father's shop. The worst pain he had ever felt till then, it has now almost dropped from recall.

In the river today he anticipates a happy event. Which must come soon: time is short. The shadow of the Tannery chimney has sunk into the larger obscurity of evening. In two or three hours he will be asleep.

The big salmon rises easily and sucks in the homemade Lady Ghost. The boy is sure that it is big not because he sees it—in the twilight he catches only the faint gleam of the cocked tail—but because it does not, in the manner of the small grilse, dash off in uncalculating panic. It balks in one spot, rather, rolling its head slowly, almost curiously, against the barely noticeable stab of pain. The fisherman will not realize till later that this is one of the rough-scaled, fresh arrivals from the ocean.

After half a minute the fish makes a languid, six-foot run upstream. The boy is poised and alert, like a sprinter waiting on the gun, for his line is but twenty feet long. There is no reel, and the staple at the end of the alder cane is touchy. He will have to move with the prey.

They feel each other out. After five minutes the salmon has made perhaps as many halfhearted runs, a few against and a few with the current, and perhaps she has sensed a weakness in the angler at the end of the last one. She lunges now—half out of the water—and lunges again—completely out this time—in an oceanward direction. Good Lord, she is big*!*

Time to follow.

The riverbed's contours are unfamiliar out here in the deep water; the boy must trust to fate. And indeed each stride seems magically to land on a supporting rock until he reaches the brink of the Black Pool, a hundred yards downstream from where the salmon first took. The stream stills here, its bottom invisible. The little fisherman, so subtly that the fish will scarcely be conscious of the effort, must coax her back. At that premature point— there is no choice—he will try to slip his tough, short fingers behind the gill plates and lift her clear. If the salmon bolts from her sulk down into the rapids, the game will be over.

The boy is dimly aware of a motor on the Tannery Bridge behind him. He does not turn. He does not see the young gentleman step down from the Model T, shutting his door with a tin click.

The alder pole bends, the line moderately tense, and the salmon, lapsed into further bemusement, moves uncertainly upstream.

She lies, long as the fisherman's leg, side-to at the upper lip of the pool. But in this light it is hard for the boy to perceive the thin breaks in the fish's forward flanks that are the gill slits. Still, he is confident, rod hand fully raised, free hand poised in the water. An inch. Two. Three . . . Now.

His fingers too far astern, he alarms the salmon. She roars downstream, wrenching the staple from the pole. In her furious final jump he sees his gut leader trailing from the fish's mouth, a long twinkle in the sudden moon.

Over the yammer of the stream the boy hears the isolated sound of hand-clapping, a sound that might strike an older person as pitiable. But as he turns and finds its source, he is merely further confounded, and a little irritated. Is the stranger applauding the prize's escape?

No. He applauds the boy's effort—as he says in his peculiarly stiff congratulation—"against all odds to kill your salmon, and with such crude equipment."

The two now walk in silence back to the bridge. A pair of cased Leonard rods lie flat on the Ford's passenger seat. The stranger moves them. The boy is moderately eager to take the ride he offers: he's been in a motorcar only twice before, and never in one so new and well cared for. Maybe this, he thinks with some disappointment, is the auspicious event he has been set up for.

The ride is brief. The driver comes from Boston, is staying at a guesthouse in Pinkham, ten miles east, is a recent graduate of a famous Massachusetts university which the boy has never heard of.

He is a generous or a very rich man, or both. In the Model T, idling before the McLeans' house, he hands his passenger one of the two bamboo rods. He gives him also a Hardy reel in its lambskin wallet.

"These will help," he says, and smiles. The boy thanks him as profusely as he can, consistent with formality—the stranger is so much older than he.

In twenty minutes the youngest McLean will be in bed, where he'll lie for another twenty, wondering what his spirit will whisper tomorrow.

This morning it had been luck.

Part One

1

"HULLO, Doc. Welcome home."

Was it a smile that lifted the scar on his ancient, ageless cheek? Edward had called me Doc from the very start, four decades back, and now I treasured the greeting, though it had once annoyed me. People would overhear the old man and take me for an M.D. Wealthy hypochondriacs, mostly, those prospective "patients," uneasy in the remoteness of the place, its evergreen-dense woods, its shifty lakes. Summer folks.

That was early, when I first came to haunt McLean. Youthful, restive, and alone—or more accurate, lonely—I haunted Edward's as well, hub of the village, such as it was. Even now, despite having used up my biblical span, I didn't "fall" into conversation with someone like Edward; talk was still hard to come by with him, took time to develop, was always terse. I can't recall why, all those years ago, I told him (or did he learn elsewhere, and if so where?) that I'd just taken a doctor's degree. "Doc," then. That's history, as they say, even if I couldn't judge even now whether his name for me implied laziness, aggression, humor, or all three. But it suggested friendship, too, I know.

I hope.

History, whose details, for all their awkwardness, point upward, or so I also hope: up, to an encoded meaning, mysterious. One summer, for example, I took a dawn walk by the stream below my camp. What was it, one of the Second World War years? They run together: it might as easily have been earlier, just after the first war. At the river's sharpest bend, where the trail flares away from the bank around an old logging yard, I came on the severed foreleg of a small deer, and right beside it, a dead grouse with its wings flattened as if to blend with the woods' floor. For as long as I've known this country, there have always been plenty of poachers to kill the slow summer deer, but how had the bird gotten there? I stood a long time pondering this, and something else I couldn't name. Where was the rest of the poacher's cast-off, the other foreleg, the hind hocks, the acrid paunch pile, the pool of blood from the rent neck?

Mystery that I observe—and make, like anyone. There are certain things, it seems from birth, that stick in the mind as signs from the heart of truth, and you attach them to what you call the self.

The self I've invented has always lived here, at McLean.

My testimony steps no further back from that place and that identity than it must: not that my childhood is a blur, though I blur it; not that my youth has vanished from mind, but I'd forget it if I could. Not, finally, that I love the self I bear witness to here, the one that has strung itself from early manhood to now. But I'd love to love it, because I love its *idea.*

The Latin on my sheepskin granted me the "rights and immunities" of a Ph.D. in modern literatures: the right, as far as I can see, precisely to call myself "Doc," the immunities a puzzle—not much to show for all that schooling. I can speak all the Romance languages but Portuguese, stiffly and formally; I have a reverence, still, for good writing. And I had a one-year stint, which my mentors considered undignified, right after my graduate training in the early twenties, as instructor in French at a southern women's college, whose classrooms smelled of expensive perfumes, saddle soap, tack leather. Can there be such places on earth anymore?

All high-toned, if not as elegant as you might imagine.

But my real story is of friendship, and a place. Welcome home. Did Edward know how these words touched me? Of course I didn't inquire.

"Tried the fish?" I asked, instead.

"Long enough to catch a cold, that's all. Can't stand up to the current like I used to."

"Know what you mean."

"Don't know a thing," Edward sneered. "Pup like you."

"Wish I felt like a pup."

"Wish I was your age."

"How about a half dozen eggs and a slab of bacon?"

"Coming up." Edward walked ramrod-straight to his icebox and paused beside it. "How long you here for?"

"As much of the summer as I can," I answered. What the hell? I went through the annual fiction, the hint that I might have business to call me elsewhere, downcountry. A fellow ought to work, and I knew it. Or I knew that McLean people knew it.

The storekeeper handed me a bag. "Good to have you," he said, absently, looking through the rear window down onto the Tannery Pool. "Tight lines," he added, over his shoulder.

Louis was standing in my campyard as I bumped in over the ruts. He'd had an eye out as always, must have seen me cross-stream at the store. As always, too, he'd made a point of being on hand before I pulled in. He had his own boy with him. The two didn't move for a minute, and I sat at the wheel, studying them against Big Falls and the woods: Louis, compact, jug-eared, barrel-chested, his son a blade beside him. Each wore a wool plaid shirt. The colors seemed weak against the lichen scrawls of Mink Rock behind them. Little rainbows of light threaded the spume of white water at the rock's near edge; the other edge faded into the deeper-than-green softwood of the west shore. The men looked small.

Louis got to me first. "Time for some new wheels, Brant." I shook his wide hand. Reunions got started indirectly here, even with him.

I ran my eye over the Buick, slowly. "She *is* a little road-weary," I admitted. The cooling engine ticked above the shoosh of the river. I looked aside. "Charles."

"Sir. Good to have you, sir."

"A little growth since I saw him, Louis."

"No smarter than ever, though." His father grinned, and the boy fluttered his hand in dismissal, blushing. He was in fact rocketing into manhood: a shock of blond hair, arms like a boxer's, six feet tall. Seventeen. This would be his last McLean summer; he had plans. Charles contemplated the moving water now, smiling.

Louis inspected him for a moment, a kind of perplexed expression on his face, before he addressed me again: "I'm soaking the leathers in the pump, Brant. You'll have to lug your water till they swell up."

"Guess I still have life enough for that," I answered, turning at last to my cabin. "The place looks good." Louis turned with me, raising his hand against the sun. His arm looked like cable. I noticed the bowed finger of his left hand, from when he'd caught for the Forestry ball team. His right arm hung at his side, bowed, too, from when he'd pitched—a drop-ball artist.

"I put the creosote to the timbers and sills," he said.

"So you did."

To look at my camp from the river side was to see a child's illustration: *House*. The wall was almost perfectly square—dead center, a plain fir door. The roof of green asphalt shingle was a square half reclining—dead center, a brick chimney. There was a single flat rock, my "foundation," under each corner post. I loved the place, right down to those rocks.

"Charles." Louis spoke over his shoulder. "The bags." The boy went into camp with my duffels.

"Yes, it looks in good shape, Louis."

"Good place to breed a woman," he replied.

"Any handy?"

"None I'd recommend."

How many years had our prologue included this meaningless exchange? Still, we laughed new laughter. Then we stepped into the cabin, where Charles was staring upriver through an insect-studded window. "That wants to be cleaned," the boy said. He was one for practicality. Often I wished for more than that from him, but I never got it. "It wants cleaning," he repeated.

"It can wait," said Louis and I, small chorus. We laughed again.

Camphor balls, dry cedar, musty bedding, mouse urine, raw soap. I could have named the smells from Boston, but it would have been names, not the same as being there. The shock of reacquaintance was pleasant, but undercut by something a little melancholy. Like all real pleasures, maybe.

"We'll go along and get our supper, Brant." Louis knew to leave me with all this for a spell. He gently shoved his son ahead of him, out. Charles never turned, but kept walking, across the yard and up the lane out of sight. Always the gone one.

"I'll see you a little later?" I asked his father.

"Right you are. You fishing?"

"No, I'll show them some mercy tonight. Come anytime."

He stood on the threshold for a moment, holding open the screen door. The blackflies broke through and rushed to the window.

"For Christ's sake, shut the door!" I snapped. He hopped out and slammed it hard. I could hear his chuckle through the mesh, and I chuckled back.

I pulled the closet curtain and emptied my duffels. Everything in its place. I circled in my tracks: plank bed; fly-tying desk built into one wall; photographs curling around their tacks; pegs for shotgun and rod; a line dryer. Then I wandered into the kitchen and groped up the ladder to the attic, bending under the roof stringers, my back twinging some. I threw my luggage into the wading pool that I'd gotten for Charles when he was a kid. He'd never taken to it, so Louis and I used the thing to store ducks or grouse at the end of a long day, when we were too tired to dress them. It kept the mice off—sometimes I could hear them up there, scrabbling at the plastic sides for a clawhold and squeaking frustration—but it looked crazy, the wry-necked gamebirds against the baby blue of the tub and its outsized yellow flowers. Crazy but right.

I climbed back down, went to the closet again, and pulled on the battered tweed jacket I'd kept at McLean since I bought the camp. Black Friday, 1929. Seven hundred dollars. I felt of the soft slickened wool. A lot of water over the dam.

I frazzled a can of beans and ate it from the pan, standing before the propane stove I'd installed the August before, tired of being driven out by the heat whenever I so much as made a pot of tea on the old wood-burning Atlantic, which, all nickel filigree and finial, squatted in a far corner against the prospect of cool nights, against my possible return for hunting. Of course I knew I wasn't man enough anymore to bust the thick brush for birds or tramp the ridges for whitetails, but the stove was still there, as if to suppress such realities. And in any case I loved it, with something like an active human affection, this relic that for so long had combined function and artistic exuberance. I always thought it looked a little like Prague.

Stiff from my drive, I ambled across the campyard to the ledge, my spot just upriver from the first pitch of the falls. A hot night, close; not much life on the stream—only small brown trout flipping at the lip. "Sandwich-sizers," Louis called them. I smiled. One larger fish rose once; I watched his dimple spread, float, break up in the rapids. He was too far out to reach unless you launched a canoe, and I've never been much for fishing from a boat. I stood for ten more minutes, and he didn't rise again. No, I wouldn't try them tonight.

This self of mine. Near McLean at least, it was at its most active and real in the first and last minutes of available light. Now, as the sun dropped behind the Tannery chimney upriver, an osprey cruised to roost the other way. Once the big birds were common, like the salmon petered out to none now. I missed the hawks in their dozens, but I regretted more that when they were here I had scarcely paid attention. They were so many, the half-light encounters in that pool by that cabin! Most people had never known the sport I'd seen in this water and elsewhere. And when the salmon quit, the brown trout took hold. Fish and Game might have stocked those stupid hatchery rainbows that the meat fishermen yank before they reach eight inches. I was a lucky man. And *sport* doesn't say what I mean, really. My breath slowed, going deep, as it had so often and would again on the rock slab I'll always call mine.

Clear water and a smart breed of trout. It made the fishing desperate hard, as Louis said, and he was right: it took finer tactics to bring a trophy brown to net than it had to kill a salmon. You could throw the worst cast of your life and it might be just what the salmon had been waiting for. The browns posed a challenge that kept the hackers off the river, drove them to the lake above, where they could use live bait and hardware.

I hadn't been on the lake in five years.

I lit a little outdoor fire just to do it, and to keep off the mosquitoes; they got vicious as the afternoon died. Sitting downwind and letting the birch smoke wash over me, holding my breath and clamping my lids when it came too thick, I sipped at an inch of whiskey, easy as I'd been in a long time, even if there was something in that smoke and that liquor that called up a few too many ghosts at once—friendly, but ghosts all the same. Not that they'd left me entirely alone for the nine months away from this little yard; from the rock-and-mortar fireplace under the bent Baldwin apple; from the great white pine that leaned over one end of the cabin; from the lollipop spruce whose underbranches I'd trimmed so as to string a clothesline from the trunk to a corner of my camp. Forty feet tall now, and the clothesline never strung: a forty-foot lollipop. . . . They had not abandoned me in Boston, the ghosts; but like the camp smells, I *felt* them here, for here I was. As the half-logs broke down to coals, the air shimmered above them. It was 1961. Louis was a man of fifty, old enough to be a grandfather, and I—at seventy—the grandfather's father.

His real father had considered me a bad influence, filling Louis's head with what he called foolishness. When the old man died, though, his son came to work for me full-time. Louis's mother had long since died, so when Louis agreed to be my caretaker in '33, he and I raised a lot of unhampered hell for a while. Not that his parents had actively inhibited him; in fact, they had never paid him a great deal of attention. But gone, they left Louis and me without so much as the pretense of an obligation, except, as we thought, to ourselves. To deer and bird. To trout. And in the old days, to salmon.

Even, once, the salmon of Scotland. The fishing wasn't any better there than it had been at McLean that summer, but the trip was a riotous success. I pictured Louis now as I sat before the low fire. Was it the McLean blood? Never before had he so much as left his native county, but now in mind he seemed perfectly at home in that foreign water, blazes of furze and heather behind him.

I poured myself another inch. He'd be down soon.

I THOUGHT back to the morning after our arrival in Scotland. The mist had been slow to lift off the river. When it did we looked across at an Empire Tory type setting up, or, rather, being set up *for*, by a whole troupe of gillies. He sat rigid on a walking-stick seat while the locals bustled up and down the beach, hoisting stones that might get in his path, unpacking hampers of cheese and smoked meats, even chipping ice into a bucket. His brush of mustache twitched now and then as he glanced at us. It was a cold, dank morning, the sun pale as a wafer. Louis was dressed in his plaid mackinaw, gigantic rubber waders covered with inner-tube patches, and his beloved crusher hat. And I, on some whim, was growing a beard, which was now about halfway, and, for all that I was yet in my forties, more white than blond. The Lord was Harumph all over, but when Louis cranked his rod arm into motion, and when one of his final casts landed almost at the gentleman's feet, the old boy retreated for breakfast kippers till we moved downstream out of his way.

Louis was a man to get up with the birds, and was on our beat the next dawn. I lingered at the inn with my porridge and coffee, that odd reluctance in my bones to face strange water. When I finally roused myself and walked down to the river, I was stopped in my tracks: there was Louis's gillie, behind a hedge, apparently choking.

"What is it, Jock?" I shouted, hurrying over. *Doc*, I thought— useless! But what it was, was laughter, and not the kind you'd associate with a dour Scot. He labored at politeness: "Please, sir," he stammered, "ask Mr. McLean." As I made for our beat, he called after me, though the tone was ambiguous, "His Lordship's a man of some power hereabout." Warning, gloating?

On his knees at the rocky shore, Louis was steadying a handsome fish in the current before releasing him. Just across, the Englishman stood, his face redder than Louis's hat. I got the story from my friend himself—a stage whisper, you'd call it, and that took some doing, the rush of the broad river loud as it was. The gentleman had seen Louis kill one grilse, land and let go two, and now three, full-grown salmon, all in the ninety minutes I'd spent dawdling at the inn. The Lord had probably thought to beat the offensive Americans to the water, and Louis's success must have been a double frustration, since he had not had so much as a touch himself. At last he had called across the water to Louis, "Where's John the Baptist this morning?" It was the beard I was starting, but who can say whether the man meant to insult or to break into familiarity? As if he'd studied the cue, though, Louis called back, "Off performing a miracle, I presume. Maybe he'll perform one for you." It wasn't the kind of thing you did, of course, but there, by God, Louis *had* done it.

The incident made Louis the hit of the local pub regulars, and he sang and danced with them as if he were a born Scot. I was welcome, I suppose, by association. I can hear the pipes at top volume when I think about it, can recall the low fiddles at their strathspeys and heartbreaking slow airs. The kind of melancholic music that the defeated cultures always save in those deep registers: the dampness of sea wind, protests from the spirits of cleared trees, sighs of the rebellious, powerless observers on their native ground. I can smell rough tobacco and malt whiskey. I can laugh out loud as Louis, mock solemn on a tabletop, recites a Burns poem that one of his new companions has taught him: "Nine Inch Will Please a Lady." I bet he could recite it even today.

We always meant to go back together, but I never returned to a Scottish river, and surely won't now.

No, the hell-raising was more and more confined to our north woods. Louis turned thirty-two and married, and our circuit shrank. We ventured ever less away from the immediate lakes and the McLean itself. I spent most of summer and autumn in camp, but I rarely saw Louis's wife, June; like her dead father-in-law, she saw in me some anarchic influence, avoided me, disapproved of me. That much was clear right off, at their wedding reception, from a look June gave me. It burns, that one, though no more than others she'd give me later. I'd see it again in the following year.

I had driven over to Waltham, Massachusetts, where Charles was to be christened, and where Louis was for the moment working in a machine shop that produced war matériel. I'll confess we got drunk. I had been every bit the sober godfather at the ceremony itself, for it meant something to me, meant that I was Louis's friend, that he'd evidently stood up to June to make the arrangement. But I'd been nervous, if that's an excuse, as the pastor sprinkled the water on the calm and unprotesting child, so delicate in my arms—nervous enough that I really unwound when church let out.

A gang of McLean Lake people had made their way to the event. They made two categories—June's special guests, and the loggers and sawyers who'd come, God knows how, for the party, the same ones who'd been at the wedding up north when I was best man: Walter with his guitar, Lem with banjo, Roger on fiddle, and the rest of the boys to croak lyrics and scuff up the floor with their clogging.

Louis and I, arms thrown over each other's shoulders, sang "The Shores of Gaspereau," a ridiculous sentimental ballad whose verses we laughed our way through (the timbermen joining for the chorus). I remember looking at my friend beside me, his voice all but gone now, tendons standing out from his neck. Then I looked away and caught his wife's eye, or hers caught mine—a stare that said, among many other things, that our forays were over now.

Louis and his family came back to McLean after Armistice, but he and I couldn't just take it in mind, say, to try the squaretails up on the Mauve water—couldn't just roll a tent and some bedding and call Dicky Mayhall down in Frenchtown to fly us into Radway Pond or wherever.

Sitting by my river these many years after, the fire dropped to a few brave embers, my glass emptied, I remembered what it felt like to land there, to coast on the pond: we'd step out on the pontoons, to which our canoe was lashed with hemp, and paddle the plane toward a beach. "That's sixty bucks when I come back," Dick said, each trip. "Twenty apiece for you guys and twenty for your booze." Then we'd swing the plane's tail, giving it a good shove so Dicky would float out past the rocks. He'd turn and wave as he cleared them, cracking the cockpit window and grinning. "Don't worry, boys," he'd shout, "your credit's good!" Then he'd hit the throttle hard, all but skimming the granite dunes at lake's head.

"What in hell would we do if he crashed that thing?" I'd ask Louis, every time.

"Live on trout till the snow flies, then hibernate till spring."

"Doesn't *sound* bad," I'd conclude. We knew the parts. We'd made a lot of tracks together. The dialogue was mechanical, the laughter never.

Of course Dick would be back at week's end. I pictured him now, scudding through the riffle on Radway, the low sun dancing off his fuselage. I could see him now, yes, even with my eyes open, gazing through the orange-and-gray haze above my campfire. Louis and I would save a drink for him and for us: the Plane Cup, we called it. Then we'd lift for home, woodsmoke on our collars and red-fleshed brookies in canvas creels on the floor. There's something about a native squaretail: he's not hard to fool, not a spectacular fighter. He just gives you that outback feeling—green-growth, clear water, tin pans, the fire. We could sit dry under the heavy spruce in a storm, smelling the woods. We could grunt at a moose through a bark horn on a late-summer evening, just to see if he was starting to get rammy. Or if it was the spring end of summer, we could paddle up on a hen duck and her brood, could laugh, but somehow, too, be tempted to cry, watching her decoy act or, that failing, her pathetic and valiant defense of the duck-lings. And all summer long, I could swear, if the wind picked up from the right quarter, you could *smell* fish in the air. Then, in the plane, we'd look down on where it all was and get the lay of it from up there, though it always seems wrong. It flattens out into a map, all the felt things out of reach except in mind and memory. There's a wrench in that or any departure from a place well loved: no matter how close you stick by it, you're always going away.

LOUIS sneaked up on me as usual: "Brant."

"Louis." There was a lull; we listened to the place together. "I was just flying out of Radway with you and Dick," I whispered at last.

"Finest kind. Any trout up there?"

"Scared to go find out."

"Like the fella says, leave it alone."

"Good times, though," I said. We smiled, sighed.

Louis went in, brought out a new jug and the cup we called Old Bluey, a tin thing whose violet enamel had long since worn off. "This still hold water?" He grinned.

"Never been tried that I know of," I said. Louis poured himself a slug and reached me the bottle. I splashed in another inch.

"Kind of young, ain't it, Brant?" He pointed at my drink.

"Because my liver isn't," I replied.

"Tight lines," he breathed, raising Old Bluey.

"Tight lines," I echoed. We drank.

I sat quietly as Louis picked up a strip of bark and a pair of birch splits. He tossed them into the flicker of coals with the peculiar, jerky underhand motion I'd noticed over the years. I was happy to see it again. The south wind had died, and the wet was going out of the air. The stars sharpened overhead as the evening cooled; when the bark caught, the smoke rose straight. Then Louis waved his hat over the fireplace till we heard a little *pop!* and the skinny splits caught too. We moved our chairs up close, and again I broke silence.

"What's the boy doing this summer?"

"Hired man at Wesley's. Mowing lawns mostly, but guiding the bass crankers some." Wesley's was the town sporting lodge, a pretty nice old camp, of a type—big salmon and brook trout hung on log walls, local girls, pretty and plump, waiting on tables. It was for the powerboat crowd now. I let out a small huff and Louis read me: "Got to work *some*where."

"Right enough," I said.

I T seems sad to me now that Charles was allowed, or obliged, to be so independent all through his boyhood. June was an unenthusiastic mother. In fact, she was an unenthusiastic person, period, though who am I to judge her? I know so little of women: just enough to keep me from speaking with the brash confidence of absolute ignorance.

And this particular woman did all she could to keep me ignorant. What I learned of her doings as wife and parent came at second hand through Louis, and occasionally their son, and neither ever offered me more than one detail or another. I discovered, for instance, that Louis had always been ordered to clean fish and game out of her sight. It seemed not so much that bloodshed sickened her. Entrails, scales, feathers, fur—these were at the root of life, and life itself dismayed her, at least in its bodihood, its biology, all the clutter and tangle it occasioned: the diapers, the dishes, the relentless droppings and leavings. Or so, however cruelly, I have guessed. In Louis's own terse terms, "June didn't like a mess." Her one desire was to stay in a fancy hotel, waited on by strangers, sealed from the distressing snarl of dailiness.

June had little time, then, for her only child. Her husband was cook, housekeeper, and cleaner, however careless, and nursemaid as well. Yet there was the brute fact of a living to be made, and Louis had to be about that too. Having no choice, Charles grew up self-reliant, reserved, and reticent. Hard to know.

Now and then I censure myself for so rarely including the boy in our rambles. Charles never saw the Mauve water, for example; indeed, Louis and I seldom waded the McLean with him. He became a more than respectable flycaster, but mostly on his own.

For years we judged him too young; and then, as if overnight, he was a young man, with his own concerns and duties, and we ourselves were older, more cautious.

After the second war, when Charles was three, I made a gesture of some kind, obscurely motivated, though on the face of it a token of goodwill or peace toward June. I sent her and Louis by train to the old Barlow House in Trafton. I expected gratitude, no doubt about it: if only for a weekend, June would have her sojourn in a hotel. It wasn't the Ritz, to be sure, but she wouldn't lift a finger. She'd go down to meals prepared out of sight; she'd come back to beds made in her absence; the bath soap would be wrapped in spotless paper. So on. I even volunteered to baby-sit, but June made other arrangements with a neighbor—anyone but Brant, I guessed. She never thanked me.

On the Sunday evening, Louis came into camp for a drink.

"Well," I greeted him, "what do you think of the big town?"

"Not much," he answered, glum as I expected.

"Didn't think so," I said. "June?"

"Oh, she'll leave me now."

"Probably." I grinned, but he didn't grin back.

"It's a fact, Brant," he said. "I had it yesterday morning, I knew it."

That old business!

WE had sat quiet then, too, I remembered, that evening back in '47, quiet as we were right now, though not the same good quiet. In time we had sipped the jug midway down the label, then Louis had started in for fair: ghosts, how they told a fellow what was going to happen before it happened. Signs a man can read. He simply *knew* his wife would desert him, from something in the high wind, in sleep, in coffee dregs, bird flight, whatever. It had been the usual voluble ramble, and I let it run down, hoping it might modulate into a joke or a story. It often had before. It did that night.

The back trail onto Louis's property passed the town cemetery, and Louis told me how once, after he and his wife and son had moved home from Waltham, he'd gotten sidetracked on his way from the store by an all-night stud game at Bill Ware's. "And me just sitting there the whole time," he said, "thinking about that jug of milk I had, and the little boy hungry, and June wondering where in hell I'd got to."

"How long did you stay?" I asked him.

"Till I bet it away. Milk and all."

"Uh-oh—"

"You don't know a thing. I staggered out of there and took up the hill through the woods."

"Past the graveyard," I said. Louis shuddered and I chuckled. "Bad country!" I added, falling in with him.

"I wasn't half by it," said Louis, "and this white thing gets up." Louis rose from his chair and looked wide-eyed over his shoulder, then snapped his face forward again. "Starts to follow me. I take off on the clean jump, but every foot I gain he gathers back!"

I shook my head and waved him away.

"Now listen," he insisted. "I play out before I get to the top. I have to sit down and get my breath." Here he fell into his chair as if exhausted, his chest heaving. "I don't dare to look, but I can *feel* him sitting next to me on that rock, and by and by he says, 'That was quite a race we had.' He has a voice like a whisper. 'Yes it was,' I says, 'and we're about to have another.'"

We laughed together till we were done. Then I said the whiskey-brave sort of thing one says: "A lot of superstitious horseshit, of course."

"I guess probably you'd think so," Louis answered. I loved to talk, but back then I had a way of shutting talk down around me.

ALL the chapters seem short when I look back, though some seemed so even as they wrote themselves.

Louis's ghosts had spoken accurately: June took a cheap room at the Barlow and lived there the rest of her brief life. Each January I'd send the hotel manager twelve postdated checks to cover her rent. I never felt easy about this arrangement; it was as if I were paying her to stay off. But I told myself that Louis would pick up the tab if I didn't—I knew him—and I'd likely have to increase his salary in the same amount I was shelling out to the hotel anyhow. My system allowed us all just to avoid the subject. Louis scarcely referred to June again, Charles soon forgot her, and in time I paid for the funeral. None of us went to it; God knows who did. Perhaps the poor woman had been, even to her blood, as much a mystery as she'd always been to me.

I'd had mixed feelings at best about June's departure. Of course, as I've admitted, I never understood her well enough to venture a fair judgment on what she'd done. And fairness forces me to admit she had her motives, not so eccentric after all. The big house that Louis's parents had left him was falling down all around her; in fact, after she went down to Trafton for good, Louis moved into the tar-paper work shed. Within five years he'd chopped down the big house for tinder. I think of that sometimes: Louis flinging up his long-handled tie axe, taking a final swing at a support post, and jumping back quickly as the hundred-year-old veranda topples. Now he ducks under the doorframe of his shed with a shard of clapboard and maybe the head of a newel post in his arms, stamping snow from his feet, flapping a glove off, and gentling the wood into his stove. Or I see the summer come on, so hot in the shack, the smutty coffeepot jigging on the same stove, fired by a scarlet coal of oaken mantelpiece.

I ponder the part of feeling in all this, wondering whether there was any pain in Louis's heart at the ruin around him, the physical ruin. My guess is that there was little. Down with it all. Chop the house apart, the shed will do! That was his way. No regard for *things*, at least as means to comfort or efficiency. So unlike me. I recall him hunting in the cheapest boots available, pea-green pacs that he'd use up in half an autumn. By November you'd see actual flesh through the slashed rubber and rent stockings. The good leather uplanders I once gave him he treated the same way, the seams cracking, entirely gone by deer time. It's unthinkable—

Louis lovingly unlacing his boots after a hunt, the way I'd do, slathering the musky mink oil into their grooves, working it along the edges of the tongues, something consuming, almost erotic, in all that ritual.

I still can't be sure what to make of Louis's willful threadbareness, his hurry. The ruin and burning and vanishing—house, wife, and all the rest: these became parts of his story, laughing matters as the years fled by.

But June, yes, she had lived with adversity.

ALL this was as gone as gone can be by '61. Here *we* were again. No women, some whiskey, and a great deal of water. Over that water's ceaseless drone, our conversation flickered on, off, on. I didn't drink much by my old standards, but more than I should have, given that I'd reached what the French call a certain age. Louis took up the slack.

Once we heard the deep hum of a night-feeding cannibal brown racing through the flat water up from the falls. "Four-pounder," I remarked, idly.

"I guess probably," said Louis. "Likely too big for a dry fly anyway."

"Late some night I'll strip a big Muddler through that pool and show you a fish in the morning."

"There you are," said Louis politely. It was just talk. I'd announced this intention for so many years that both of us knew it meant nothing. I'd caught enough big trout in my lucky life to prefer a moderate-sized brown on a floating fly to an invisible brute on a streamer like the deerhair Muddler. And if Louis had challenged me, I'd have admitted that now the notion of night-fishing the pool, no matter that I knew its every ledge and dip, chilled the man of a certain age. What was it Hemingway had said? "The fishing would be tragic." I had an idea what the old swashbuckler meant. I wondered if he still fished. You didn't hear much about him nowadays.

We kept on talking till the fire died, our words wrapped up in the water, small talk—how many partridge broods were showing up? what about a Catholic President, and so young?—which by this late in our lives had the feel of intimacy and importance.

* * *

IT was almost nine when Louis came into the campyard next morning, surprising me as usual by the outdoor fire. It irked me, this habit, the way he'd stalk me like a deer. It embarrassed me, just as my early retreat to bed the night before had done.

Seventy years old, for the love of God!

Unable to resist, I was finishing a third cup of coffee, and my nerves were a little raw. I had my gear spread before me on the plank table, and I turned back to it pointedly. There was no wind to hamper my work out here, and I was tying up some Pheasant Tails for the first mayfly hatch, the Red Quills. In time, they'd jewel the air, banded wisps of cherry. They were late this year, but the day looked to be shaping up well—a rising barometer, clear, still air, the sun already taking some chill off the stream. By one or two o'clock there might be some action. A trout can be predicted to some degree; he's looking for food in that river, unlike the vanished salmon in their spawn.

Louis eyed the neck feather I was fingering, dyed so expertly it might have been one of the old Indian naturals, illegal now.

"Where'd you get the hackle?" he asked.

"You know . . ."

"Snake," Louis said, and spat behind himself.

"Oh, leave it alone!" I barked.

"Tarantula," he said. I glared, and he went into the camp to fetch Old Bluey. For a moment I wished I'd lied, then thought, The hell with it! This was the finest damned material you could get anywhere, and the price was right. Johnny Morse was the best feather merchant in the East. I'd given up buying my tying materials from him for a little spell years back, but nothing else I could find would float as well as a fly made from one of his hackles. Besides, I thought, what was between Louis and Johnny was their business, not mine.

There'd been a time, eleven years earlier, when it might have been my business, and I'd stood off. I didn't like to think about it. Long back, but it lived on.

I'm not sure I've made out my story's conclusion, but I know its beginning—the *real* one—was then. I know it began in '50 with a fight. And then another fight. And then a change.

2

"LET's go find the trouble," Louis had said, poking his finger at the little roadhouse. I pulled in, already wishing I hadn't.

"Too old for trouble," I answered. I was in pretty good shape, pushing sixty, but how would I not have slowed down some?

It was only five in the afternoon, but through the closed windows I could hear two-beat French Canada music over loud conversation. The panes were sweating. Somehow even the crunch of the fat Buick's tires on gravel sounded gloomy to me: the day had been perfect, and I didn't want it spoiled. I sensed something here I knew I wouldn't like. Jesus, I thought, I'm getting as bad as Louis. But the air was wrong. I sat at the wheel for a spell before killing the engine.

We'd come back late that morning from the Mauve water in Dick's plane. The heavy brookies had risen from daylight on. We'd only kept a pair, and were eating one when Dick flew into the pond. It was plenty for all of us, and we shared it with the pilot, lolling in the sand till almost noon. During the flight out I looked down on the ridges, where the popple leaves were the size of a cub fox's ear, and the old burns and the elevations looked like fields of daffodils. We'd sat unmoving for several minutes when Dick tied up to the Frenchtown wharf. This was a different stillness.

"Well," said Louis at last, abruptly pushing open his door, "never can tell when there's trouble to be found." I followed him.

I don't know whether he'd seen Johnny's truck in the lot or this was another instance of his famous second sight. It wouldn't have meant anything to me either way. We went inside, and I felt a rush of warm air, burdened with male sweat, wet wool, spilled liquor. My heart sank another notch.

Loggers, millhands, drivers—by eleven o'clock, somebody'd likely get nailed here. An idiom that has nothing of the metaphorical about it in a joint like this one. I've seen men with their faces slashed raw by hobbed lumberjack boots. Even the truckers wore them. Fun. It wouldn't be any place for a quiet drink by late in the evening. It wasn't now, I thought, and started right off figuring how I might get us the hell out of there—soon. I didn't seem to have much gravel left in my crop these days. I don't know that I'd ever had enough for this kind of company. The thing was, you weren't quite sure what the line was between acceptable and excessive violence here, and while you were wondering, you might get a boot sole in your mug.

"Biscuit's Place," it was, named for an old camp cook who owned it now. Here's where the young bucks came after supper upriver at the Brookfield Diner, or, as everyone called it, Big Ed's. There had been so many scraps in the diner that Ed finally imposed a rule of silence on his customers. Big Ed was a man you'd take orders from. It was the damnedest thing you ever saw: a roomful of rednecks eating, quiet as Trappists.

There wasn't any ban on talk at Biscuit's, and I had to raise my voice for Louis to hear me. He wouldn't look at me, just kept running his eyes around the room. It was one of those back-road honky-tonks cut from a pattern. Wherever there's country, they're there. Mothy buck's head over the bar, a tie or hat or glasses on it. The joint's first dollar bill in a greasy frame on the register counter. Photographs stuck to the bar's mirror—dead wildlife and fish, splayed on tailgate or trunk.

In the so-called lounge section, someone's idea of Beauty: a big, vulgar oil painting—Hollywood Indian, backlit elk, whatever. The felt on the undersized pool table is worn everywhere, full of rips and divots, stained with blue chalk and old beer suds. The cues are out of line, even the sawed-off one for the tight corner. But I've seen as much passion seethe around such tables as around the great green snooker cloths of Irish pubs.

I couldn't make sense of Louis. He seemed so determined somehow: head down, bucking the crowd, he pushed toward the table, where Johnny Morse was picking up some winnings from a small trucker I'd never seen before.

"Candy from a baby," Morse repeated four or five times. The little loghauler looked ready to cry.

"About your speed." Louis's voice was clear in the lull, which stayed on and thickened. It seemed that a minute passed.

"What was that?" Johnny asked it quietly, conversationally, but the tops of his ears were red as the three ball.

"About your speed," Louis announced, slapping two quarters on the table's Formica edge. "Want to pick on someone your own size?"

I looked over at the trucker. He was smiling, ruefully.

"All shots called," Johnny whispered, "kisses and rails included."

"Finest kind," said Louis, whispering too.

Johnny was one of those backwoods boys with a big paunch, but not a hanging one; it jutted, riding his red-and-black tartan shirt up over the navel. On the left shoulder of the shirt was a patch. *Keep 'Em Flying!* it said at the top, and at the bottom, *U.S.A.F.* It was the time of Korea, and Johnny was a patriot.

The skin of his gut was a rind, a hide. Johnny was my feather merchant. A merchant of *feathers*—I'd have chuckled if I'd thought about it in a different place. Yet sure enough there was a delicacy in the way he moved around the table, made the circular bridge with thumb and forefinger, cocked his broad elbow. It was almost pretty.

They flipped a coin, Louis won and broke, and Morse just ran out the frame, flamboyantly banking the eight ball long to end the game.

"Man enough for another?" Louis grinned. A few subdued guffaws sounded from deep in the cigarette smoke.

"You?" said Johnny, with an evil, lopsided smirk.

"Man enough for *you* in anything you *do,*" Louis cooed. I waved at him, but he didn't see me. Or else he ignored me.

"You shut your fucking mouth, McLean!" Louis's little couplet seemed to infuriate Johnny. He dragged his shirtfront down with one hand, the other gripping the rail of the table so hard that the rough knuckles mottled themselves. They scared me.

Louis stood in his tracks with that half-smile, looking Johnny up and down. Finally he laid another pair of coins on the felt. "Rack 'em up, champ."

"Loser racks, pissant," said Johnny, grinding the chalk cube onto his tip.

And of course Louis *was* the loser. Again and then again. I grabbed him as he went up to the bar with a dollar: I was tired, I said; I was an old man. "Well, go along then," Louis answered, staring me down. "I'll get a ride somehow." He turned and carried his change back to the table.

"A sucker for punishment," Morse announced to the crowd. The little trucker slipped out the door. I heard his rig throw a bit of gravel in the lot, then chirp as his tires hit blacktop. There didn't seem to be a small man left in the lounge.

"Man enough for *you* in everything you *do*," Louis intoned. Again.

Johnny screwed up his face, more in contemplation, it seemed, than bad temper. "But not man enough for the Kraut," he said at last. Johnny had been with Patton's bunch, and the war remained the high point of his life. Afterwards, it had been these cheap little roadhouses, these endless bouts of whiskey and eight ball, and raising roosters—the best, to be sure—whose neck feathers he sold to a handful of East Coast flytiers.

Louis had worked a civilian's job in a strategic industry, had never thought to enlist. Now, as he bent to the table and leveled his cue, he muttered into the utter silence, "Yep. Must have been hell frying all those spuds."

Louis found a nerve, as he knew how. Some down-on-his-luck old army chum of Morse's had drifted through the country a few years before, shortly after Armistice, claiming that Johnny had been an army chef. Johnny had denied the claim ever since, violently sometimes.

I can play it back the way I still see it—as if in slow motion, the short stick in Morse's hand comes down, cuts a swatch from the hanging smoke, takes Louis low behind the big left ear.

Louis sprawled on the slick felt, a thin rope of drool running onto it. Everybody who knew Louis McLean knew that he was a match for anyone—even a big man like Morse—in a fair scuffle. But this one wasn't going to be fair. I watched, nailed to the sticky stool where I sat. I should have protected him. I should have helped him. *Something!* I shouldn't just have watched.

Morse turned, almost casually, and put the short cue back in the rack behind him. I should have made a move before he turned again.

Louis had gotten onto his feet and was peering at Johnny quizzically—he didn't know he was in this world. Then his wide hands came up together by instinct: he looked like a child, his eyes, at half-mast, peeking through the cracks of his fingers while Johnny walked quickly over, swinging his meaty legs in a stiff march. "Man enough for *you*," he growled, dropping a heavy hand on Louis's shoulder, like a field worker stabbing a bale with a hook. Louis shook his head feebly, then lobbed a weak left at Johnny's nose. Johnny blinked, as if the punch had been a distraction, a nuisance. Somewhere someone laughed.

Johnny took off at a trot toward the door, Louis's jacket collar locked in his fist. I saw where my friend's heels dragged two lines through the swill on the café floor. I looked frantically up and down the bar and around the lounge. No bouncer, of course; and everyone a stranger. Biscuit paused, his hand on the tap, waiting for Johnny to haul Louis clear; then he lifted the handle and blew the head off the draft.

I burst out into the lot. Three men were smoking cigarettes there, the only other spectators. Their conversation droned behind the sounds of bone on bone, the spat curses of Morse, the moans and grunts of Louis. Johnny had wrestled him into the cab of his rusty Scout and wedged his head through the steering wheel. Knees against Louis's chest, Morse held him there, swinging one punch after another from below the wheel. The car wheezed on its springs.

I ran to the three smokers. "For God's sake, man," I shouted, to none in particular, "pull him off! Enough is enough!" The one closest to me paused in his chat with the others, looked up at the sky, where the moon hung now like a sickle: "Seems like it's *their* business."

In those days I used to carry a shotgun in the Buick's trunk during the hunting months, even if I were headed on a simple errand. But these weren't the hunting months. I pictured my Model 21, gleaming with oil on its pegs in the camp, and I squeezed my trigger finger on air. I wanted it to be autumn; I wanted to run over to the car and fish out that shotgun and put a charge of number eights into each of those indifferent bastards' asses. After I'd sent them howling down the tarmac, I'd put the warm double barrels through the driver's window and right up against Johnny Morse's left temple. I wouldn't kill him. I'd make him flop those fat feet on the gravel and leave Louis alone. Then I'd make him lie facedown on the tar, I'd click off the safety, I'd turn the gun and pound its stock into his head. Then I'd let Louis do the same.

But the imagination is bolder than the will.

Instead, I flapped around like a marionette, playing out these fantasy moves at a ten-foot distance from the cruddy Scout, where Morse was ruining my partner. How could I be so useless?

I shuffled around to the other side of the cab and flung open the door. Someone fell out on the ground, half-righted himself and blinked like an owl: Heath, the McLean town drunk. He shivered slightly, and passed out. I dragged him aside like a box. I was going to shout something at Johnny, but what? I couldn't threaten him. Not an old fart like me.

There was a double blotch of blood on Morse's pants legs, below the knee. The stain was symmetrical, as if he had used some of his hackle dye above either cuff, in a pattern. I felt my gut turn over. I opened my mouth to scream, but my tongue was cotton-dry. I tried again, and a squeak came out. Johnny looked over at me and frowned, the way you do at a little kid who's always asking *why?* Then I saw his face seize. Louis had run his hand up between Morse's thighs and was squeezing for what he was still worth. Not much. Johnny let out a shriek like a stuck rabbit, wrenched Louis from the wheel by the hair, and hefted him out of the car. I got dizzy, glimpsing his face as Morse unpacked him.

Johnny was dragging Louis again, this time by the scalp. He got down on the gravel, Louis across one knee. They looked like father and son, the old man helping the boy get sick on the ground. Louis, all the grit whipped out of him, seemed tiny, deflated. Morse drew the head back and slammed it forward on the hub of the Scout's front wheel. Once, twice.

I found my voice and bleated, "I'll never buy another feather from you, Morse!"

What a pathetic old bastard!

Morse snickered. He knew what I was. My heart nearly cracked open with terror, but I threw myself against him in a kind of creaky cross-body block. Johnny, without even looking back, threw an elbow and knocked out my wind. I sat, gasping, on the gravel, while Louis did get sick, puking all over Johnny's hands and sleeves.

There were scraps of our Mauve water trout's pink flesh in the vomit. One world to another.

Morse growled disgust, flapping his hands like a man who's been burned. He stood, gave Louis a careless kick, got into his Scout, and bucked out of the parking lot toward Pinkham.

Heath still slept where I'd left him; the three smokers had vanished.

I struggled to get Louis into the back seat of my car and lay him out. I didn't want to look at him up close. I turned the key and rolled out onto the hard road, uncertain where to go: a doctor? home? I asked Louis himself.

"Snake," he gargled. Then he fell quiet, or maybe he fainted. I shuddered through each mile back to McLean. Every breath he gathered seemed to come from under filthy, shallow water.

I HAVE said that my story begins with that old fight, and perhaps it does. But what followed next day was more crucial.

When we'd arrived back at McLean the night before, Louis had sat upright; I tried to persuade him to bunk downriver at my camp, but he'd managed to get out of the car, pausing only to say, "I'll stay home, Healey." It was the first time he'd ever called me by my last name. I thought it was over between us friends, and I thought I deserved no better, though what might I have done? It had made no difference that my silly body block came so late in the game; it would have been useless at any stage.

I remember how I lay in bed through the night, not sleeping till a few minutes before dawn, and then being jerked right back awake—in dream, I'd swung the gun butt at Morse's head, but had missed and struck Louis, hard, in the chest.

Weak with nerves and exhaustion, I'd sat on the edge of the

mattress, ribs aching from the shot Morse had given me, and playing over the gruesome and incredible details of the beating. Louis had taunted Johnny, yes, but not enough for so crazy a response.

I recall dragging on my clothes and going to the ledge to ponder it all. There I'd stood, the blackflies ravaging me, as Louis sneaked down through the alders. When I noticed him, he was leaning into the Buick.

He emerged, holding the cloth sack with our spare Radway trout in it. "Ought to have gotten this fella on ice," he said.

I shook my head as I came over next to him. He was lolling on the car's open back door with one arm, and I can still smell the stench of fish from the floor mat where the sack had stayed through the night. I'd forgotten all about it, with Louis hurt so badly. The last thing I'd expected was to see him this morning. His cheek-bones and eyes were blackened, his lips ballooned, but he had all his teeth, and his hand was steady on Old Bluey.

Now, the breakfast fire snapping before us, he said, "You and I have both seen better." He was filling me in. As if I hadn't betrayed him at all.

"Yes," I said.

"Sometimes it's the way she looked at something. I don't mean me. A rock. A bird."

"Yes."

"Johnny goes down to Trafton to get one of his goddamn bags of chicken feed or something. You were here, and I'll admit it to you. I was supposed to be guiding. You thought I *was* guiding. I meant to be. But he's gone, and I run into her at Edward's, and next thing you know we're out at George Bailey's camp on Middle Lake."

Good place to breed one, I thought, but the joke seemed sour and I kept my mouth shut for once. "I know the place," I said.

"Sure you do," said Louis. "We caught a few chub off the beach. Twisted their necks for the fish hawks. You know how they'll come if you're quiet."

I stayed quiet.

"Then we're over at Finnegan Point," he went on. "Picking berries. This is August."

"At the mouth of Unknown," I muttered. "Blueberries."

"Very same. She picks one and holds it out on her hand, and she looks at it that way. It was how she talked too. She said something oddball. The berry was the shape of the world, she said, only blue. They're not blue, of course. More like purple with white dust . . ."

"Go on," I urged.

"I don't know. I couldn't get her back to George's quick enough to suit me, or her either. I don't know what to say. How a man could explain it. I mean, I knew I liked her well. We had the sparks going for a good long time before that."

"Yes."

"And who in Jesus was out there to see us? But somebody was. Funny part is, I had it that morning something was set to go off wrong. Even before we went."

"Yes."

"Maybe I forgot, or I wouldn't have taken her out there. Not then. I sure as hell forgot when I *was* out there, Brant. But I don't know but I'd take her out there again. Right now I would. Like I said, we've seen better, but back a few years . . . There was just something."

"A pretty woman to this day, I bet," I added, though I'd scarcely known Velma Morse. I was just slowing down the talk, which was making me uncomfortable.

Listening to Louis's story, I hadn't known how I felt, exactly. But it wasn't good: I recall how I had to force concentration, because something in me kept rising and ebbing and eddying, tossing me six ways to Sunday.

"Not just looks," Louis continued, unmindful. "Something else. I mean, I had it. It wasn't a good day. I can't get over that. I had it, but still . . ."

He took a drink of coffee, gingerly, his lips drawn back as far as the pain allowed. He was watching the last of the cook fire. We wouldn't talk for quite a spell.

What was bothering me? That I'd been such a washout the very night before? That would have made sense, but it didn't feel accurate. What was it?

"In a week," Louis said finally, "he just picked up, birds and all.

Over to Pinkham, and that's that, her along with him. Never a word from her."

"You didn't see *him* all that week?"

"I did, and I knew he knew all he needed to know. Somebody told him. But he didn't say a mumbling word to me. Didn't have a cue stick, I guess."

3

Louis had flared for only an instant when he saw I was using one of Johnny's hackles. But he let the matter drop.

We watched the ribbons of river mist fade into bright air. It would be a bluebird day, but I meant only to fish a few afternoon hours, close to camp. I needed to harden into the harder fishing. It wouldn't do for the old man to wade too long right away. Louis began to pace up and down the ledge, stooping now and then to lift a flat piece of the schist and skip it, like a kid, across the calm surface upstream from the riff. Maybe he was replaying the old fight too. He wasn't a man to sit around in any case. I'd tried years before to get him interested in making flies, but he was too restless for anything more complicated than a big streamer. He got fidgety even to watch me tie, irked, I think, at my stillness, concentration.

I, for my part, could never work properly while he shuffled around the place, picking things up from my bench for idle inspection, chattering, whistling, sighing. This morning, though I'd just arrived, I felt, as always, I had to get him out of there if I meant to finish a single fly. Some latecomer might be looking for a guide at Wesley's, and I told Louis he was free to go find out. You could tell he was relieved.

"We'll have a real visit tonight." Again, we spoke at once, the same words, and laughed at once too.

Come evening, we could share a little tap. He'd keep a lot stiller.

I offered to drive him up to the lodge, but he told me he'd just as soon walk. "The sports don't get going as early as we used to, Brant."

I watched him stride up my drive, and almost called him back before he disappeared. A few years before, I thought, I wouldn't have let him go. We'd have fished together. I wouldn't have sent him off to help the lake fishermen in their powerboats. But I turned again to my work.

I went on laying in the sparse dun fibers for the tails, erecting quill wings, wrapping the slim pheasant herls up the body, twisting the fine gold wire and, at last, the delicate hackle that would float the fly. It was an art grown automatic, instinctive, over the span of my life. My mind should have been free to turn where it would. Yet, though Johnny's name had not even been mentioned, though the old fight had been recalled only for a second, and obliquely, my thoughts kept retreating slavishly through the years, as sooner or later they always did at McLean, to Biscuit's Place. To Louis's tale of passion just after.

I seemed to rehearse it every year, and still do. On that morning in '61 I thought back to 1950, and back even further, then forward again. Like it or not, it was a habit of mind, one I sometimes wished I could check, for it seemed to make the world a cumulus of retrospective detail, overpowering. My life became the story of a man who remembered himself remembering.

I, too, knew something of passion and something of its violence. But for years Louis didn't know that I knew.

JE VAIS, tu vas, il va—I still hear my voice, and the antiphon from the class. Every day I'd plod through each drill till it had run its course. I'd scribble French words on the chalkboard along with their English equivalents, the students waiting in the most courteous silence as I did so. Routine, reiteration. Then I'd erase the English translations and ask the students to write sentences based on the French words. Only here was the dullness broken. The sentences were always awkward and sometimes hilarious: *Le bec de M. Larocque s'appelle Pierre,* just for example.

I closed each session with work on pronunciation, directing one mortified girl after another to read aloud from our elementary text. Soon, giving up the chore of weeding sonorous Charleston or

Richmond or Raleigh accents from the French inflections that now and then surfaced, I'd wool-gather, turning my ear to the *snick snick* of a horse-drawn sickle bar taking the last of the hay from the college meadows. Otherworldly, this place, where as much attention was paid to the steeds as to the undergraduates who rode them. Grasshoppers leapt ahead of the mowing. The scent of cut timothy reached even to my upstairs room. Ground birds shuffled in the clay paths of the quadrangle.

Yet how polite my students were, how timorous! They would sit unmoving, while in my mind I flicked a fly or swung a shotgun. I find myself touched, after all this time. It was somehow sad, how they went through motions, and to what end?

Once, during the pronunciation exercise, I leaned out the window. It was a gray, cloudy day, the final hay had been gathered, and bits of chaff and leaf were tumbling across the green. I noticed a woman leave the deanery at the far corner. She came the way the wind came, her overcoat's tails blown before her; like the wind, too, she gave the impression of speed, her stride buoyant and long. Yet she came, in fact, very slowly.

I vaguely heard the chapel bell signal the end of the period, but continued to observe the dawdling approach of the figure below. She reached her bicycle, propped against a redbud under my window. Depositing something in the basket, she mounted. Suddenly she looked up through the branches of the tree, directly at me, her expression stolid as she raised her hand in a chopped salute. Then she rode off. I watched her out of sight, then dreamily turned. My blushing reader persisted, though by now the period was several minutes over, and her fellow students apprehensive. I blushed, too, and dismissed them all.

It is one of many images that couch in my old brain, a touchstone of my history: a face, rather stern, looking up through branches—leafless with the season, almost oriental, abstract—and the wind-raked world around it suddenly still.

I SAW her next in November. I remember exactly: the opening of the quail season, though hot weather had returned and lingered. I was all business as a hunter back then. Not from competitiveness. In fact, I was secretive about my hunting passions, shy of my colleagues' presumable reactions. My obsession was instead a lust for absolute competence, that adolescent yen to be somehow extraordinary.

But the languor of that afternoon had infected both my dog and me. I'd already run through my customary responses to bad conditions: anger, frustration, resentment (as if someone had plotted the weather against me), and finally a crackle of guilt—the hunt was keeping me from . . . from what? Oddly, I felt in those times that I ought to be *writing,* for although I had never put pen to paper, I fancied myself a poet-in-waiting. Now I see that fancy as part of some quest for self-justification, some radical Protestant streak, perhaps inborn. To be an extraordinary sportsman would not, I thought then, redeem me in the eyes of the world, and already, if redemption were an issue, I knew I wouldn't find it as a teacher. I was passing through. I recognized that much very early. There had to be something else, something beyond. So, I must have imagined, one day I will be an artist, after the hunting falls off. I had no idea yet how far into the future that ideal might take me.

I broke through a tangle of sweetbrier, cobwebs festooning my hat, and stood there picking burdocks from my clothing. My pointer, Minnie, gnawed at the burrs in her feathers, pausing to pant in the dust, that squinty half-smile of tired dog on her face. When she whined I looked up. A bicycle. A woman on a bicycle. Another image.

She spoke: "Mr. —"

"Healey. Brant Healey."

"Anna Graves," she announced. "We've met, after a fashion."

"Informally," I murmured, feigning an easy smile, my chest tight. "Through a window."

"Exactly," she said, looking me up and down with disarming frankness.

"Well," I stammered, "what brings you out here?" She pointed into her bicycle's basket. I saw a sketch pad.

"Painting?" I inquired.

"Drawing," she corrected.

"A hobby of yours?" I felt like a rube; the question sounded silly before I completed it.

"More than that," she said. Again she inspected me boldly, even fingering the cloth of my battered vest. I read her.

"Less a hobby," I explained, "than a passion."

"I imagine there are worse." She smiled.

My dog had wiggled over to her and now leapt up, her front paws streaking Anna's skirt with red dust.

"Get down, Minnie!" I shouted, my embarrassment keener with every minute.

"Oh, let her alone," Anna said, scratching the bitch's ears. "It's not as if I'm dressed for the ball." True enough, there was an almost studied inelegance to her clothing: a gray muslin house-dress with diagonal stripes of gunmetal gray, broad-soled shoes such as nurses and librarians wear, laddered stockings. Something about her dishevelment suddenly eased me.

"This *is* a passion," I said. "This and fishing with a fly."

"A fly?" she asked, a quizzical smile slightly bending her mouth, showing large teeth.

"You know, an artificial one. Made of feathers. It's supposed to look like the real thing, the thing the trout are eating. A deception."

"How naughty," she teased, arching her dark brows. The smile opened and lingered.

"I had an impulse to call this my 'special academic interest' at the reception for new faculty last month."

"Oh!" she blurted. "I wish you had!"

"I doubt the president would have liked that."

She rolled her eyes: "Oh, *him*!" she huffed.

"I've heard dull academic speeches," I began, but she cut me off.

"The finest traditions of this great institution! The fellowship of scholars!" She called out the same ponderous clichés that the president had cast among us. But it was less the accuracy of words than of voice and gesture that stunned me: like the president, she bounced on her toes as she spoke, drawing back her lips in a grimace, as if she were frightened; and when she made an emphatic point she raised her arm and brought it down, fingers fluttering, onto her crown.

I had to wipe my eyes. "By God, you could have given his speech *for* him!" I cried.

"I just did, didn't I?" She smiled.

"Indeed you did," I responded.

"What is your department?" she asked.

When I told her she leapt into a takeoff of Fratti, a harmless middle-aged colleague who favored soft Italian shoes, silk kerchiefs, boutonnieres. An oriole among sparrows. Anna had his voice exactly, too, his postures and gestures. I had to sit down. Her eyes sparkled with pleasure at her effect.

When I recovered the world seemed eerily quiet. "Where have you been painting?" I mumbled, uneasy in such stillness.

"I've been *drawing* at the cottage," she said, after a wait.

"Cottage?"

"Ours," she said, looking westward. "Or my husband's, really. He's dean of arts." I remembered him, William Graves. A stuffed shirt whose British locutions and pronunciations clashed with his deep-southern drawl. Gangly fellow with a brush mustache. A painter. I'd met him at the same reception.

"It's out there," Anna said, her back to me. "The cottage, I mean. By the lake." She turned and studied me for another long minute. I felt the blood pressing my ribs and forehead and cheekbones.

"By the lake," I choked.

"Yes."

"It sounds lovely."

"I could show you," she answered, her voice so firm, compared.

4

I FIRST made love to Anna a lifetime ago in a small southern cabin; yet she has been with me since.

She was surely with me that morning in 1950 after Louis's beating, and somehow her presence deepened the odd anger I'd felt as he spoke. I did not bid her, but she leapt up, as if from the fire I'd piled high with brush to ward off the blackflies. I would not ward off Anna. My old compulsions swarmed about as thick as smoke itself, once Louis had spoken his tale of infatuation.

Infatuation. Even these long years after, when I think back to my friend's story on that dizzy morning, something in me snarls or sneers. I find myself, as if by instinct, speaking of his moment with Velma as a childish fancy, though it's easy for me to conjure the particulars, to sense how real they must have been: the old quilts thrown to the board floor, the glassy lake outside, the yellowlegs bobbing on the sand beach by a canoe, nearly afloat in the shallows where Louis had carelessly left it in his rush. But I make these details parts of a mere story which I trivialize as so much adolescent passion, willfully forgetting that Louis was older in that moment than I had been when I burst into Anna's cottage, as if it had been fated.

Fate. Infatuation. *Ignis fatuus.* Will-o'-the-wisp.

I don't mean that I came to these recognitions easily. I'm a stubborn man. On that morning after Morse pummeled Louis McLean, I now know that I was on the brink of some enormous sea change in my judgments of self and others, but whenever I recall that day after the fight, I still must struggle against an old irritation. I'll catch myself thinking that Louis and Velma's instant on Middle Lake came and went almost at the same time, while my craving for Anna carried on, carries on, it seems forever.

But if in me, why not in Louis? The spirit rising up from the blueberry barren on Finnegan Point and driving him and Johnny's wife across the dead-calm lake like a gale—who was I ever to imagine it would not persist, too, in my friend? My best self now believes that spirit became part of the ghostly voice Louis claimed almost daily to hear. I scoffed at that claim for years, but I look back on my own story and I see, in all my time with Anna, that I also behaved as if choiceless. I say to myself, Step back, old fool, if you can. Who was the possessed one? Whom do you presume to judge? For I know what it is to behave as if some whispering demon were bullying *me*.

Even now.

I bent to the half-finished fly pinched in my tying vise, but straightened immediately: a picture of myself in 1950, angry beside the camp fire, crowded my mind. Each year—no, each *day* when I'd been with Anna, each day since, had been an effort to say something, if only to myself, about what she *was*. And every effort a failure. I couldn't name them, the motives to follow her, as they say, to earth's end. Not even to myself; and who else might listen?

I loosened the vise and tossed the hopeless fly in the grass. It was clear my thoughts would go their own way for a spell. Maybe that, after all, was why I'd sent Louis off guiding so soon after this, my latest return to McLean: not so I could tie my Pheasant Tails, but so I could fail, could allow myself to be distracted by reminiscence—and purged.

I remembered a nasty desire to pummel Louis myself, as if Morse had not done an adequate job of it. I had gone into my cabin to brood, the blackflies too vicious for me in spite of the fire. My cabin. My ledge. My pool. My river. I had made them that way; I had invented a home ground, and with it the version of self that I would need, *and* need. For without the home the self is a cipher, as I had been, panting beside Anna's cottage near that lake. And whatever Louis had been, bloodied and battered in Biscuit's gravel lot, he wasn't that.

I came outside again, almost immediately. The smoke was still rising from a stone hearth built by my hand; I stood in a place that had become a habit of body and mind. Yet I felt the little water feeders under the granite on which Louis and I had so often stood, together, the very rock that held up earth and house. Beneath it water was sifting its way to the river, and the river was running down to ocean.

Perhaps just now, these long years after, Louis was off on the lake where he and Velma had watched their ospreys and picked their berries. Lake of detail. He knew that water, its every keel-busting rock and every cove, its mood in all winds and all absence of wind, the color of its sand in Dark Bay and off Norway Point. He balked only at more abstract vision: "You and I have both seen better," he'd said. "There's just something," he'd said. "I don't know what to say" is what he'd said at last.

And I?

To have seen how alike we were should have been to forgive him. But I remembered how the anger grew, bullying my thoughts.

"Some friend!" I had shouted aloud. Just a fool. Like me. In-fatuated.

ANNA's hair was so dry, I was afraid to touch it. It might break off like late-summer stalks. It stuck out from her temples, whatever her efforts to smooth it—casual; she didn't care.

Her nose was lovely, aristocratic. But you don't lose your sense over a nose.

She had rabbity teeth.

She was long and lean. A surprise, then, the flesh of buttock and upper thigh—slack, fishbelly.

Her walk was a lope. I think of a coyote's canter, its subtle speed. But even that first time on the dusty lane to her cottage, she covered the ground slowly. We hurried, clutching each other, breath short and shallow, but I took pigeon's steps, to keep from dragging her.

How seldom, after our first breathless meeting, she laughed.

You and I have both seen better. . . .

I think that for all I craved her, Anna must have represented something not of the body. She was no one's beauty, but she had a look of *composure*, though she was often in disarray. I don't know what to say. Maybe her indifference to physical looks suggested composure in some other dimension, where there'd be a way of finding the world shapely. Was it that dream that drew me? That Anna, minute by minute, might give sleekness to my life, which otherwise seemed so random? There we were, on a November day that felt like July: a man with a dog and a gun and leather-faced pants, a woman with a bicycle and basket, a sketchbook and charcoal pencils. There we were, in a tree-shaded lane where it was cool enough for birds to stream back and forth in their hundreds, and where I, the hunter, heard the two-note whistles of bobwhites. *Here* was where they had come! They called outside the windows, so loud they might have been wolves, it seemed. They would not quit till after, and then they would quit as one. Then there would be only the rustle of leaf, pinestraw, and needle, and far off the ceaseless locusts. Which would all seem a silence, after.

We had fallen together on the narrow bed. The dust of disuse billowed around us. The rough hunting clothes had tumbled onto the floor's dust, the muslin dress following. The timid words of first-time lovers had drifted up into the cobwebs.

A scent like grass stain settled into the heavy air. My sweat had cut its small paths through the chalky dust on her face. I pulled her to my chest, her face out of sight.

After, I felt so distant from anything familiar that I shivered, once and violently. And then, because I could not breathe long at that distance, something had to be said: "I'm sorry. I seemed to rush things a little." As if what I'd shown were a kind of bad manners.

She stuck out her tongue in response, and I giggled like an acolyte. Then the giggle gave way to a laughter I'd never known before, immense, rising up and out of me. She went on studying me as she had when we made love—curious, her knitted brows running together above that stately nose.

There was composure in her manner, yes, but something of irony too. My words fall short. In the year to come I'd congratulate myself for discerning this indefinable quality in Anna, telling myself a coarser man might miss it. But I was a smug little fool, even a liar: there wasn't anything refined about my passion; it turned her every trait into something that *burned* me. She spoke, and I craved her. I craved her when she fell silent too. When she walked, sat, lay down, knelt, smiled, frowned.

But what burned me most were those impersonations. And the one that almost maddened me with lust was her imitation of *me* in my awkward imitations of others. I had no gift for mimicry. I'd try to take off poor Fratti, his liquid consonants and airy vowels, his butchered English syntax, his exquisite gestures of hand and arm. Then she would mimic my mimicry, and my lust would erupt, whatever the hour or place.

My only successful imitation was of her husband, and by that I mean no cruel double entendre. I had his pretentious intonations and mannerisms perfectly, or so I once discovered—as if by accident—standing before my mirror to shave. The bathroom in my dreary apartment was no bigger than a closet. Stooping to see my face through the steam, I reached to wipe the glass clear, at the same time raising the hand that held the razor and beginning a fulsome praise of the Georgian poets, one of the dean's enthusiasms. I rubbed quickly again at the mirror, half-fearing what I'd find behind the vapor.

It was the first warm night of April, and I was preparing myself to be with Anna. We would celebrate the end of a winter filled with furtive rendezvous. My nasty landlady lived just above my apartment. The town was small, its single hotel right on the edge of the campus. We had had to settle for frigid trysts in the lakeside cottage, stripping from the waist down and burying ourselves in the musty bedclothes, our breaths a chain of clouds in a darkness we didn't dare light up. Rodents skittered under our bed, more at home than we. So now I was longing to touch the length of Anna's body, to feel the heat of her stomach, her breasts' small dents in my chest, the high ridge of her spine.

An hour later we sat, the plush of the ninth green under us, on the college golf links—bare, apart, protracting our yearning for as long as we could bear it under the first warm-weather moon. Musical from his distance, a farmer's hound saluted its rising. The howl flowed into the far whistle of a night train. I imagined myself with Anna, headed slowly northward in a Pullman, the jackpiney delta country dropping away, the Blue Ridge ascending. On and on we went, till daylight brought us the catarrhal mutterings of old porters in the corridor, and we slept.

Anna reached for me, the soft light sliding along her arm, but I slithered backwards and stood. I would hold her off. I would hold it off, ridiculous as I must have appeared, erect by the limp ninth flag. I turned away until I had subsided. Then I turned back and began my imitation of her husband. I had done it better in my tiny lavatory; still, she gave me a look. How can a look be so neutral as to overpower? I stopped abruptly.

Dismayed, I walked off, eyes lifted skyward, so that I stepped over the edge of a sand trap and pitched into it, somersaulting. I bit my tongue and it bled. As I cursed a small spot of blood fell on one of my arms, already covered with the trap's fine sand, a drop of red among the sparkling grains.

I climbed out and lay facedown on the fairway, squirming to brush off the grit, then rolling over to wave my arms and legs, like a child making snow angels, wiping the flecks of dirt from my shoulders and neck. Standing again, I felt the dew run down my belly and back, and I hurried to Anna. When we threw ourselves together, the far hound began again its soulful baying.

WHO was the husband, the rival? *William Graves.* A dean, whatever that meant. A painter too; so he styled himself. But how often I longed to storm into my closet, pull down my Winchester, literally *shoot* one canvas of his. It hung in the foyer of the arts building, so that I passed it daily—*After Claude,* the fool's attempt to transform the tobacco and bean fields near the college into pastorale. What must they have thought, the snuff-dipping couple he'd hired to pose as swain and goodwife? What mix of rage and contempt must have coursed through the stooped black cleaning lady who every morning swept that foyer?

Anna had married William when both were art students, he in painting and she in sculpture. He alone had completed his studies. She had withdrawn early, perhaps, as I once ventured, because she was the only woman in her program, a pioneer.

"No," she said flatly.

"Why, then?" I asked her. We were conversing in high, shivery whispers, having made love on our feet in that cleaning lady's closet. New Year's Eve: our outrageous celebration.

"I got pregnant," she said, breaking into a speaking voice. I put a hand across her mouth—the words seemed so loud—but she jerked her head away.

"Pregnant," she repeated, still not whispering.

We jumped at a noise in the hall, then dug our nails into one another's arms as we waited. But there was nothing more. A mouse, maybe. A draft.

"My doctor sounded the alarm," she went on. This time she did whisper. "I needed to rest. Some structural defect in me, it seems."

"And so the child . . ." I began.

"I lost it in any case," she said, terse, informational.

WAS there no refuge from this turn of mind, from these tumbling recollections? How heaped and random the way they came, how perplexing so much of what they blundered onto!

I blew the scraps of feather and thread from the table, snapped my kit shut, and carried it back inside. I twisted the dial of my portable radio. A handsome young leader was urging different ideas, another spirit, new frontiers. I tried to attend; it was a message I could use. But the voice became a crackle, a blurred undersong to the hum of the stream past my ledge.

I'd have done better to keep Louis with me this morning, I thought. I was getting too old to confront the rush of the McLean alone. The white water over Big Falls looked daunting. If I lost my footing upstream, I would float helplessly into that tumult and be borne off out of anyone's sight forever. Who would mark my going?

ANNA was gifted. I base my judgment not on any credentials she had, for there were none the world might honor; I base it only on what I saw. Anna always carried that sketchbook in her bicycle basket, wrapped with the box of charcoals in a canvas sack. She drew quickly, nervously, almost it seemed without looking either at her subject or the paper.

I remember especially a sketch of the stubble field near her cottage. Moss-bearded cypresses stood at the lakeshore along the meadow's far edge, and there was a silhouette in the foreground—a man's head, from the browline upwards.

I begged her for that drawing. I had watched her as she faced the field, shading in that strange detail of the head with the flat of the pencil. A hedge-choked ditch behind us hid us from any bypasser.

I would go on begging her for drawings, but everything she completed she quickly destroyed. She was pleased to the point of vanity with her own work; yet, having finished a picture, she'd coolly fold it into quarters and rip it, slipping the tatters into her sack without a word.

Did she feel impelled to give shape to her world, and, that world being so fragmented (especially now that I had wandered into it), did she find the shape of one moment irrelevant to the next? So I speculated, but she would not comment on her drawing. A momentary shape, then gone.

And just so our time, it seems to me now, was always momentary, except for one four-day trip to Savannah. Her husband had trained to some northern colloquium. It was December, early in our love affair; we met circumspectly outside our hotel, after travel in separate coaches. I was too nervous even to bring my Ford.

We never left the room, even took our meals there. Our lovemaking was interrupted only by sleep, and by the midmorning arrival of the chambermaids who changed our linen, fluffed our pillows, and removed our dirty dishes. We sat bashful then on the cold balcony. Or I did, imagining the maids clucking at the stained bedclothes, at the slovenly heaps of our clothing, always the same, on the wicker armchairs. As we huddled outside in our worn robes, Anna seemed unrattled.

During these interludes I tried to observe. Anna would speak at length out in the chill air, sometimes rising to pace back and forth in her black outfit. She was not given to darts of intuition, the supposed female mode, but to formal, general thought. She had what I then considered a European mind, inclined to broad concept. I remember being both irked and shamed by my limitations, compared, so that for all my fantasies of running off with her forever, I recall a strange satisfaction at having had such little time together and devoting so much of it to sex. For what might my feeling of inadequacy become otherwise?

One morning, for instance, Anna launched into a discourse on modern anxiety, which she said the artists had initiated by discovering perspective. A bizarre theory, surely a wrong one, but she was persuasive, well informed—where did she *get* her information? The humility I felt almost gave way to real anger.

WE think of a romantic affair as involving minutest details, specifics of hand or gaze or lip, the gestures of physical love. I can summon all these even today—in Savannah, her back arching under our canopy, her flyaway hair a canopy itself, shadowing the perfect nose and prominent teeth; the great gray eyes narrowing slightly inside that shadow; the slight *huff!* of her breath at the last. She sinks forward onto me, the mixed rhythms of our pulses in chest and neck subsiding when she dozes. My upper leg goes numb. My feet tingle, short of blood.

But what were her mannerisms of *speech* out there, as the chambermaids secretly smiled or frowned on the other side of the high French doors, as the paper mills spewed their foul, beautiful smokes into lilac air, as horse carts passed below in the cobbled square and songbirds thronged the vast oaks? "It was how she talked too." So Louis had put it, providing instances, however broken, details.

Anna took small pleasure in detail. Even her drawings were remarkable for a kind of abstraction—rendered as they say from life, they somehow rose above life's clutter. You couldn't claim exactly that she rendered a scene, because her pictures would be at once larger and more minimal than the word implies—but I don't have the vocabulary to be precise.

So her diction, too, was abstract: polished, dispassionate, lecture-like. It was as if she read a prepared text. I see her now, standing like a don, or perhaps a judge, in that black robe, her back to the balcony's grillwork. Her long arms hang inexpressively from the hunched shoulders, her stance is broad and stolid, her mouth alone moves.

In time she will reach her conclusion, as if a cylinder's lock had clicked. Then she may see me here, the white iron of a chair digging into my spine, a look of discomfort on my unshaven face. And then she may (in pity?) break into a takeoff of someone, and it will suddenly animate her—the president's bounce and grimace, Fratti's Latinisms, the whining drawl of the provost. I'll peek quickly through the glass door into our room, praying in that instant that the lumbering housemaids have gone off to other duties and gossips.

WHENEVER I think back to that time of stupefying passion, I drift to that mimicry of hers, to the stammerings of desire it evoked. But why should desire have so ruled me?

I had learned many things in the course of what's called a classical education, but I could not make them fall into an integrity. Against her synthesizing mind I had only lust, however cheapening that word now seems as I say it. It was the one coherence I knew. Things came together in my craving, as from time to time they have come together for me in the field or on the water. The analogy must seem so oblique. And yet I make my way on a river, the current with or against me; there is a rock or a ledge or a pothole here, another, others, there and there; the sky is a welter of cloud, of blue, or gray, or rose, or dark. Then, the water eddying, tumbling, washing by, one bright fish, of the many imaginable, kisses the surface to suck in one fragile fly of the millions low in the air or on the moving film, and the world is for that instant a formal, an elegant place.

Or, stubborn hardhack a chaos around me, the wind all wrong, the landscape a map of uncertainty for as far as I can see, my dog locks on the scent of a hidden grouse, which then explodes out of its cover and meets the center of my shotgun's pattern and, before crumpling, suspends itself forever in mind against that backdrop, so shapely all of a sudden.

BACK then, though, in my twenties—nothing more than a boy— the world in my hours away from Anna was growing more unmanageable every day. Students had begun politely to complain to my superiors. The spring semester had just started, and so had

Fratti's tenure as department chairman. It was one of his first duties to summon me for a conference: he was chagrined, maybe even frightened.

"There is," he began. "I am told . . ." He struggled to go on, and I felt a surge of sympathy as he sat there in his neat flannel blazer, picking imaginary spots of lint from its lapels, his eyes averted from me. "It is said, or I am learning," he began again, "that you are—what?—*distratto, distrait*. . . ." He gave a mock-hearty chuckle. "Dis-*tracted*, isn't it?"

I stood and went to his office window: dead January, the prospect outside bleak as my own, but I could not find it in me to feel threatened. I tried hard to feel that way, anything to quell the recall of Anna's imitations of my colleague. I bit my lip to hide laughter, turning my back to hide the fact that I was, as they say, in the manly state. He would think me crazy—and wasn't I? The urge to laugh finally fell to a smile, my erection fallen too, and after several minutes I returned to his desk. Still smiling, I lied. "You are right. I've been careless. I'm working on something, and I'm not giving my classes enough thought."

At last he looked directly at me, returning my smile, which I suppose he took for one of pride in my own scholarship.

"Though we, too, are proud, Brant, to have here our scholars," he said, "we are as proud of the reputation—isn't it?—for the teaching that is here." He took my hand in both of his, exhaling.

It had been a painful interview. I had resorted to tricks against my own giggles, had imagined the rock visage of my father over his stiff collar; the death of my good pointer, Minnie; Anna leaving me. But for poor Fratti it must have been worse: he never called me in again, though I went blundering on, *distratto*. I babbled. I forgot the most commonplace French words. I proposed boggling grammatical rules.

One Wednesday I walked out of my so-called advanced class, having mumbled sentimentalities about Lamartine's "Le lac" for the full period, to ever denser silence from my students. I looked up from my feet to discover late spring. I'd arranged to meet Anna after dark, and, compared even to our first post-winter tryst on the golf links, tonight's would be downright balmy. The redbud beneath my classroom window was so swarmed with leaf and rotted bloom that I couldn't reconjure the face of Anna glancing briefly upward through its spare branches, as it had all the way back in October. I hold that instant more clearly now in mind than I wish I did, but it fled me just then. I stood, dizzy, heart palpitating, breath labored. I stared at the redbud. Judas tree.

"COULDN'T I *what?*" A chill in my soul, I asked it again.

"Couldn't you take a trip yourself?" she repeated, levelheaded, poised.

For an instant I tried to picture the slate ravines of a Rocky Mountain river, blackhawks riding its updrafts and screaming; steelheads struggling upstream from the north Pacific coast; summer Atlantic salmon running toward headwaters; bright gorse above a Scottish firth. All charged, quick images, but for one of the few times in my life I think I saw in my fly-fishing passion what others must see—a kind of bizarre quest, involving sacrifice, discomfort, meticulous care. All for the sake of water creatures, their brains the size of nailheads.

We had made love on the golf links again, under another full moon. Warm spring wind had pasted our hair to our scalps. She was urging me to travel. She had just announced her own intention to go to Paris with her husband from mid-June till the last of July.

"And what kind of a mess do you think Paris is now?" I tried to sound knowing.

"A mess?"

"So soon after the war." It was 1921.

"It's for my husband, really. He wants to see an old teacher who went back five years ago—some patriotic impulse, you know. The hour of the fatherland's need, and all that."

For an instant my heart leapt: "I'd like nothing better than for your husband to have that visit." I smiled significantly. "Let him go for as long as his little heart desires."

And Anna again: "Couldn't *you* take a trip?"

I wince to remember what I said, but I said it: "My heart wouldn't be in it."

She chuckled. "How's that?"

My heart, I explained, would be with her. This time she gave a little barking laugh, which terrified even as it angered me. But I was prepared to be hung for a sheep: "Don't you love me?" I asked. A whimper. The little town and the country beyond and the world were suddenly teetering on a perilous edge.

"I shouldn't dignify that question by answering it," she replied, "but as you very well know, the answer is yes."

Grateful, I reached for her. She stiffened: "The answer is, of course I love you, but since you seem determined to lose your head, one of us had better not."

The composure!

And then, speaking very slowly and deliberately (as if, I thought in a moment of bewilderment, she were mimicking the college president), she outlined all the advantages of the separation. Thrown together for a month and a half, she and the dean would be forced, as she put it, "to sort things out." The dean was devoted to the pettifoggery of his office; for the entire past year he had brought home stacks of paper and busied himself till midnight each evening. Anna had simply slipped out to meet me, had had no need to invent pretexts. He and she had been living completely disparate lives, each—thankfully—without the least notion of what the other did.

"In a sense," reasoned Anna, "our separation is already in progress."

The formality!

"Well . . ." I muttered, but she cut me off.

"We'll both see what I've known for a long time."

"Yes?"

"That we aren't of any use to one another."

"We?"

"My husband and I."

Did she mean, I asked, to tell him she was leaving while they were overseas? She did. Did she mean she'd come to me, that she'd tell her husband so? She did. Would she do it all soon, would she come home early, alone?

She deflected me: "We couldn't possibly stay here, of course."

"We don't have to stay here. I'll resign."

"And what about finding another position?"

"I don't *need* one, Anna. I have money." It was the first time I'd let on about this. She looked at me quizzically, perhaps, I thought, even resentfully. Did something turn here? Now I don't think so;

back then, I hurried to defend myself, explain it away, but again she cut me off.

"So much the better," she sighed, looking into the distance. The wind had matted her hair to her temples.

"How so?"

"For us," she explained, without, however, looking back to me.

5

THE college village took on a different character in the summer months back then, and under other circumstances I might have savored the emptiness, the quiet. I could imagine gradually working my way into the company of the old men gathered at dusk in the town square; they sat on benches as the last of the sun threw long easterly shadows behind them of courthouse, shade tree, pitted Confederate cannon. Small birds flitted back and forth in the twilight's coolness, chasing mosquitoes and gnats. Doves chortled sweetly from the eaves.

The men would pass a flask or bottle—without a sideward glance—along their ranks, squinting as they sipped. Several doubtless still felt the sting of defeat from six decades back, felt their long field hours, their anonymity, the disappointment, vocal or quiet, of snuff-streaked wives. And so they came here to drink their whiskey. As I walked within hearing I recall one leathery farmer's comment, offered to the air: "Now *that's* a jug with some time in it."

For what but time do the vanquished save?—the whiskey that has sat for a long spell, perhaps in the ruins of the family place; memories (many, I noticed, of hound and hunt and game); bygone characters, rough or gentle, skilled or awkward; weather; crops— stories in all.

I was very young, but I might have insinuated myself, learned something. Instead I passed them by, picking up a word here or there, insinuating myself, after half the summer, only enough that certain of the old folks would nod as I crossed the square.

I passed them moping, then passed the neat houses of the professors, rich compared to the clans squeezed into their shotgun shacks farther out. Night coming on, I walked more and more into open country, where the blacks lived. Where they *hid*. It wasn't lynching country, but on those long, depressed evening marches, I had the sense of a people sequestering themselves from pale me as well as from anything else. As though I were the demon against whom the bottle trees stood on each low knoll. I shiver even today as I think of the silver moonlight coruscations on the glass shards in the branches; of mule hair and mica and china fragments on a graveyard's crooked stones. Whiffs of resinous woodsmoke reached me from roadside cabins. Some sound would come and go inside an open door; I fancied a family—grandparents, parents, relatives, round-belly children—in a single dark room, motionless, speechless.

I knew I was watched.

One evening I jumped when a shape spoke softly to me. I had thought it was a stump, but a large old man, sitting on a stool by road's edge, addressed me: "Cap'n," he said, the deferential salute of the time. There is no sibilance in that word, yet it sounded like wind.

I'd always end at the rutted dirt lane beside the lakeside cottage, hearing the pinestraw shift as small animals scurried, hearing the clucks and exclamations of night fowl by the shore. I might have gone somewhere and fished hard, but I had not. For fear of missing Anna's return. For she would return at any moment—or so I literally prayed—and then I'd take a trip right enough: away with her, away from this alien place, its deserted streets and fields, its lonely dot of a campus. Even the students' horses had disappeared.

I was a wreck. I took a meal whenever I remembered to. I swung between bouts of whiskey euphoria and melancholy. There were times when I knew, as if by revelation, that she wouldn't come back. I thought of her steely will, how it might order life into shape and then annihilate it, like her drawings. I tried sometimes to take heart from that same willfulness: she had pledged to force a crisis with her husband. It would need more than that prig's objections to undo the resolve.

Wouldn't it?

Meanwhile, by the first of July, I had nothing to go on but an unsigned postcard:

> *Unbelievably hot. Soldiers, beggars, nasty*
> *Parisians or depressing. Writing from Lux Gardens.*
> *Wish you were here.*

Over and over I scrutinized the card front and back, for some encoded message. Nothing. All I could cling to was her wish for me to be there. And where did I wish myself?

There. Paris. The presence of her note—for all its noncommittal contents—seemed to call up the savors, the odors, of *there.* Spilled wine, sawdust, oyster shells, urine, and rotted orange peel, as if I'd been transported to one of those Left Bank *caves.* But no, I had willed this miasma into consciousness; she wasn't in it, nor was I. Instead I smelled the pitchy scents of southern summer, and she wasn't there either. The frying smells from the town's open kitchen windows: not there. The sweet-sour tang of compost and pig dung out in the backcountry. Not there.

Sometimes, too, I imagined Anna and her husband together, his gestures of romance—Montrachet in a bucket by the frayed table-cloth; a stub or two of candle; the bone-weary *patronne,* her place otherwise empty, looking pensively up at the wall clock. The dean's romance, his postures, failing. Mustn't they? But I could as easily imagine Anna in a lover's grip: a piece of moist bed linen balled in her fist, her teeth biting down on her lower lip, almost enough to make her bleed, and her gray eyes asquint with a look like pain. He would be doing things to her, his thigh compacting the loose skin of hers, so that it bunched and dimpled, and as he withdrew, their flesh would stick together, annealed by the sweat of the dank summer afternoon, despite the cat's paw that cuffed open a balcony door, revealing the corroded metalwork of the railing outside, admitting the squawk of birds in the market. Sunday.

The worst, the most unacceptable thought: the lover was her husband after all.

IT was a fight to swim up through the thick afternoon sleep, each breath a sedative, as if the warm air from my lungs went inward along my bloodways, bearing its drug.

This wasn't what I'd hoped for, the heart-stopping instant of reunion after long absence, fire in our eyes, flesh trembling. I could feel the disappointment, the lethargy under my relief that, at least and at last, she was here.

"Oh, darling! For God's sake, come in," I mumbled, blearily.

She'd come home only two days early after all. I thought the yellow jackets had awakened me, tapping against the screens in the heat. But it was Anna, flicking a fingernail on the window above my bed. How hopeless, how torpid, I must have looked.

I met her just inside to embrace her. Though it was gentle, a press of her wrists against my shoulders told me a change had come. Still weighted by slumber, I needed a moment or two to care. "I thought you'd never be back," I whispered, in truth.

"Behold me." She laughed, but not easily. Her laughter had always been rare enough that now it alarmed me. I longed for sleep again.

"And your husband?" I asked. Despite myself, I was awake.

"Back on Monday," she said, turning with a jaunty motion to inspect something on my shelf—a coin, a newspaper clipping, whatever. "He's spending the weekend with his mother in Asheville," she went on, the voice still offhand but loud, as if there were no news to disguise.

I spoke with false bluster myself. "How did he take it?" Perhaps if I treated our old plan as a *fait accompli* it would be one.

"Take it?"

"How did he take—us?"

"I'm afraid he's still in the dark about all that." *All that*—the words sounded too dismissive.

"I thought you were going—"

She cut me off. "Something's come up." The heartiness was gone; Anna knew she couldn't fool me. She looked at the floor.

We were in the dog days of a Deep South summer, but I felt winter in my soul. I walked deliberately to my hot plate, the way a drunk tries to walk a straight line. I turned a jet and struck a match. It went out. I struck another, shakily.

"Some tea?" I offered.

"No," she said. "I can't stay."

"Can't stay," I echoed. What obligations could she have, and why?

When I don't know how to respond, anger has a way of doing my thinking for me. Confusion stood aside to hear rage speak: "Oh yes! Something's come up!" She raised a hand, but my voice ripped onward: "The romance of Paris! Of course! The light! The deep, wonderful chimes of—"

"Brant!" she shouted. Then, more softly: "Please don't be a complete fool."

"I've already been *that*!" I spat, jostling the kettle, sloshing water down its sides. The burner hissed, its flame gone purple.

"Brant," she said—one word, her tone noncommittal.

I plowed on: "I suppose I should cheer the return of marital bliss."

She winced at my clumsy sarcasm, gathering words for a speech which she gave up immediately. She simply said, "I'm pregnant."

I dropped into a wicker armchair. The threadbare rug's oriental design doubled, rejoined, and doubled again in my stare, in my study. It was like the first response to news of a friend's sudden death, the response to a blow.

A dog, barking downstreet, brought me back. "It's mine!" I cried, full of sudden hope.

"His," she replied.

"How in hell could it be his?"

"Believe me, darling, since I lost the other, I've made a science of these things." If it was not irony, it was the old composure again.

"What did you do," I snarled, "study the entrails of Sorbonne students?"

She gave a huff of exasperation. "It's a simple matter," she said, "of reading a calendar."

She could always make me feel like a child; and sure enough, I heard my next words go pouty: "But I thought—I didn't know that you and he—"

She interrupted again: "Once a month only. It happened in March. I'm due on Christmas day." Everything so ordered.

"You wanted a baby."

"Very much."

In the next few moments I postured for another outburst; then for tenderness, or complaint, or question, or challenge. I marshaled words, swallowed them, and finally looked to the carpet again. The burgundies and ruined beiges swam.

What brought me back this time? Some unearthly sound. I'd never heard Anna weep, had never heard *anyone* weep as she did now. It began as the far-off rush of wind across a plain: it's still calm where you are, but even in the dark you can feel it coming, an immense soughing. Then the trees and grasses go mad.

She let me grasp her; she let me hold her for half an hour, grief or relief or joy or pain all rushing out of her—rolling, cresting, receding like a wave, then arriving again. She coughed; she choked and shuddered. I felt storm in the bone of her spine, in her small breasts against my stomach. Her saliva and tears coursed on my chest. But if it was fear or revulsion I felt, even as I murmured consoling small talk, it was not a physical kind. I wouldn't be able to name it for a while.

Another wave came. I clenched her through it and braced for the next. But as if she had watched the salt in an hourglass, Anna stopped her crying with that final tumult, as quickly as she had begun. She backed from my arms and said, "I have to go."

I was too stunned to react. I watched her leave, pushing the screen door, not looking around.

THAT night I would go myself—into the deepest country, farther, more aimlessly than I'd done all summer. If I was not wise in the world's ways, and I surely wasn't, neither was I a complete babe in the woods. How had Anna managed to persuade me that the child she carried could simply *not* be mine?

It didn't matter, either way. I knew that Anna and I were done for. And so that night I meant to revel in cancellation. I remember standing at the edge of a cypress swamp, thinking that inside it I could leave all light behind. I don't know what kept me from entering that snake-laden dreariness, except the sense that its muck would slow me. I meant to get to blackness by getting away, to walk forever, to pass beyond the humped mountains above her lake, to be where I couldn't look back on the glow of the wretched little town.

I even cursed the full moon when it rose. Under its beams I could see the incidentals of a world now repulsive: an opossum's smile among the windrows of a late mowing; a foul-odored black-snake glittering in the clay where a wheel had broken its spine. Bitterns bumped in the ditches—I leaned into those gullies, eyes wide, knowing the birds' reputation for pecking intruders blind. They didn't strike; they waddled off, heavy-bodied. Everywhere the drone of locusts, whose abandoned husks littered the tree trunks.

I broke into a reckless run, face starward like a possessed man's, till I caught a toe and sprawled. The red grit ground into my chin, and I ground it farther, howling, pressing my whole body against the road. But I wasn't gone: dogs bawled; they could hear my tumult from town. What could I do?

I could burn it all! I jumped to my feet, patted my pockets, imagining flames flying on the easterly breeze to the village. The parched grasses and softwoods of the plain would seethe with fire! I wanted the terrors of the earth.

My feet and my body turned, as if they had wills themselves. I made for her house.

THE brass knocker was a racket in the night, and the yard dogs took up again. Let them yammer, I thought. I rang again. Nothing. I moved to the back of the house, half-shouting my curses as I stumbled over loose flags. I saw that a single nail held the basement's scallop window to, but I broke a small pane with a kick anyway. Let them wake in panic upstairs. Let them *be* upstairs. Let all hell break loose, and let me be its devil. Pulling the nail out, I flung it against the fence behind me. It made a flat little whack and dropped clinking on the stone walk. I grabbed a shard of the glass and threw it: better. I heaved all the other glass I could find, then I dropped to the earth floor inside and groped toward the staircase, ears keen for a footfall upstairs. *Wanting* to hear one.

But at the landing I could smell abandonment, dead air; and along the kitchen corridor, dust hovered in the glimmer of dawn, flushed up by my movements.

She was surely gone. But even if I'd believed otherwise, I'd have done what I did, wandering, thinking: so this is *their* place. What does that mean, what *is* it? My anger was turning into overpowering mystification: I had never been here.

In their parlor a stopped ormolu mantel clock; a shelf of books, leather-bound sets of Meredith and some Scot's treatise on natural philosophy; a Princeton bachelor's degree; a portrait of his eating-club fellows covered in scrawled valedictory messages. Kickshaws, curios. A Turkish gem box with ivory inlay, a bad reproduction of David's *Horatii*, an oak-framed discharge from the Navy, needlepointed hassocks, a brass spittoon holding a dead zinnia. Again I looked for stairs.

I first passed a room so tiny it went by in a glance, its contents wrapped in the dark. Down the corridor I pushed into another— broken wooden chairs, rolled canvas, a derelict box spring. Retreating down the hall, I paused, sucking my teeth. Through the open door I could see, in a gleam now of real sunlight, that this was their bedroom, and that I'd be alone in it.

She was not there. Not there again. I sat on the bare mattress and ran my eyes over the place. What, if not her, was I looking for? Perhaps a drawing, one she might have saved? But no: the only picture on these walls was a water-stained daguerrotype—white horses snoozing in an ice wagon's traces. On the near side of the bed three cough lozenges, melted onto a table beside a library copy of illustrated essays on Holman Hunt, much overdue. On the opposite table a red-jacketed copy of *Tamburlaine the Great*, foils of tissue marking a page. Not a clue. I didn't even know which side was hers.

The day's heat was creeping under the window blinds, a dove was chanting. Just as a dove, one of the few recognizable birds, had sung that evening as we staggered down the lane to her cottage. "I could show you," she had said. "Show me then," I murmured, lips gummed.

I remember rising, as if with new purpose, whose occasion I cannot imagine; I went to inspect the room at the head of the stairs, closet-sized, stifling, windowless. Sweating, shaking, I found a lamp cord. I saw a pile of infant nightshirts, collapsed on a cot, the tiny round collars yellowed with age. Another image. I can see it now if I choose to.

I ran down, twisted the front door lock, and rushed into late July's sun.

The six o'clock alarm had run down when I reached my rooms. Why on earth had I set it? My hair matted with clay, chin raw from my fall, eyes red with fatigue, I muttered a greeting to my landlady as I shot by. Safe inside, I looked out at her, motionless under her clothesline, a gray sock in one hand. She squinted my way, the kind of person who had been well satisfied to hear my clock's bell go untended, and to witness my return, confirming her dear dark surmises. I pulled the shade.

My poor dog Minnie, abandoned, had fouled the apartment; I paid the mess no mind, fed her, forgot her. I could count my pulse in my teeth, in my calves. Again I had that queer sensation of studying things as if they were on display behind thick glass, as if my apartment were a tawdry museum: this is what a man was, how he surrounded himself—this was his woeful furniture, jerry-built bookshelf, coin-thin carpet, and folding bed.

I gave myself elementary instructions, as though addressing some lackey with little command of English: *Make coffee. Eat something. Wash your face.* The lackey followed the first command, scalding his tongue and cursing loudly—but he would not eat or wash. Instead, he knelt for a moment, as if in prayer. Then he sat heavily on the floor by his liquor cabinet; each of three bottles held an inch of liquid, as if the menial had resisted finishing any one bottle, had sought by that small restraint to prove his self-control. Well, the hell with it! In quick order he gulped bootleg gin, rum, and whiskey. Then he stood again and stumbled to his listing armchair.

I say *he.* It seemed as if some utter stranger had come to do these random things, and I to behold him. I stared across the room at the mirror and raised a hand from the chair's arm; the stranger raised his own and let it fall as I did, disgusted. I yawned, he yawned. I insulted him, and he mouthed my insults back.

And then our hooded eyes snapped wide. "The cottage!" we shouted, jumping up, flying through the door, nearly capsizing the landlady with her heaped basket of clothes as she lingered on the stoop outside.

If I had stayed in that chair, I'd have sunk into sleep. But I'd decided to find Anna out by the lake, sure she was there, in my certainty passing *through* exhaustion. I might march, if I wanted, to world's end, disembodied.

Here and there were the mad signs of the evening past. Another wheel had run over the putrid snake, and the crows had tugged at it. Its eyes looked like rice grains. Farther on, tracks along a ditch where a man had courted injury from huddled bitterns, where now he saw only a discarded work shoe. Then the turmoil in gravel, where he'd flailed on his stomach, where now a beetle was lugging some corpse.

"You look terrible."

I lifted my gaze from the road and its dated news. She was dismounting next to me.

"I've been all over," I breathed, my shoulders going slack, as if the worst were behind me. I made ready to tell her all about it, but I held off: let her wonder at those muddy meanderings through her house; let her husband wonder; let the shattered glass pierce them if it might.

"Brant."

"Anna."

There are details I can muster—where she put her bicycle, how we got behind the sod hill in a hot field, what she wore. They aren't important. My recall runs now to abstraction: when I bared it the subtle swell of her torso struck me as achingly sensual. Today it returns less as an aspect of Anna than as shape itself. I ran my filthy hand up and down her midsection, and I watched my fingers slide there, but no matter. Our act of love was passionate, vocal, almost angry in its heat—almost violent, for *this* was the real end. I knew it, I thought.

As we sat there, bug-strafed, stubble-pricked, covered with dust and the red streaks we'd painted in handling each other, my words were passionate, too, violently uttered. Useless exclamation, cliché—everything spiraling into the next thing.

Then, in a shock of bewilderment, I noticed her expression. It was as if, in hearing my mad banalities, Anna had been listening to something "interesting," had wanted to catch it all in full. I understood what I would do and was waiting the moment out.

She sighed shallowly: "Aren't we being a bit dramatic?"

I hit her.

She scarcely seemed to notice. I hit her again, harder. The whack was loud above the snoring insects in the grass. "Don't give me that calm-and-collected bit!" I spat.

"Oh?" she said, fingering the pink welt on her check almost casually.

I could imagine a bone breaking under my closed fist. "What about all winter?" I whispered. "All love and passion, and trying to start a child with that son of a bitch who—"

"Can't we for the love of God discuss this like—"

"Like *what*?" I snarled.

"Like reasonable, mature—"

"Oh Jesus Al*mighty*!" I raised my hand again. She seized it, kissing the knuckles; it fell back, open.

I watched her try to cover herself with bits of clothing, snatching each one up with quick little motions. So vulnerable, so patently improvising. I touched the rosy line on her cheek. I had loved her so much.

"I lost a baby once, Brant," she said. My softness vanished again, but she hurried on. "Seven years back," she said, her voice rising out of the whisper. "I wanted another. There wasn't anything in my marriage—"

"There still isn't!" I hissed.

"Wait." She put a hand to my lips. "I wanted another so badly. I tried and tried. Hoping can be a habit. I'd close my eyes when we were in bed and I'd see a baby."

"When *we* were in bed?" I challenged. Then suddenly I saw the two of us there, like naked savages on some savannah, and I laughed noisily. *In bed:* the silly politeness of euphemism.

"Of course not. Not when *we* were in bed," she said, unmindful. I remembered my rage, I came back.

"Well, just what did you picture when *we* were in bed?" I mocked her inflection.

She looked at me sadly: "Nothing, Brant. Nothing. I didn't need to."

"Oh, I see! One bed for passion, one for procreation. How neat. How reasonable. How *mature*!"

She raised her palms against me. "No. No. I just fixed on this child. I *dreamed* of him; I thought I knew him. A boy. It made sense to me. It made things make sense. Then you came along."

"How thoughtless of me," I sneered.

"Please. I'm trying to tell you. I wanted this child, and I wanted you. But I couldn't expect you to want him, and so I just went on, and I kept on. I was blind. It was—what?—Russian roulette. I wanted you and I wanted the baby, but I didn't like my marriage, and then we went to Paris, and I found out . . ."

It was her turn to run down. I let her go, the composed look vanished, the studied diction. Her turn to babble, mine to be the collected one. It would all be a kind of pointless formality, and I resolved to get it over as easily as I could, to say what was meant to be said: "Here's the plan. You'll have the baby *and* me. I have money. I'll just take you away."

"No," she answered. "I'm just not made like that." She looked off briefly across the field, then back at me: "Can't you *see*?"

She was suddenly the little girl who answers *because* when you ask her *why*. She had no self. The truth of it finally reached me: she was an impersonator.

6

I THINK of this now and I feel an old chill. Surely we all invent ourselves in some measure, but now I believe such fabrications must somehow connect with a substance, whatever it is, in the murky depths of our real characters, whatever they are. I don't quite know even yet what this means, but back then I recognized that if I might be a fraud, I was more genuine than this woman who stammered before me. My world was full of improvisation, but less so than hers.

In that instant I convinced myself that to live without her was to be well spared, that her hollowness would be, perhaps had already been, a kind of contagion. I haven't again felt quite so certain about this as I did on that small earthen hill. But sitting there in 1921, I was ready to laugh again: Look at us! Listen to this stupid debate in a summer field, bare to the eye of heaven. See her put on her ridiculous clothes. See me here, a grimy Buddha, haloed by furious gnats. I took my disenchantment for a sign of the freedom to come.

Those nine months at the college, I'd reeled through my days like a lost child. Enough and an end of it! Hell, I said to myself, she's no more composed than I am—I, who knew and had known for a long time that I had no mastery of my life. Out of which, as the saying goes, she walked. With her long slow loping strides.

I WENT to her husband's office the next day and resigned. The dean stood and sniffed, emphatically, several times, his wisps of sandy brow lowered. "The semester starts in just over a month."

"I know," I answered.

"I'm certain you do." The tone was gruff, but he didn't meet my eyes. He slouched in his swivel chair, turning his profile to me. The brush mustache worked up and down as he sucked his teeth.

After a moment he tugged on an ear and rose from the chair, drawing himself to his full gangling height. "Rather short notice," he intoned. "Bound to play hell with the schedule." He pronounced that last word in the English manner—*shedgel*.

As in my interview with Fratti, I bit my lip to ward off laughter. It was the solemnity of petty officialdom, which always has that effect on me, but my expression must have struck him as nervous. He took heart, looked me directly in the face, and announced that my quitting was "most irregular."

He cast down his eyes again when he saw my broad smile. A demon was prompting me to trot out my one good imitation or to fill the dean in on the year just past. The wretched paintings on his office wall seemed to float back and forth in my vision; I was giddy with the temptation. What would his face do, what would he say?

But no. However much I wanted to recite my saga of desire to someone, he wasn't the one.

RESOURCELESS, I made my way back to Boston, where I found that other recitations had understandably come into vogue. Our soldiers had been demobilized, and I sat through long nights with some of them. I, the outsider, had obeyed Wilson's summons to democracy's salvation, only to have the army doctors dismiss me from consideration because of a spot on my lung, one that my own physician wrote off, rightly, to childhood whooping cough. In any case, I would be no use to the national effort, would miss the mammoth conflict, just as it seemed I would go on missing everything.

My old undergraduate crowd met every Thursday evening at Benton's elegant speakeasy to trade accounts of life on the various fronts. We were a discreet bunch, well dressed, well mannered, and young, though I recall a kind of wonderment that these men were the college chums I'd been friendly with so shortly before. We drank a shocking lot of brandy, I guess, but our conversations remained in the main as polite as the tinkling piano by the far windows on Charles Street: a coat-and-tie crowd, for the most part, precociously earnest and somber.

The soldiers had good reason for the somberness. It was the first war, more than the next, that changed the world. I could read it in their faces better than I had in the *Globe*'s newsprint, better than in the photographs so lately seen in the weeklies.

A person passing by would have had no reason to single me out. Yet what could my function be, other than to ask questions, open the floodgates of anecdote and reminiscence, smile blandly at the occasional trench humor? They were my friends, I would have said, but they had gone, I had stayed, we were different. Out of all that pain and chaos in Europe, they had constructed narratives to make life cohere as it could. I had hunted and fished, and would go on doing so, even as some of them, old gladiators by then, would manage to re-enlist; even as certain among them would be blown from the earth, along with their war stories.

7

TODAY I'm ashamed to think that in those evenings at Benton's club I truly believed I'd been through something like battle myself. I don't remember feeling such shame, though, on that morning in 1950: my mind was too crowded by the rush of associations occasioned by Louis's story of passion. The story had made some things clear—it had explained Johnny's rage, for instance. It seemed, though, to have muddied a lot else, and it had set me seething, there by my campfire, in my favorite place.

Then I had it.

I leapt from my chair, as if bee-stung.

I'd had no one to tell.

When I had been foundering, Anna gone, my own passion unfocused; when I was bursting with the need to disburden myself, to testify, to discover a sympathetic ear—there had been no one.

I hadn't known it till that very instant, but it was an old agony and confusion that had swept me again as I'd heard Louis tell me of Velma.

No one to hear me.

Leaving the professor's life, I had thought to come "home." I'd taken a new apartment in the Back Bay, and had begun the stewardship of my modest inheritance. I had written my first and last poems, each at its maudlin, dense center a lament for the Lost Southern Love, had published five of the obscurest in a thin journal edited by a Bohemian lady friend of my late parents, and had given up the literary life right after, mortified to read my own scribblings. But I'd needed to so *something*, I suppose. I'd had no better way to purge the thing. Unlike my supposed friend, Louis McLean.

I remember how I raced to my woodshed, hauling down a tumble of logs from their pile and whacking them to shingles with the double-bitted ax. Maybe I chopped into the memory of Anna, trying to sliver that haunt into nothingness. That would make a kind of sense. But I know I saw Louis's face, too, as the chips flew. I'd had Anna and lost her, with no means of testimony. Louis, losing Velma, might have had a confidant in me. Yet he hadn't said a thing, and then not much, till Johnny Morse's beating had prompted him to, all this while later. And I, old fool, had up till then believed us the closest of friends.

NEXT morning I beat the alarm awake, nervy, unrested. I wasn't hungry, so I made a pot of coffee and took my cup out to the ledge. I sat contemplating the broad current above Big Falls. I had always thought the McLean a permanence in my life, but today it seemed that each fleck of foam, boiling in the rapids, was a gloomy icon. The surge of water was an uninterrupted and useless utterance.

The first birds began. Little skipper trout above the break splashed at bugs, or maybe at nymphs just under the surface—it was still too dark to tell. My osprey came by upriver, wingbeats silent, and faded into the obscurity northward. A mink darted out from behind his boulder on the far shore, patrolled around it once, shot back under cover as I heaved a rock at him. It was the finest time of day, all right, but it damned well didn't feel it.

Somehow I knew to turn so Louis wouldn't catch me. There he was, still not out of the woods at the end of my drive.

He walked up, miffed, I thought, at having his stalk detected. "What do you see?" he asked, standing beside me and looking out to the stream.

"Not much."

"Not much doing this time of day," he commented. I turned my back, positioned the chair toward the river, sat again.

"How's the coffee holding up?" he inquired.

"Well, why don't you go in and find out?" I said. I could feel him looking at me, wondering what was bothering the old man. He shuffled off, though, and returned with Old Bluey.

I kept my mouth shut till, after a minute or so, Louis broke the silence: "Party with Warren took a hell of a bass yesterday," he began.

"To hell with a bass," I growled. "Dumb bastards." I kept watching the river.

We fell quiet again, stone quiet. A Canada jay lit at the tip of the ledge, five feet from us, cocked his head, then hopped forward, between our chairs. I kicked at him. Louis grunted. I waited at least another full minute before I asked him, "Ever think of Morse's wife now, Louis?" I made myself call her that.

"Now and again."

"*What* do you think?" I twisted to face him.

"I told you yesterday," he said, peering up at the jay, who had fluttered onto a low branch.

"You told me about some goddamn blueberry, some fish hawks, some flick in the sack at George Bailey's camp. That's *it*?"

"I don't know—" he began.

"Don't start with that crap!" I snapped, lurching around in my chair to stare at him, hard. The bruises in my rib cage burned like coals.

Louis put Old Bluey on the flat arm of his chair and bent forward over his knees. Breathing heavily, he began to pluck the heads off shoots of long grass.

"That's it?" I repeated. He kept picking at the stems, whistling through his teeth, more like a hiss. His lips probably still hurt.

"Doesn't sound like much to me," I plowed on.

Louis looked up, his stare full of menace, his whistle stopped dead. Perhaps we weren't friends. I studied him for a long moment, his eyes narrowed, the crow's-feet and laugh wrinkles gathered, his jug ears like bristles on either side of his face, and his neck tendons showing. I was the one to blink, leaning over to relace the top three eyes of a boot. I could hear him breathing again.

There was a small inside voice that kept trying to interrupt me, to get in the way of the reckless anger. But I wouldn't hear it out, not till later. I felt it coming. For the first time I was going to hide behind rank: Louis knew a good thing; I had nothing to be afraid of; he wouldn't lose his job for the satisfaction of beating an old man.

I peeked over at him, a little more cautiously than I wanted, and this time he was the one to look away, upriver. A trio of sheldrakes was splashing around at the head of the pool; the sunlight caught the sheen of the males' heads. Two men squabbling over one woman, probably. Louis took a great final breath, held it a moment, then let it out in a rattle of small snorts, like a buck deer blowing.

"Courting time, I guess." I nodded at the ducks, spoke quickly, because I'd changed my mind about this talk after all. Too late.

"Better get a new man, Brant."

"Yes?" I asked.

"That's right. I just got done." I'd been wrong about the job. I got mad all over again.

"I'll get my checkbook," I announced, rising.

"Truth is," said Louis, "I don't want your fucking money."

I waited till he'd disappeared into the alder run. "Good riddance," I said, but the words came out unsteady.

I'D fish, by God, I thought. That's what I'd come here to do, wasn't it?

I took a spade, carried our spoiled Mauve brook trout out past the outhouse, and dug a hole about a foot deep. I lay the fish in the trench, all its bright hues neutral now, its eye flat. Sad. But if I wanted visitors, they wouldn't be skunks, or coons, or bears.

I didn't know what the rift with Louis meant to me, whether it had a remedy, whether I wanted one. But that inside voice wouldn't leave me peaceful. You let him down, too, it said. In your own way. The voice wasn't talking just about the fight, either, and not even about my nasty comments a moment before. I knew that.

But, I protested, that business with Anna was so long ago.

Yes, came the answer, and it lives on. It's you—partly, anyhow. What had I done?

WAS it not enough that Louis had been my partner in a kind of companionship that so often seemed not to *need* words, explanation, justification? I'm not talking the kind of crap you read in the sports magazines, clichéd rhapsodies on the Sportsman's Code. There *is* such a code, but most of it is inarticulable; there's a way you can hunt or fish so long with a friend that articulation's not an issue. That's part of the point.

As I came back to my ledge the three sheldrakes flushed from the surface upstream, winging low to the water toward me. I raised my imaginary shotgun and swung on the lead bird. Left-handed, my natural swing, the opposite from Louis's. For years, tramping the draws and ridges after grouse, he'd covered to the left of the dog, I to the other side, so that I almost felt a physical pull on my body if we momentarily switched positions. We didn't say a word, but I knew he felt the same pull; we'd cross without a signal back to where we each belonged. And when the dog came on point Louis knew where he needed to be to get a clear shot if the bird busted out his way; I knew where I needed to be. He knew I knew he knew, and the other way around.

We never said a word; we just got there. And when one of us brought the bird down with a papery crash, the other would say, "Good *boy!*" Always. How to comment on, how define the satisfaction and love in such a dumb oath, in such a place, when the world makes something clear about *itself,* no help needed? A plain mystery, and a mystery made plain.

I had tied more flies than a man could use if a hundred hatches came off at once, but I went back to my vise and pliers. What else might I do till fishing time? Ten minutes hadn't gone by, and I'd come from rage at small talk to recalling it with a glow.

At eight o'clock in the evening I looked up, fingers cramped and back on fire from my meticulous labor, dry flies heaped like drifted snow on the plank table. I gazed out at the river. I could tell from where I sat that those were Hendricksons towering out of the camp pool. It had been very mild all afternoon, and the water had needed to cool down a few degrees. It was the kind of moment my mind plays over and over, that hour in spring before full dusk when the ground birds are restless, when the nighthawks veer back and forth overhead in anticipation, and a pregnant stillness creeps into the air above the flow. You can feel something.

I watched the early stages from inside, stringing my rod, then sorting the Pheasant Tails in my fly box. I selected a number sixteen, dressed as sparsely as possible, a still-water fly, one hackle. You could get away with a single hackle even in heavy water if you used one of Johnny's, as I was doing—I had no choice. I got the tippet through the hook's eye after several tries. The air was full of flies. The fish were rolling in the camp pool. Louis was vanished. I had more than enough cause to be shaky.

I pulled a bandanna from the closet, wet it with bug repellent, and tied it around my neck. I grunted into my waders and put on a vest. Squirting another line of dope on the underbrim of my hat, I put it on too. I slipped the cellophane off a big cheap cigar and lit it, then dropped a bottle of ale into my creel.

The mayflies crowded past me in the breeze. Everything aloft was chasing them, into the wind. It was still early enough that a dragonfly was hunting; I flinched as he grabbed a dun just before me at eye level—*click*! Like the pulse in a charged fence.

Small trout were slapping the water in undisciplined rises. I picked one out to sharpen my eye, shuffled through the shallows below my ledge, checked for eddies, dropped the Pheasant Tail six feet above him. It rode high and sure; the fish took, tail-walked like a miniature bass toward the near shore. I played him in an instant, not to exhaust him, reached in and grasped the shaft of the hook to let him wiggle free. He lay finning for a moment after I released him, right at my feet; I moved a boot, and he darted out of sight.

Shaking off, he had slightly bent the curve of the hook. I held up the fly and began to squeeze it back into shape.

Whoomp.

A good one. I saw his ripples pass the lip of the falls and break up. I'd put on a new fly. The Lord knew I had plenty. I wouldn't take chances: I went up a size on the Pheasant Tail and cut back my tippet. As dark came I could risk the stouter gear, the trout's backdrop of sky dulling with every minute as he looked up.

Whoomp. I marked him: two feet upstream from a whitish rock across from me, about three out from the bank. A yard and a half above his feeding station an alder leaned low over the current; I'd have to cast beyond it, throwing a lot of slack so my fly would drift under the sapling. It mustn't drag. You need a long float for a big trout.

Whoomp.

I dropped the cigar; it hissed and slid over the falls. My knees quivered as I stepped quietly back into the river. Like when the dog used to go on point. How many times, I'd wonder, have I walked past a point to flush a hidden grouse? But I was always all nerves, my heart pounding, ears pricked for the quick bird's explosion. Every leaf and stone and bush seemed etched, perfect. And the same as I studied a big brown's rise: how often must I have done so? Yet here I was again, quaking, unblinking, watching the lie, single-minded, the world confined by a sapling and a stone. Three square yards.

The small ones still flipped in the shallows close around me. "Little bits of bastards!" Louis used to say. "Where the hell's a decent fish?"

Whoomp.

"*There's* a decent fish," I answered out loud, inching toward him, water rising to my waist. I imagined Louis, impatient, doing the same thing, but too quickly, putting the big brown down. Had I done so myself? No: the trout came again, and he was a *hell* of a decent one, as good as any I'd ever seen in that pool.

I made a practice cast, a few feet short, to watch the float. It looked all right.

Whoomp whoomp whoomp.

Now he was as active as he'd get; time to try him. I stripped two more big loops off the reel, snapped some false casts to dry the fly, then released a loop at a time, aiming above the bent alder. I checked the last cast, leaving six or seven feet of slack, to be sure the fly wouldn't skitter across the river just as it reached his window. It sailed smoothly under the trunk and branches, and I leaned forward, switching the rod from right to left hand, extending my arm. The fly was on top of him now, and I stared at the surface. The fish should come; I had a lot of faith in that little Pheasant Tail.

Splash! The trout cocked his broad tail and slapped at the end of my leader.

"Goddamn fly's too big!" I cursed aloud, angry not to have stayed with the size sixteen. Once a fish makes that move, humping his back and slashing at the lure with his hind end as if annoyed by its presence—once he's done that, he usually won't look again. I watched for several minutes, then turned upstream, to the larger world that had been there right along. I was a little disgusted with myself. The fish would be here all summer, of course, but it was unusual for one this big to be rising so freely to surface bugs. Oh God, I prayed, give me another hatch this good!

I pulled my hat brim down to blot out the last glare of sky, and tried to see another promising swirl as the swarm of mayflies thinned. It had been a quick hatch. I stood with reeled line, left hand holding the fly and tippet out of water. A beaver climbed up on the east bank, changed his mind, and got back in the swim, crossing again to the west, giving up some latitude in the current. It took him a minute.

Whoomp.

"Well, I'll be damned!" My words sounded louder; the dark had fallen with a swoop. The hatch all but over, I could just see the mayflies' shucked cases drift against my waders, spin, float free toward the falls. All done. The birds were gone, the breeze stilled, just a few quick bats pivoting in the gloom.

But my trout was still hungry.

I squinted to find the dead alder upstream from his lie. I couldn't see it, couldn't even make out the white marker rock. I'd have to trust to luck.

Whoomp. Louis liked to call it sound-fishing. Nothing to see, so you listen hard and you do some guessing. I pulled off a few cranks of line, cast it directly upstream into a narrow belt of light at the river's center. Then I ripped it from the surface so I could see how much I'd stripped in the dark. I compared it to what I thought I'd need to reach the big brown, and listened for his next rise. It came. I made my cast, and when I heard him sip again, I set the hook.

He shook his head a moment, as if puzzled, stationary. I took my slack back onto the reel. I still had on the 4X leader; I could boss him some if he tried to dive under the bank. I'd keep him taut, so it would be a surge if he made that rush, not a jerk.

Sure enough, now he bulled toward the undercut and I bulled back. It was risky to hold him so, but if he got in among the roots and rocks it'd be over. He came out, upstream. Good.

Picking my way, I waded farther toward him. The water rose above my midriff, a drop or two splashing over, chilling. I could feel the river's drive against me, but I wanted to get outside the trout, to scare him back into the shallows on the camp side. We were both in midstream, and at this angle I could just see the small

V the current made, breaking on my line: the brown was sulking, yawing back and forth no more than half a foot at a time. He made one more little run at the far bank after a minute, but I raised the rod tip the other way and brought him back.

Slowly he began to sink downstream toward me. I had to get him out of the deep stuff: I kept working him, working him, working him by inches over to the campside shallows. I reeled carefully. My body worked its way back too: I could feel my heart again; I could hear the water. He was dropping backwards, tail-first, his runs just feints now. His dorsal broke the surface once or twice. I would have him.

The crucial moment was at hand, when you have to reel the butt of the leader through the rod's top guide. Was he played out? I couldn't risk another good burst from him then. If the butt bound on the guide, the smallest final rush would break him off. I thought to let him fight the current for another minute or so, but on the other hand I wanted him to have enough left to keep himself upright when I released him. I wanted him to recover when I let go.

I stood there debating with myself. I didn't even have to hold him now; not to speak of. He was a minute vibration on my bent rod's line, a bizarre tap-tap from great Elsewhere.

He was too quick for me to respond. With a final explosion of will, he turned and dashed downstream between me and the ledge. There was only half a foot of water in that sluice, and I could hear a hum as his upper parts flashed past in the sudden moon, like a shark's.

He was below me now, in the deep part of the riff. Maybe I could hold him steady, feel my way downstream along the bank, come up again from behind. He was stuck—I didn't think he'd drop through Big Falls. He had some sense after all—he wouldn't have gotten that big without it. He knew he was exhausted. Exhausted enough, too, that he wouldn't swim back up through the rapids.

I made for the bank, the sweat cooling on the nape of my neck. I felt older all of a sudden; I didn't want to be tripping around in the middle of that white water. Not in the dark, moon or no moon. I stopped above the rapids and began to horse him toward me. I knew it wouldn't work; I knew it was over.

I reeled in, fly and all.

I was sure I'd never been into such a trout on the dry fly. I put my rod deliberately up on its pegs in the camp and rolled fifteen feet of line onto the dryer. I thumped into the kitchen, a runnel of river water behind me, and fired the coffeepot. Then I stepped back outside, hooked my heels in the jack, and drew off my waders. Watching the tumble of the falls in the moonlit air, I peed, shivering, in the campyard. Then I went back inside, put on my jacket, dry pants, wool socks, and moccasins. I lifted down the jug and returned to the kitchen. I filled half a cup with tarry old coffee, the other half with bourbon.

"To sweeten it up," I explained to no one.

I took a big yank at the whiskey-and-coffee mixture. Years back, I'd have sat there in solemn rage, replaying it all, cursing myself for screwing things up at the end. For ruining a story. But I was old. The fish had gotten away, God bless him. If he'd gotten away, well, lots of other things had gotten away.

"To the big brown trout," I said, raising my cup and drinking to the dregs, toasting him. Alone.

8

THE ones that escape have a famous way of growing in memory. Almost twenty years old now, that episode with the lunker brown. But that was a fish, that was a battle! It stays with me, and so does the other battle, even more vividly.

That evening I didn't stop with spiked coffee, but knocked down the bottle a little farther than I intended to. I meant not to think of Louis. I meant to stay busy. I meant to get up early. I didn't expect any action on the river at dawn, but I didn't plan to sit on my ledge and think all day again, or to tie another bunch of unneeded flies. I'd be at it.

Past midnight, despite myself, I did tie a couple of good-looking attractors, using fine silver wire wrapped over a herl from a blue heron I'd found dead some time back by the Big Eddy. I told myself I might beat up a fish with one. Then I tumbled into bed fully clothed, reasoning that I'd save a little time, gain some extra sleep, if I didn't have to dress in the morning. All this I did as I sat on the edge of my cot, too drunk even to fiddle with belt and shoes.

At about two-thirty I jackknifed to a sitting position. The dream was of the biggest salmon I'd ever seen, and by God I had him on! He was too much fish for me to act proud: I yelled at Louis to grab the gaff and get below me. But I couldn't seem to work the salmon in close enough at the Black Pool's tail. Louis was wading deeper and deeper, and of course he couldn't swim. I had to call him off. It was a fish all right, a hell of a fish, but I'd

rather lose him than Louis. I'd give him a long line, let him slip
one pool down, try to kill him there. Louis read my mind, fought
his way back ashore, then started off, stumbling downriver over
the grapefruit rocks.

The line I gave was *too* long. I saw the silver flash off the reel's
spindle, all but my last few yards of backing let out. The salmon
sounded in the deepest part of the whole river, made one great
splendid rush to the surface, putting all that drag on my gear, and
dropped free back into the current.

"Better the fish than Louis." I spoke to no one, aloud and rueful
in the dark.

The leathers in my pump were getting old and dry, so that now
and then—just as sleep seemed ready to come over me again—I'd
hear a little sigh of air in the kitchen, like some other troubled
sleeper's. There was no regularity to the noise, so I couldn't incor-
porate it into all the age-old insomniac games: counting sheep,
logs, or merely numbers; it would come between leaps and sawings
and digits, and, the more I was irked by it, the more the insomnia
gained on me. I looked over the meager collection of magazines
and books on my headboard shelf, but I couldn't concentrate. I was
still fighting with the anger that had possessed me earlier. No, I
was fighting with the way it had taken me over. Its disproportion
shocked me.

I shuffled through the stuff on my shelf again, finding a copy of
Carlyle's *Past and Present,* which I remembered buying on one of
my Scottish sorties an age ago. Had I read it since? I couldn't say.
But I did call to mind some of the old raver's terminology, and I
wondered if I hadn't behaved like one of his mammonites, whose
relations are based on the cash nexus. I thought of my Winchester
Model 21, my Leonard rods, my perfect hackles from Johnny
Morse, and I pictured Louis wading bare-legged in the McLean or
shooting that godawful Marlin over-and-under sixteen gauge. But
all this was only a small part of my torment.

I remember seeing the clock reach four. I felt too old, had let
myself get too drunk to get up in an hour and a half for a fish. I
fought to my feet and headed across the room to push down the
alarm's pin. Then I stopped in my tracks. I had made a wacky
mental progression: alcohol—alarm clock—Stubby White. I was

too old for a trout at five-thirty, but I'd get up by God for Louis. Better him than the fish.

"STUBBY White was well liked," Louis had said. I sat there on my rumpled bed and told the story to myself, silent, hearing his voice. "Everybody liked him," I could hear him say, "but he had a little bunch on his shoulder, which you'd call a hunch-back."

I laughed aloud. Poor Stub.

"And the other trouble was, he couldn't tell time. That's what raised the devil. The boys would take his alarm clock. He always carried it with him, and he'd put it somewhere when he was cutting. He got his daughter to fix it for lunchtime. The boys would take that clock when he wasn't looking, and set it just anyhow—ten in the morning, four in the afternoon—it didn't matter. Never lunch, though. Old Stubby! He never knew what time it was."

I could see Louis, his shoulder cocked, an imaginary alarm clock in his hand, a bemused expression on his face. There, in the middle of the night in my tiny camp, I dwelt for a moment on the fact that Louis had my old lover Anna's gift for impersonation.

Why would a man find *acting* so attractive?

I'd think that through another time, I pledged. I wasn't up to it now. My head was throbbing, and this little detour had flushed so many rabbits in the woods that for a moment I felt I might keel over on the floor. I was sweating, my breath shallow. Just the booze, just the booze, I tried to reassure myself. But in that second or so it was as if the very bed, the floor of the camp, and the ledge underneath were about to yawn open and let me fall forever. I wondered if even this physical world, this one solid little chunk in my life, was somehow *composed* of falsehood and deception. I made myself go back to the story.

"Old Robbie Ross ran the store," said Louis, "and he was an awful drinker. You'd see him slicing salami up on the counter, and soon as he cuts a piece his cat's up there and drags it off somewhere. He makes a swop at him: 'Go 'way, kitty!' "

I savored the details of Louis's digressions, the way he'd clutter a narrative with them, accumulating so many, wandering so far afield, I thought he'd never get back.

"Red Loughlin came in one day with some butter he had from Robbie. 'This butter tastes of the cow,' he says. And Robbie says, 'What in Christ do you think it'll taste of, the *bull*?' Oh, he was a miserable bastard."

Robbie Ross had had a cleft palate and a harelip. I'd been told by the old-timers that Louis mimicked his diction exactly, though he'd never seen Robbie; Edward had run the store since before Louis was born. When they heard this yarn, then, Louis's listeners were in the presence of art, not history. Or perhaps at some point they merge.

"Robbie lived at Little Falls with this Mrs. Spencer, and she was more miserable than he was. They had these parties, you know, and they'd get into the home brew, and then the fur would certainly fly."

I can't give Louis's moves and grimaces, the very things that turned a platitude like flying fur into comic genius. I should have bankrolled a movie long ago. It could have been done.

"One night Mrs. Spencer gets ugly and picks up an alarm clock. She wings it at Robbie, takes him right over the eye.

"So the next day he's sitting in the store with a big bandage on his face, and who comes in? Stubby White. 'What time is it, Robbie?' Stub says.

"Robbie says, 'What?'

"Stubby says, 'What *time* is it?'

"And Robbie looks at him and says, 'You go to hell, you humpback son of a bitch!' "

WHEN I got to the guides' lockers at the landing, Heath told me I was too late; Louis had already headed out with his party. Just two nights before I'd watched Heath fall out of Johnny's truck, but it was clear he didn't remember the brawl now. He probably didn't even remember being at Biscuit's.

"Christ, there was about *ten* of them," he said now. "All in a Christly big yacht!"

I felt like hell. Gone again. Well, I thought remorsefully, I guess he figures he has to make a living somehow now.

"Great big long thing. Jesus Christ!" Murray suddenly chimed in. I supposed it was one of the new powerboats that the bassers dragged in. They weren't so common in the fifties as they are nowadays. And I supposed that there were about four or five fishermen, because Heath and Murray made a habit of exaggeration; it was how they spent their time, hanging out by the landing, spouting local color. I felt a moment of resentment. I wasn't some damn tourist, after all.

The two drunks were sitting on a railroad tie playing cribbage and drinking vanilla. Edward had begun to sell beer and wine then, but Heath and Murray stuck to the old ways. It was a wonder, I thought, they could live and breathe.

"Want a little tap, Brant?" Murray spoke. I felt my hackles go down, and I gave a wan smile. What the hell? It was sociable. I was hung over, and maybe it would settle me. I wiped my hat across the neck of the vanilla bottle and tipped it. The liquor burned all the way down. I knelt and scooped a handful of lake water to chase it.

"Thanks, gents," I said.

A drake loon, half tame from being fed dead shiners at evening when the guides dumped their bait buckets, chortled briefly. Murray looked over at Heath: "Laughing at *you*, you son of a whore," he said. He was winning the cribbage game.

"Never mind him," said Heath, turning blearily to me. "After the fish, Brant?"

"After the fish," I said.

"Doing 'em any harm?" Heath had been one hell of a salmon fisherman back when he was a kid, before the liquor ganged up on him. He could cast right down to the backing, and I remembered the huge forearm on his rod side, like a bricklayer's. I looked, but his sleeves were down, for all the morning's summer warmth; a gray cuff of long john poked out of each one.

"Well," I began, "last night . . ." But I wasn't going to sit around swapping fish stories with a couple of old roughnecks who wouldn't remember I'd been there five minutes after I left.

"Went down last night, but couldn't fool one," I said.

"Getting used up, Brant," said Murray.

"Been here since Nineteen-Froze-to-Death," added Heath.

I looked at them, bristling again, then calmed. "Used up," I agreed, recalling how I'd bounced off Johnny, how his one elbow had lifted me.

I walked over to the locker row. It was a low white shed with numbered green doors. Each locker was about five-by-five—good enough to stow paddles, motors, fishing stuff, gasoline. It had its own odor of gas fumes, wet canvas, fish scales. I liked the smell, for all of me. Louis was number three: I wrote a note telling him to come down for a drink, folded it, and stuck it in his padlock. I looked over at Heath and Murray, but they'd already forgotten about me. I ambled back to the Buick and slid onto the seat. It was good and hot now, and a cloud of blackflies followed me in, herding themselves against the windshield and dancing on the glass. It's the one good thing you can say about a blackfly. He won't bite you indoors.

I got as far as Bill Ware's bait tank on the canal before I turned around and drove back to the lockers. I would come again at evening and wait; I'd invite Louis man to man. I crumpled the note and threw it into the barrel, among the bottles that Heath and Murray had dumped there. Then I drove home to pass a long day.

You take a log and brace it against another, set perpendicular, with a foot. Then you swing down hard, flicking the blade sideways just as it hits the wood in order to throw the split, to keep the bit from binding, and to prevent cutting your own toe. It sounds dangerous, but it's not; not if you know how. I learned the technique fairly late in life, from an expert, Louis. Whose salt was in the handle of the ax I used.

I scratched a redhead match on the fireplace and lit a curl of birchbark, dropping it in. Then I lay one split of cedar slowly after another on top, building the blaze as I went, like Louis. In three minutes' time I had a nice kindling, so I went back and got the hardwood, a lot of it. I was making a big fire for some reason, or for none at all. There I stood for a good spell, kicking a log here, lifting another there. I like to fool with a fire too. I love it when the draft is all just right, and the wood is dry, and the kindling is wild, and the whole thing takes off. Love it.

Once the fire got beyond even the remotest excuse for further fiddling on my part, I simply beheld it, the tiny red ants pouring out of one log to escape, the wisps of bark curling up quickly and puffing into flame, the skinnier splits breaking into squares that would tumble to the fireplace floor as coals. I stepped forward at one point and yelped. My pants legs had gotten hot, and they burned my shins when I moved. I retreated four feet and let them cool, then went inside and peeked into the icebox. I brought out a pork chop and slid it into a basket broiler, which I propped in front of the fire, its handle resting on the piece of grader blade I had laid across the fireplace's arms. I would turn the meat in eight or ten minutes, and would have a meal in fifteen. The fat started to drop right away, sizzling in the ash. It smelled good, but I threw the chop away.

I drew one of Louis's half-collapsed chairs out to the ledge, the same one I'd sat in the morning before. The bugs were too bad, so I dragged it back to the fire. I had an idea. I got as close to the coals as I could; I wrote three checks to cover some bills and stuck them in envelopes. It was a hot day, and I was soon sweating.

I took off my shirt and trousers. Old wet bag of gut!

I waited till I was wet all over, then half-trotted down to the alder run below camp, where I took a frigid stand-up bath, at the mercy of the deerflies. A turtle heard me shiver and yelp; he labored out of the thicket.

"Go to hell, you humpback son of a bitch!" I shouted, laughing.

I STOOD off till Louis's party had settled up. He had seen me at the landing, but he shuffled back and forth between the Chris-Craft and his locker, ignoring me, carrying small loads of this and that. There was a smear of what looked like oil on the sleeve of his T-shirt; I couldn't tell in the light. The evening sun was throwing a long shadow off the locker shed.

One of his men walked by me to get his car, a fat fellow in cutoff Levis and no shirt, about thirty. I felt a little better seeing the milky folds of his belly lying over his belt buckle, streaked with red from the day's heat. He wore a cap with *Bass Chaser* inscribed on the visor. He backed his station wagon down to the shore and got out. Three other sports were waiting for him, and one immediately got into the car, leaned over and came up with a can of beer. I saw him through the rear window—a tall and muscular boy with a mean-looking scratch on his jaw and a shiner. He caught me studying him and glared. Probably took a little fall today, I mused. Probably went a little heavy on the drinks. I looked away.

The fat man was wrestling a wallet from his pocket. He handed several bills to Louis as his companions winched the metal boat onto the trailer. Then they all got into the station wagon and bumped away from the landing. They turned left at Bill's bait trap, spinning in the gravel, the big boat fishtailing, heading out of town. Loud shouts spilled from the car. Bill came out his door— long, lean, scowling; he shaded his eyes to watch, then shook his head and stepped back inside among his knicknacks.

"What's that all about?" I asked, walking up beside Louis.

"Oh, the boys are having themselves a good time," he answered, pretending to count the bills in his hand, snatching each one taut between his battered fingers. There was a pause. I was waiting for him to look up. He didn't, just counted the money, twice, three times.

"How about a little tap?"

"I guess I better go see if Charles is home."

"He's a big boy, Louis. I'd like to talk."

Louis surprised me, walking swiftly to the Buick, still not meeting my glance. We rode silently down to camp. He sat himself on the kitchen table, half turned from me, as I poured him a stiff one in Old Bluey.

"There," I said. "See if that still holds liquid."

"Much obliged," he said. Then I noticed his upper lip. It had gotten worse.

"You take a fall today?"

"I got up fast," he quickly answered, the ghost of a smile on his face.

"Jesus Christ! You didn't!"

"Not much," said Louis. "He didn't have much side."

I walked over and gave my friend an awkward hug.

"What are we, Brant, a couple of lovebirds now?"

"What in hell happened out there?"

Louis told me that they'd pulled the powerboat up on Jake's Island at lunchtime. He had filleted a half dozen bass and was cooking them when he heard screams from the back side of the island. It was Margaret and Sophie Ware, the bait man's wife and daughter. They had paddled out for a picnic. The fat sport and the muscular one stood dripping on their blanket, naked; they'd been swimming around the island when the fat man played out and came ashore, blundering upon the women. When he heard the shrieks the other guy got out of the water to join the fun.

But Louis had heard it all, too, and now he stood on the little spine that runs down the center of the island. "Go get your clothes on, you ignorant sons of bitches!" he yelled. The younger man, he allowed, had landed the first punch and knocked Louis down. "He wished he hadn't," Louis added.

"Gave him a thrashing, did you?"

"I guess by Jesus I did!" Louis crowed. "When I looked around for the fatso, he'd lit out. Didn't show up again till after lunch, either. Not that lunch was much. Those fish was pretty well cooked by the time the dust settled down."

"Back in fighting form already," I said. Louis looked away. "Maybe we ought to head right back to Biscuit's," I added.

He made a chopping sign of dismissal. Then I saw him clench his hands for a moment, whether at the memory of Johnny's beating two nights before, or at this scuffle with the bass fisherman today, or at the squabble we'd had ourselves that morning.

"Thought I'd got done down here," he mumbled at last.

"Louis," I said.

"Brant."

"I want to apologize. You know that."

He gazed uplake, but I could see his big ears move slightly. Smiling, I figured.

"You'll stay," I said, half question, half announcement.

"Well, you're just miserable enough that I like the challenge," he answered at length, holding his hand out.

"Finest kind," I said, grinning.

We went outside by the fire, and I told him about the fight with the big brown, each detail sharp in mind. Each is still as sharp, all this time after.

"It's the ones that get off you remember," he said.

"That's for damned sure," I began. Then, after a long pause, I began again: "You know," I said, "a married woman—"

"Don't start," Louis warned, standing quickly.

I put a hand on his shoulder and moved him to a chair. "No," I said, "I want to tell you about it. I never told anyone about it."

9

I DIDN'T fish in the afternoon after all. I'd meant to, all right. I'd figured to fool a trout or two and call it quits in time to be waiting for Louis as he came back from his bass outing, or whatever he'd found at Wesley's once I sent him off. But I'd gotten caught up in my fly-tying, so to speak. What's more, I told myself, the late-day hatch was spotty. A wind, small enough at first but right in my face on the McLean, had kicked up to scatter the mayflies. Three separate times I'd struggled into wading gear, and once even put a foot in the shallows by camp, but I backed out. It wouldn't be worth it. Underneath all the rationalization, though, I knew that the river somehow scared me. I didn't want to go it alone. But what had I sent him off for, tied these handsome flies for, driven north from Boston for—what, if not fish?

In the end, it worked out. Louis came sneaking down through the alders to catch me, dreaming on the ledge, after my third try at the water. Even the birds had failed, the flycatchers and swallows bucking the wind for a while as it grew, then giving up, rolling with it, departing.

"Hell of a fisher fella you are," Louis said, startling me, grinning.

"Goddamn wind," I answered.

"You ain't got to tell me. You should have seen it upcountry."

"I imagine."

"I was thinking of you," he finished. "I mean, with the wind and that."

Louis had brought us a bass apiece, leavings from his sportsmen. "Didn't want to eat 'em, goddamnit, but didn't want to put 'em back neither." He scowled.

"Sports," we said, as one.

The wind kept on building as I poached the bass over the outdoor fire, the bubbles blowing over the rim of the smutty pot and hissing in the coals. By the time I cooked the fish and melted some butter, the smoke was sideways in the blow.

We took our dinner inside, ate it, and got tight. The conversation—plans, memories, adventures to come, or just plain *talk*—lasted into the small hours. It took time to get our bearings, even for the coming summer. Summer of '61! The number seemed to me suddenly vast, the turn of a new century close at hand. I wouldn't see it, and yet I remembered the turn into this century—God help me!—as a shy, chubby schoolboy.

At last we lapsed into silence, in which two minds—I'm sure of it—went back to certain dogs, to eddies and rapids, ruined orchards where grouse and deer fed. Perhaps Louis summoned that time in 1950, when we fought and reconciled. Perhaps he thought of Velma, just as I thought fleetingly of Anna. Or just maybe he clung to the same notion as I did: that out of seeming waste may emerge a completeness, even peace.

I MUST have pushed my alarm clock down, but I didn't remember it. I didn't wake till almost eleven next morning. Louis had stayed the night, but he made no answer when I croaked a greeting through the door to his room. Up and out. Of course. Again, as on that morning eleven years gone, I turned to the world late. 1961. I still couldn't get over it.

Just a few hours before, for all that we felt the velocity of the years, we'd been flush with reunion—with the return to person and place, with conversation. And now I had slept through the liveliest time of day. An old man late to awaken. I must not resign, I said to myself, slapping my leg for emphasis. A fellow has just so many hours of conscious connection with whatever he is and wherever, and I had passed through a handful of them asleep. My head buzzed with the booze I'd drunk, a lot more than I needed. I made a resolution about that as well.

The floor was cold to my feet. I shivered and pulled the prop from my window, wincing as it slammed. A pair of houseflies tumbled off the panes, so numb they almost fell to the boards before rallying clumsily and disappearing into my closet.

After coffee I stepped into the campyard. The wind was, more than ever, steady, urgent, and broad, with that whitecap smell from the northward lake. I could picture Mason Island, three miles up that way, standing in the funnel where the lake thins toward the river. I could imagine the tops of the island's pines bending landward, as if in some obeisance. It was the kind of day, as Louis liked to say, when it took two men to hold on one man's hat. I planted my feet and leaned into it all, straining a bit to gather breath. A limb, big around as a human leg, had cracked on the dooryard oak. Still hinged to the trunk, it screamed with the wind. I'd begun for a moment to feel revived, as if this rushing arctic air might hone the edges of my drowsy mind, but now I felt a certain gloom. I had slept so soundly! I might have perished in bed, and that struck me as wrong, especially now. The first crack of the big limb must have been loud as a pistol in the night outside my window. Some woodsman! I played my sloth against a matinee image of a scout bivouacked on the trail, a twig, broken in darkness, rousing him to the ready.

Behind me, near the privy, I watched another limb drop to earth, deadly, soundless till the thump on the earth. They call them widow-makers, even those who have no wives to widow.

I was morose again, no doubt about it. The wind blew tears into my eyes, and I turned back-to, facing the cabin, where—through the evening past—we had spoken words we both needed.

Fighting the wind, I squatted on the granite, imagined myself in a youthful crouch to dress my fish or fowl, while Louis dressed his next to me: a partridge crop full of haws like scarlet jewels; the coral roe of a hen salmon; the haloed spots on a brown trout's flank; glint of a knife blade rinsed in the quick spangled shallows at our feet; feel of the meat—clean, weighty, dripping in our hands.

YES, the air had first been cleared by our palaver that night long ago, had gone clean as this air today, this cold, naked, windblown air; clean as the dressed fish and game I had for a moment just felt in my hand; clean with the moving water of the swift, dear McLean. Detail on detail.

It had taken years for Louis McLean to step out from behind his barricade of northern reserve, for Brant Healey to show forth, undisguised, that old southern wound that had driven him to these woods and waters, that in so many ways yet drove him over whatever track this was.

Even now it took time for us to get back to that frankness. But having sailed past our little sophomoric jokes, our almost ritual indirection, we could reach to a kind of straightforwardness. If then our conversation slid back, still the tone would have changed, as it had been changed by a fight in a honky-tonk. Hard to explain. I'll say only that Louis and I could return to particulars, which now had the value of metaphor.

Once my wounds and Louis's had again been uncovered or at least referred to, they could be dropped from speech, which— whatever its audible content—was in fact about ourselves. Our selves, rolling on like the river, it seemed, forever.

Now Louis was up and gone. What, I suddenly wondered, if he should never return?

BITTERNESS that had ushered in affection; disillusionment with Anna that had prompted a lifelong illusion, or delusion, or ideal. Everything so mixed, difficult to grasp. Standing in a high wind, I beheld that ceaseless river of mine. I should have felt fine; I scoffed at omens. But if the clouds that hurtled over were clouds of fair weather, as they dimmed the sun they made mammoth checkered shadows on the McLean's surface. My sight blurred by the gale, those shadows had the look of great water creatures, each racing my way.

10

SOMETHING in the weather had spooked me, right enough. Why has there always seemed that doubleness to things? The redbud tree beneath my classroom window, for instance, through which I glimpsed Anna's open countenance, had struck me even then as a tree that boded betrayal. Or am I blending the sad later developments of our brief life together with the earliest ones, as if I had been a seer?

Whatever, a gloom-freighted loneliness dropped on me just as Louis and I had crossed our annual paths, reasserting a bond that any two humans might crave. I couldn't know how Louis himself felt right then, gone as he was for the day.

How often, come to think of it, he was gone. If his presence spurred me to reminiscence, so did his absence.

The plain fact, in any case, was that I was jittery, and not only with the nerves that sometimes attacked me after heavy drinking. I needed to be moving.

I put on a light jacket and a pair of boots and headed out the gravel lane. I looked back over my left shoulder at the McLean. 1921 to 1961: forty round years. If on one hand there was a kind of satisfaction in the roundness, the fullness, of that figure, the speed with which it had arrived must have borne down on me. I suppose my restiveness involved some yearning not merely to mark an anniversary but to forge a summary. I didn't know that then, and I doubt that to have recognized it would have eased me much. You can't will yourself, exactly, to conclusion—life keeps coming at you too fast.

It did occur to me that I might have gone wrong in choosing a river for the locating image in my life, even if over the years that water had charmed me—in every sense—by its very changeability. I might wade it toward the Tannery at five in the afternoon and, wading back to camp two hours later, discover the patterns of its flow to have altered altogether—though its progress was always down, down, down.

Yet it was surely too late to choose a new scheme. I hustled over the washboard of the camp lane, scared by my own turn of mind, and onto the town road. I was too jumpy to hike the woods. What if I dropped? I'd be someone's mystery: how had the old boy come *here*? My fear was real, all right, and bad: I'd been frightened to die in the water the day before, and in bed last night, and this morning on a trail.

I decided to make my way to the village, maybe to Edward's. But when I arrived at the store I kept to the dirt street. If I were going to talk, it had to be the sort of talk that Louis and I had had the evening before. Something straight, direct. For once the idea of cramped dialogue with Edward was a pall. I swung left, past Wesley's camp, up the short knoll to the Tannery Bridge, where I leaned on the rail for breath.

For breath, great God! I looked behind me, down the tiny hill I had just mounted. For breath? But there it was.

The McLean tightens under the bridge; back in the log-driving days the rivermen had needed an extra head of water from the dam to move the boom over the up-jutting ledges there. It was a little dizzying to peer down into the flume.

It was there that I began, I believe, to understand the motive I understand now: I'd walked out in search of a way to see four decades whole.

The wind kept howling down from the lake behind me, chilling the sweat on my neck and back. Louis was probably up there, headed away from me, holding his bow into the whitecaps.

There was, after all, another constant in these forty years than the moving river.

"Let me claim it," I suddenly said, startling myself, even though the words were lost in the roar below.

Claim what? Louis had worked as my caretaker for a long time. But the advantages had always cut both ways, and not just financially.

There on the bridge, its shake beneath me oddly soothing, the long seasons came at me as they would, after all. But their order was not of the calendar, would never be.

Strange to say that Louis's absence in my past—chiefly those dreary winters in the Back Bay—had been nearly as compelling to me as our companionable time. The anticipation of our reunions, and their recall, had engaged me almost, if not quite as much, as savoring the reunions themselves. We never missed each other, even if our hours together were restricted to the fishing months as age came on me. The McLean sang through these hours, except twice. The first time was during Louis's stint at Raytheon in the second war.

SOME months after Charles's christening, I'd had time on my hands, nothing much to do, and I decided to surprise Louis. I drove over to Waltham to catch him at his lunch break. I never told June about the visit, and I doubt that Louis ever did. Maybe that speaks a volume. In any case, I found the machine shop just as the noon whistle blew. In the din of the place, it was my turn to sneak up; I watched Louis wrench his goggles off and fling them into a metal bin. I was shocked to see the swatch of skin that the glasses had protected, pale as my own against the grime of dust and filings on the rest of his face. Then he threw off his safety gauntlets—his hands showed the same perch-belly white. He stood for a moment, pouting babylike.

When he lifted his gaze the smile came slowly. "Look who blew in on the gale," he whispered as we shook.

"A fella had to be desperate," I answered.

Louis surveyed the shop. "I judge he'd have to be," he said, running a rag over his brow. "Probably was, if he landed here." The whistle had stopped, but the machinery clanked on. More nuisance to shut it down and restart it than to let it roll all day.

The shopmen were filing out. Louis nodded and exchanged a few words with this one and that. A lanky black man shouldered him aside at the doorway, flicking a playful jab at his chin. "Care-

ful now, Piney," he laughed, his half-closed fists held low, a tooth-
pick wagging from his mouth.

Louis chuckled, sadly. He tipped up on the balls of his feet.
"Wouldn't want to harm you, son," he said, doing a little butterfly.
The black bounced on his bent knees, bobbing and weaving. Then,
dropping to flat feet, he shook his head. "Shee-it," he whispered,
and walked out, smiling.

I let go a breath, then managed a sneer: "Piney?"

"Seems to be," Louis sighed. "Not a bad bunch," he added.

"How about lunch somewhere? My treat."

"Finest kind," said Louis.

We rode a few blocks. Deep into January, the wind had authority. Soot and sand clattered on the Buick's windshield like stiff
rain. "The last place God made," Louis grumbled. He waved
vaguely to a pair of workmen, leaning into weather at the curb.

"Pals?" I asked.

"You could say it, I guess."

"Shall we ask them along?"

"No," said Louis, flatly, to my relief. Right or wrong, I've always
felt at ease with the rural poor—I can generally steer conversation
to hunting and fishing. A link. With these factory boys there'd be
no common ground. They'd likely wonder at Louis's friendship
with his upcountry Boss. Which I wanted to think was natural.

We sat—the Boss and the Boss's friend—for a brief half hour
over gray hamburgers and coffee at Ginger's Diner. Behind the
register, Ginger herself sat on a long stool, black roots vivid at
the base of her girlish ponytail, a roll moving under her bra as she
leaned this way and that, making change and predictable conversation with her clients. Above her was a clock with the Raytheon
logo, beside it the inevitable gag sign: "In God We Trust. Others
Pay Cash." You could replicate this eatery all across America.

A big, ham-handed fellow leaned over the booth and tipped
Louis's scarlet crusher down onto his nose. Louis snapped the
brim up abruptly, as if alarmed, and eyed him warily. "Look who
blew in on the gale," he repeated. The big man giggled like a
schoolgirl, his high laughter a shock from that immense body,
which jounced with pleasure.

"Old Piney!" he crowed. "You in for Friday night?"

"Let you know then, Dick."

"Chrissake, Piney, live a little!"

"See what the wife says," Louis answered, raising his hand in my direction. I tensed slightly. I didn't want the introduction. But now the shopman made a chicken sound, or what he meant for one, then turned swiftly and slapped a bill in front of Ginger, as swiftly reaching up to chuck her chin. She feinted to slap him, popped the register, and handed him some coins.

"See you later, sweetheart," he crooned.

Ginger gathered her penciled brows: "Thanks for the warning." Dick raised his wide palm as if to strike her back, his giggle exploding. Then he made for the door, glancing at the clock, buttoning his jacket as he went.

"What's Friday?" I asked.

"Stud game, Dick's place."

"You a regular, are you, you old thief?"

"Been twice. Come out about even." Louis seemed distracted.

"Something to do," I ventured.

"Something to do." Louis was preoccupied.

"Rough bunch?" I asked. I imagined someone like big Dick gone mean on liquor.

"No, a good gang," Louis answered. Then, after a pause: "They all think I'm from Mars."

I chuckled. "I bet they do."

"And that goddamn place of his—seven floors up. If there was a fire, I'd have to step out on a cloud."

I looked away, amused but touched.

"It's the third place he's lived in since I knew him," Louis went on. "Not married. Always has to be on the top floor or damn near." His words came in a tumble now; his lunch break was hurtling to an end, and all of a sudden I recognized that that mattered.

We abandoned our watery coffee, paid our check, and drove back breakneck: we were almost late.

I stood by Louis for a minute after he took up his stance. Just as the 12:45 whistle wound down, a streamlined chunk of dark metal burst through a heavy asbestos curtain at one end of the shop. Louis raised a phantom gun and swung on it: "Black duck over Unknown Stream," he shouted in a rush, then bent to the belt. I raised my hand, confounded; then I laid it gently on Piney's shoulder.

"Good-bye," I said.

He didn't turn to me. Couldn't.

I drove back slowly to Boston, blue with that last speechless instant, intent as usual on trying to make things make sense. I imagined the next something—I didn't know what—that would come down the shop line to Louis, how he'd put his gloved hands to it momentarily, and then it would be gone, and then another something, the same, would follow. The same and the same.

Every trout or salmon Louis had ever fingered, each he had hefted and cleaned, every dressed deer, plucked bird—every one of these was in some way, too, the same fish or bird or animal. But they came from lake or stream or ridge or woods that had been there forever, and Louis depended on that permanence, a permanence that made him, on the other hand, an improviser, forever changing his method to meet the locale, the season, the prey's evasions. I was getting at something about routine. I was trying to.

The Raytheon bunch knew nothing of all that: Dick could pick up today and live somewhere else tomorrow. Yes, Louis could chop apart a house and move into his shed, but that was something different, and I struggled to see it. All around Dick and the rest of the poker players, buildings went down and came up, streets butted through neighborhoods, shops opened and closed. In a few weeks, Louis had told me, the factory could retool for a whole new line of manufacture. At the same time, nothing changed: nine to five, half-day on Saturday. The machinist might stand in the same position on the same floor for twenty-five years, and then receive the same good-bye watch to tell his hours.

My caretaker's life was steady as opposed to routine. That's what I said to myself on the bridge, and I guess I'm willing, still, to claim in this sense that it was Louis's salvation. For one thing it held through the winter, an obvious advantage. A McLean man could work in the woods, but that meant leaving the shack with lantern and bucksaw (or in recent years flashlight and chain saw), needing the light, too, for the return after dark. It was all piecework: you were paid for what you cut, or for what you hauled, if you were a teamster, or later a trucker. Thank God Louis never learned to drive! Caution wasn't his strong suit, and the twisty secondaries of that country are bad enough when they're clear and dry. Once the ice and snow come, the downhill road from Cotyville to the pulp mill is plain suicide. Someone wrote a song about that, I recall.

I had always kept my property plain: no lawn, no power, no plumbing. So Louis only had to see that the cabin stayed upright during those bitter winter blows, and that no poor hobo stayed past a reasonable time. He was simply on call, and I believe the unpredictability of the call was part of its pleasure. I know it was for me. Whatever the season, I could phone Edward with the old message: I'm on my way. Then Louis and I could wade the river together, shiver together in a blind, tramp the whitetail ridges, bust the puckerbrush for partridge and woodcock. It was a companion I wanted, not a guide. I could set my own decoys, dress my own game, rig my own gear, net my own trout. When the time came that I couldn't do these things, I vowed I'd quit, as indeed I had done, one thing at a time, till it came down pretty much to fishing now. That was only half lament, though. Fishing was and would ever be more than fishing, after all.

As I got on, there'd be more days when I'd ask him for a run into a back lake, supposedly after bass, but mostly to reexplore. We'd look for moose in the warm months: we'd flail our paddles like madmen when they sank their huge heads to browse the lily bulbs, and we'd sit still as herons when they surfaced to chew and blink in an aura of greenhead flies. Now, as I wandered off the Tannery Bridge and homeward, nervous little bunches of spring birds hop-scotching autumnlike before me in my path, I recalled how once we caught an ancient bull swimming from Gull Island to the mainland of Unknown. Before I knew it, Louis had jumped onto the animal's back. I laughed and prayed at the same time, and still laugh just at the thought of it. Louis couldn't swim a stroke. It was a day like this, if a month later, too windy to cast a decent line. The moose was huge and full of hell for all his years. One stubborn tatter of velvet trailed from his antlers in the water, low on the huge rack, where he couldn't get at it to scrape. He thrashed back at the rider with those horns, his eye wide and white, but Louis stayed far astern, whooping like a wrangler. Just as the hooves touched solid ground, though, Louis had the sense to slide off into the shallows. The moose clattered onto the beach stones, then turned lakeward, where my friend's head seemed to float like a delicate ball. The bull pawed the rocks and snorted, the eye white with rage after all, not fright. He took a long time to wheel, and then to wade chest-deep into the young popples of the Unknown burn, crushing them as he went.

IN spring we'd spy on the loons, their nests all but adrift among the duckweed. One pair got so used to us that in the spring of '57, even after the chick had hatched, they'd let us paddle up close. At lunch on a warm day, when the shiners flashed in the sunny water over a bar, we'd corral a dozen or so into a smelt net, twist their heads, and toss them for the gander. He'd sweep out to fetch them from underneath, rise for a second, black eye on us, then dive back gracefully as an otter to his mate on the nest. With a full mouth, unable to pull at the reeds, he struggled to get ashore, hobbling like a cripple to the hen's side, his feet set so far back on his body he couldn't balance on them. Like the mariner's albatross, I remember thinking, water and air his elements. If you were looking to be cursed, you could shoot a loon as well, but I was a compulsive enough narrator without needing any supernatural help. God prevent Louis from shooting one!

This was all sport, too, and would be again, precious as what bass fishing we did on those trips. I'll confess that in later days I had come to fish for bass with something like pleasure, using the smallest of my old salmon rods to fling the surface bug far out, even whooping when a smallmouth smashed it or when he managed in calm weather to tow the canoe some. It was all inelegant, unsubtle, yes, but the water was still clear, and I could enjoy this fishing, especially when my joints had stiffened from wading long hours in the quick, cold McLean. And there was the McLean to return to, always. All those blessed evenings.

BY the time I got back to camp from the Tannery Bridge, my nerves had passed. I looked out on the river, the earlier clouds gone, the faithful skipper trout cavorting just upstream from the rapids' breach of the river's otherwise seamless syntax. The sun began to set.

My hunger surprised me. Still wearing my outdoor clothes, I opened a can of soup and put it on to boil, then turned off the jet on the propane stove; I would fire the Atlantic. I went out to gather a few logs from the pile, the sound of the wind spooky in the treetops.

Waiting for the old wood stove to warm, I concluded that I hadn't in any case been a demanding employer. I was satisfied about that. If Louis's pay had been low, he could supplement it however he wanted. There on a bedroom wall hung a rusted leghold trap from the line he ran when I was away. Sometimes he made paddles with ax and drawknife, or chopped modest lots for a logger. As I slowed down, he was free to work even when I was at McLean. The odd jobs had the benefit of keeping him busy. If that comment smacks of the plantation, I'll only say that I was there. Idleness, I knew, wounded Louis even more than routine.

Yes, the outside jobs had been a boon to both of us, especially since there was none he couldn't drop when I arrived. Whenever the alternative, as Ishmael puts it, was pistol and ball, I could light out of Boston and find a home and partner. Sometimes in May, sometimes June, and at any stage of the gunning season till 1958, when at last I quit hunting and Louis became a free man after first frost. He could let the dog pen rot now; the cord of wood he cut for my summer cook fires would be enough; he could heft the iron Atlantic into its new corner, leaving only the six leg dents to show where it had served me so long and well.

That Atlantic, and how I loved it: the cedar kindling popping under the oak and maple logs as we lit it, the wood smell blending with the odors of wet wool stockings on their drying wire overhead. A drop from a sock's toe splashing and dancing on the stove top, skating over the surface, running down the edge—all steam now.

I can remember filling the firebox, fingers numb, with nothing but the fragrant cedar, wanting a fire so quick and hot I could open the oven door and see the sheet metal turn cherry. A good moment, the finest of any winter day. Winter wasn't my season—I never kept a hound; we used Louis's or a relative's. I didn't give a damn about snowshoe rabbits, really: a young one's edible, but that's the best you can say. And I shudder even now to think of night dropping early, the hound still ragging some long-winded buck hare down in a black swamp. I can feel the chill rise foot to shin to thigh. How many evenings did we come back, happy-drunk at eight o'clock, to hear the dog yet howling down there? And the same at ten, eleven, midnight. In the small hours we returned, the happy part of the booze gone. At least from me. Now it was a dreadful lucidity—too obvious now, the black of the black swamp, the horror of frost and ice in wheel ruts, rebounding the stars' remote fire.

Not that I didn't, not that I don't, love the fresh smell of winter air; it seems to go so deep into the lungs. When Louis and I were younger we swore that to breathe it, early on an ice-locked lake, was to cure a hangover. Drilling through seven inches of freeze, bustling around with the sapling tip-ups, splitting wood for the bob-house stove, you would sweat, and then the wind would blow out the cobwebs. Then you could start again. Hard cider was our ice-fishing drink; we'd sip it as we watched our flags, Louis and I. For years he kept one skinny alder pole that he called Old Drunken Arthur, for the way it swayed in wind. We always pulled for Arthur, soul mate, hoping he'd get the first touch and many more. And I can summon the scents of smelt and yellow perch in hot grease. We'd eat the smelt bones and all; we'd cut out the rib cage and chew a perch like cob corn.

How long had it been since we'd ice-fished? Five years? Ten years?

Winter fishing once had its points, I thought, peeling off my jacket and pulling my chair up to the Atlantic. But there came a time—like everything, an apparent rush—when suddenly I couldn't digest fried fish; suddenly I couldn't hold morning cider; suddenly I thought those foamy jugs had served all along less to warm the body than to blunt our spirits to the blank reality of what we were doing—sweating in an overheated box, watching rags on sticks, shivering as the gale blew the sweat to crystals, our wet hands aching as we unhooked some common school fish or skimmed the slush from our auger holes. Suddenly everything failed, out there in winter.

Then I remembered little Charles. What else would I call him? I saw him so seldom when he grew up that I think of him even now as four or five years old. He loved to fish through the ice, though

Louis rarely seemed to notice his pleasure. "A yank! A yank!" the boy would shout, running out to inspect a waving flag. Louis would nod absently after Charles returned with his catch.

I sometimes wondered at this seeming ambivalence to the boy: did he remind Louis too much of his own failures, of his wife's absence, of the fact that Charles was motherless now?

Louis's mood could be the blackest thing amid all that white. Perhaps for that, I remember loving the child myself. And I don't think I delude myself—it may not have been love that Charles felt for me, but it was at least a kind of closeness and familiarity that would go out of our relation too soon. Neither of us had said or done anything to make this so—indeed, it was the absence of gesture and word that troubled me now, sitting bemused by my stove. Was there anything I could do, this late? Would I see him at all this summer?

The thought of the boy—or more properly the man—momentarily rekindled my uneasiness, my jitters. I felt a pipping in my chest and my eyes burned. What was Louis's part, if any, in the failure that bothered *me*?

I tried to imagine my palms again on the bridge's rail, the calming hum of the water running up my arms. Maybe it was natural in a man of my years, yet, in fact, I'd been this way for all of my life: a sudden notion will come across me, and before I've given myself an instant to think it out, I'm lost in a vision of blankness.

Charles never exactly resisted my awkward avuncularity. It was just that he couldn't be held in my company long enough for me to—what? Counsel him in spiritual matters? I had been the godfather, but I didn't have the right kind of capital for that. The boy would grow up like Louis, a pantheist if anything, and I couldn't have helped it if I'd wanted to: there wasn't even an active church in the village after the war.

What then could I give him? What besides the fried perch, which out on the sealed lakes, long ago, he said were the best he'd ever eaten? What besides the joy he took in little jobs I assigned him? I'd send him over to shore for dead softwood twigs, low on the trees; I'd tear a paper sack and stuff it under a small tent of them; then I'd let him strike the match. The wind would blow it out as soon as it flared, but what was our rush? The fire would come in time. Then he'd grin, and he'd grin again when I told him to spit into the hot fat. If it sputtered and jigged, that little white bead, we knew we could turn a perch or smelt crispy brown. We didn't say much, but who knew what the years might bring? His father, whom I loved, had been a man of few words, too, when I first met him.

Once I remember dispatching Charles to wood duty just as Louis got into one of his harangues on the spirits. Distracted, it took me a while to notice that the boy had been gone too long. I bolted from the bob-house. I couldn't see him on the near shore, and panic blew through my bones like snow: had he fallen into a spring hole? Where was he? In that moment nothing seemed bleaker to me than the thought of the child remaining forever the same age in mind, never growing into the future he barely surmised. Louis and I raced over the ice, our terror easing when we came on his tracks, plain in new powder. They led into the woods a few yards: we found the boy wrestling, proudly, with a spruce limb bigger than he was. His old man's son.

The squall of fear came back that night as I lay in camp, wind hooting in my chimney. I could too easily bring to mind that terror at lake's edge. The world had looked so abstract in the late afternoon light—so hard-edged and symmetric—and Charles so tiny. I could not sleep, flinching to recall him in his tiny wool mackinaw, a soft uneven smudge against the lake's white booming expanse.

I winced to have that picture, even now, the wind outside howling downstream, and the water.

11

THE summer of '61 blew by. I choose the words exactly. The months were nothing but wind, and then disaster, whose signs, had I been more like Louis, I might have seen in the air itself. The gale that had ripped the limb from my oak in late June was a portent. The lulls were so rare, I bet I didn't wet my line for more than five hours altogether. "In all my years, I never saw *this*. It never used to do *this*"—so Louis said, over and over, as if sensing some vast and incredible change in the order of things.

And why not? I remember how, with the dwindling of July, the gale screamed even at night, till the village people tired of their own banality. No one said anymore, "Well, it'll change in time." It was as if we had accepted the most bizarre aspects of the blow. Walking up to Edward's one morning, I leaned into the air like a sailor, spying a bewildering patch of yellow on the gravel ahead: squash blossoms, torn from Bill Ware's garden, strewn across the road and blasted onto tree trunks across the way. There's an expression in the north country—"wind enough to blow owls from the trees." It had always seemed fanciful before.

Everything climaxed on the last day of July. At least for me it did. I was peeing in the high weeds by my ledge, like a small boy gleefully watching my stream turn to spray. Then I heard a crunch. The deadhead popple near the privy, long shorn of its widow-makers, had toppled over entire. It broke in two on the ridge of my camp.

I gazed unblinking at what I'd witnessed, what I couldn't believe

I'd witnessed. At last I stepped inside with the same fear and fascination I'd felt in boyhood, rambling through the woods and clearings in search of trout holes, when I explored a collapsed hunter's cabin in the Adirondacks. But this was here, this was mine.

Old bits of nest were scattered on the bed; cinnamon ants, dislodged from the popple's punky core, raced for cover under the baseboards; lichens shifted on the windowsill like dust, and dust itself swirled in the downdraft from the roof's huge rent. All this bustle and ruin at once, as if death were a kind of action.

I crept like a burglar up the maple ladder. The first thing I came on was the blue wading pool I'd bought for Charles, filled now with crude insulation—corncobs and newspapers that the old teamster who built the place had stuffed into cracks. Idle, I sat and read a yellowed article: STEAMBOAT FOUNDERS IN ST. PIERRE BAY. When I felt that little pain in the vocal chords that means you're set to weep, I stood up.

Most of the attic was open to the scuttling air, but I needed a flashlight to inspect the corners. The crossties looked sound, but there was a frightful interruption in the ridgepole. I saw the jagged jaws of that break; where part of the wane had splintered off, wood borer trails wandered across one another; a strand of wire that had been buried in the heartwood crumbled as I touched it.

I went down to the Buick for my tow rope. Its ends were frayed and it was full of ancient mud, but otherwise it felt solid. How like me, I mused, to carry a rope and not a chain. Well, I used a silk fishing line too. If a rope breaks when you need it, you can tie up the break; if it's a nuisance to dry it each night, you can fish that silk line for years, because it won't crack and sink. I was looking for things to feel good about, assuring connections.

I worked the rope under a beam at the bedroom end, then tied it off in a fisherman's clinch knot, one of the few I know. Next I uncoiled it, ducking past the hole in the ceiling and jamming the butt under a beam at the opposite end. I snubbed it as tightly as I could, bracing my foot against the brick chimney. I prayed that the top half of the cabin wouldn't fall out in the wind. I would not think of it falling *in,* wouldn't let myself.

I spent that night in the main lodge at Wesley's, awake. Timbers shook whenever the wind turned meaner. Twice I headed downstairs for the Buick, and twice I retreated. If my past on the river was being blown to hell, I wouldn't stand there and watch it go, the gale sweeping away all my dust.

The winds quit dead the next morning, as if my catastrophe were the one they'd been planning all summer. It was the first of August, and the weather stopped still, October-cool. I caught Louis at the landing above town, just before he was set to push off with some late-season trollers, man and wife. They were sympathetic, God bless them, and after Louis had set them up with Walter, we went down to inspect the damage.

"No worse than I expected," he offered.

"No better, either," I answered.

"We'll make the best of it," said Louis, after a time, proposing— no, announcing—a plan. We'd spend five or six nights in the old Forest Service cabin by Middle Lake Dam. We'd paddle out to the rocky islands in the mornings, casting for bass in the chill, spying on an otter slide that had been on Finnegan Point for as long as either of us remembered; toward dark we'd come off the lake and angle with worm and float, like kids, from the dam's apron—there were perch there all summer, and we'd eat them, Louis promised, till they came out of our ears, poach them, fry them, chowder them. Huck and Jim stuff. Two men of a certain age.

"But what about the *camp*?" I whined.

"Charles is the boy," he answered. "You go on up to the store, and I'll meet you there after I talk it all over with him."

I followed his orders like a zombie.

An hour later we picked up a key from Edward, who seemed pleased by our project. He hummed as he worked a spot of tarnish from the brass with his thumbnail, attaching a tag to the key ring with FOR. SERV. neatly written on it, meticulous, proprietary as ever. "You boys stay as long as you like. Long as it takes to build her back up." He was almost voluble.

Louis was no carpenter: he insisted on making those wooden armchairs for my camp, but at best they'd last three summers, then would lean in the woods around my camp like dolmens. Charles, though, was handy; he could do the job, and Blanche would clean up. As we stood in the campyard, all our gear loaded, Louis eyed the saws and drills uneasily. Anything more than a single, simple blade struck him as unnatural, dangerous.

We left Charles and Blanche to their business. The boy had already braced the gable ends, erected a scaffold, called lumber up from Pinkham. He waved to us from the roof, and Blanche smiled bashfully from the ladder, one hand gripping a rung, the other a bucket of nails.

Blanche waited tables at Wesley's, where Charles was man-of-all-work. There was something between these two local kids, and they'd hopped on the job with gusto. Wesley had released them both from chores: even as I mourned, I felt a glow; it seemed that everyone in town was compassionate to the old guy when he needed it. The old guy with the ruined house.

While we dodged the ruts of the Middle Lake road, I smiled to recall the expressions of Charles and his girl when we departed. Sanctioned time together. I was too old to worry about anybody's sanction, but too old also—so it seemed—to have thought up a holiday like this one without the prod of bad luck. In fact, I wasn't the one to dream it up even then.

We rode in silence past the sugar orchard west of town and into deer country. Rambling around one bend, I had to stomp the brake as a doe and two lambs bounded out of the brush in front of us. Louis and I gulped air together; then, still not speaking, we moved on.

We passed the Dougherty burn. It was gone by, but I could remember a few years after the fire, when the berry vines and gray birch and popple had come up there. A hot hillside for small game. The grouse would stay coveyed there right into late October, I can't say why. Now the popples looked immense, and the twisty birch limbs were like a mess of wire. The understory was going sparer by the season; cabbage pines invaded the gritty clearings.

When we got to the Mason Stream turnoff, I touched the brake. "Now where the hell was the turn to Brookson Slough?" I wondered out loud. We used to jump-shoot wood duck in that marsh, creeping over the oaky ridge to catch them feeding. The drakes were beautiful as they lifted against the still water behind them, and in the right wind you could hear their sad little squeals. Often we let them go.

"Brookson? You passed it."

I stopped the Buick dead. "Didn't see it."

"Hard to see now."

I turned back; I needed that landmark. Louis didn't say anything till we reached the old intersection. "There she be," he announced. I blinked; the road was almost invisible, grown up in jackfir higher than the car's hood. I looked at Louis, opened my mouth to speak, then shut it as he nodded.

At least Old Crow Spring was still there. I nosed us up on the shoulder and we got out. Back in the footloose days, we'd hide a cup by that spring, and hide a jug, too, sometimes, under the brush. We'd dip the cup into the bubbling water and then fill it with bourbon. A fellow could do that, no matter what the time of day or night, when he was younger. I remembered sitting once in the browned ferns after a successful morning's hunt: it must have been nine o'clock or so, and the sun bore down on that patch like a spotlight. We stayed half an hour, the warmth bathing us, the liquor a glow in our guts, a fork-horn for me and a six-pointer for Louis strung up in the woods by Middle Lake. We'd need someone's truck to fetch them. We chuckled in contentment, and lolled.

Now we laughed again to find the dented steel mug we'd drunk from all those years ago. It was the color of the leaf mulch that had covered it, but we scoured it and waited for the spring to settle. In the chill, there wasn't a bug, and once more we sat easy, trading the cup. We drank a lot more water than liquor, but we got feeling good anyway. It may have been an hour before we moved on.

The Forest Service cabin was tight. Edward kept the place up, so the inside was orderly. Bedrolls hung in a strict row from a roof beam. Coffee cans, wrapped in brown paper and labeled KNIFE's FORK's SPOON's, for God's sake, stood side by side on a shelf. The wicks in both oil lamps stood out of their mantels at identical heights. I shook my head. How was it that Edward was caretaker here? How did he round up all his perks? Louis didn't know, but didn't begrudge him. "There's a lot who run him down," he said, "but he always used me right. Carried me through some winters on the books, and not a word."

I turned in my tracks. "He takes a job, the job gets done," I added, laughing at the understatement.

"Old Scarface." Louis smiled. There probably hadn't been a soul besides us to come inside this shack in a year, but you'd have thought it came with a live-in housekeeper.

The forest rangers all flew planes nowadays, so I wondered: "Why does the service hang on to a place like this?"

"To shelter poor old homeless farts like you," Louis began, but when I looked at the floor he added, "Don't brood now; the kids'll make it right."

WE caught fish by the bagful. We'd no sooner toss out a night-crawler than the red-and-white float would bob, and we'd yank in a fat perch. Louis would fish for a spell, and I'd fillet; then we'd switch jobs, he driving me almost mad with rendition after rendition of "The Eddystone Light," but whenever I turned to complain, I'd relent. There was something right in the way he plied the knife and sang, nothing on his mind.

We threw back everything too small to fillet. By the time we had six or seven good fish apiece, it was cold. We cooked on the wood stove, another Atlantic. Its nickel shone so much more brightly, though, I made an idle resolution to do something about mine. Louis had pocketed a lemon at Edward's; we squeezed it into melted butter, which we poured over each poached strip of perch. We boiled a potato apiece and two small onions. Food tastes good in the woods, famously, and it tastes different too: the fish was a little like lobster. Even the small grains of smut that chipped off the pot and into the onions had a savor, and not bad.

We sat full-bellied after supper, breathing whiffs from lamp and fire, the door cracked just enough to let in some sweet cool from the night. I was thinking back on autumns—boots drying by a stove, the dog's fur stinking slightly as she stretched next to them, now and then kicking her legs in dream; I'd speak her name and she'd stop, lifting her head for a moment, laying it gently back on the floor. A jewel or two of frost on a northerly windowpane. . . . "I could cry if I thought about it," I began.

"Did you ever think of letting me put you on a deer stand?" Louis asked. "By Jesus, you ain't too used up to have me *drive* one to you!"

It was good and warm in Edward's cabin. I stood, peeled off my shirt, and walked to the door. Leaning out, I inhaled the tart air, recalling the doe and her two grown fawns in the road. "Must be a buck around here somewhere," I said.

"Yeah," Louis chuckled. "Thinks it's November or something."
I kicked the door all the way open. "Nice night," I breathed.
"They'll be moving in this weather, Brant. Something to think about."

WE pestered the bass with popping bugs next day. A few had come inlake in the cold snap; we raised a fair mess, but we let them go. It didn't seem fair to take them after they'd gotten this far through summer. I fished in the forenoon, then we went ashore to eat a last little cheese and bread, neither of us hungry after the past night. Then Louis sat casting on the forward thwart, my turn to paddle. By late afternoon there was that pinch between my shoulder blades that feels *hot*. And I hadn't even had a wind to fight. Used up. We fried some more perch inside that night, the weather still calm and cold. Sleeping weather.

Morning broke into supernatural blue. We suited up warm, as if for still hunting. I always preferred that, sneaking from tree to rock to tree, eyes peeled, waiting ten minutes between moves. Louis didn't have the still hunter's temperament. He'd travel fast till he came on sign, and even then it had to be pretty fresh to slow him. But if he found it, I swear he could walk right up on a deer. He'd step out of his shoes for the last hundred yards; once we spent more time looking for his boots than he'd spent on the stalk. We finally gave up. I remember the buck went 207 pounds, dressed. Following Louis on the trail to Finnegan Point this morning, I remembered him standing by Edward's scale in stocking feet.

We saw the otter slide all right. It was clearly active. No otters, but no need to complain, either. They'd be there another time.

Then we staggered along the rocks on Finnegan's west side, down to the foot of the cove, where the sand beach is. When the paper company blew up the Mason Stream Dam, they dropped the lake's level about five feet and left this spotless stretch of sand. We used to leave our canoes here all summer, back when it was safe to do that, before the company dozed a road from Pinkham to the lake's south shore, back when you used to have to carry if you came from that side, up over the stone dam in Cook Stream that was gone now too.

All the change had brought a crowd, but we were alone on the lake today. We picked a hatful of blueberries apiece from the little heath by the beach. We ate them slowly, tossing the green ones at shiners cruising the shallows. Their flanks flashed through the tannin-brown water as they startled and regrouped. Then we lay back against a mossy deadfall and napped.

Eyes closed, I wondered at the airplane whining overhead. Fire or game wardens, I figured, too shiftless and easy even to lift my lids. Then I felt a quick prick on either cheek and came awake. Mosquitoes: I'd never seen so many this late. I was sweating; they like that. Maybe they'd been waiting all summer for the break in the gusty weather and the late cold.

Louis was already down by the water, flailing his arms. "Go to sleep in the goddamn winter and wake up in summer," he snarled, scraping a shin on one of the rocks as we hurried off the point. The weather was still out to baffle us. A humid south wind had sprung into that astounding blue as we slept. The ridges across the lake were milky with haze. Our collars buttoned and our pants legs tucked into socks, we were steaming like cart horses when we slammed the cabin door.

Coals still throbbed in the stove. Louis carried a pail down toward the dam for sand to damp the fire. It took him some time to gather it; the sand kept coming up wet, and we didn't need a stovepipe explosion to cap our fiasco. I could hear him swearing.

Battalions of mosquitoes clung to the windowpanes. They seemed to have followed us from the bog at Finnegan Cove, and were whining to get in, no matter that I was grimly eliminating the ones that had entered with us. The fire was out, but the stove top still shimmered. We couldn't open the door, and we couldn't leave it shut. I rustled through boxes and canisters: extra wicks, nails and staples, hinges, even nail polish. Everything but repellent. Not like Edward, I thought. Of course, the weather in the fifties, too cold for bugs when we left McLean, we hadn't brought our own.

Not a screen on a window, either, but then Edward was a *real* old-timer. I've stopped and had tea with him in his kitchen, deep in August, the heat so fierce it drew pitch from pine panels a century old. His kettle huffed and peeped. The funeral-home thermometer above his stove strained at its peg.

"I had it this morning." Louis had come back with the sand bucket.

I braced for it. "Well," I feebly offered, "it could be worse."

"It will be."

I knew what could make things worse; I didn't need to be a prophet. I shot him the severest look I had. There'd be no spiritualist monologue if I could help it. Here we were besieged in a stifling room by the biggest army of insects God ever made, nothing to eat on the shelves but a box of rolled oats, our bread and cheese and potatoes gone. We had counted on fish.

"I told you we should have kept a couple bass," said Louis resentfully. He hadn't, of course, but I let it slide with another look. We'd be hungry, and that was that. It seemed too appalling a prospect to fish below the dam in what would surely become, as evening deepened, an even greater horde of mosquitoes; then to light a cook fire in the swelter, to try and sleep afterwards. Yet my home was a shambles; I pictured arriving to shards of shingles, dropped nails, sawdust.

We sat there suffering for an hour, Louis whistling "The Eddystone Light." It sounded like a dirge now. He paced back and forth at brief intervals, his shirt, like mine, drenched; he kept looking out the window as if he expected to see something that would alter our fix.

I was coming to the end of my tact when we heard the crunch of tires. Louis hopped to his feet and rushed again to the window. A gray International panel wagon drove out on the dam bridge and loomed above the pool like a displaced hippo. A boy of twenty-five or so, in army fatigues, stumbled out of it, waving arms through the mosquito cloud. Someone pulled the wagon's door shut behind him, and we could just hear his jocular curse. He ran around to the other door and began a tug-of-war with someone inside, finally winning. The wagon rocked as he dove across the front seat, and again as he got out, a can in hand. He circled the rear of the car and took a few steps onto the bridge, looking our way, squinting into the late sun. I don't think he could see us. He sprayed himself with bug dope, then turned and waved his companions out.

They were an attractive woman, about his age, and a rough-looking man—someone's uncle?—with several days of gray beard, a bandanna cinching his wild hair. We could hear a hubbub, broken by bursts of laughter, most loudly from the woman when the young man sprayed her bottom. The stocky young fellow faced the older one, pointed at where he'd sprayed, and wagged a finger. Stay away, you old bastard! Or some such thing, you could guess.

"There's a start," said Louis, glumly as he could manage.

"Well, in this case," I replied, "I don't mind the company." I looked at him hard again. "Maybe borrow their dope." Louis shook his head. We saw the girl walk around to the back of the International, lift its hatch, and pull out a huge portable radio. I looked at Louis, softly all of a sudden; we nodded as one, then began to slap our gear together. We hung the bedrolls on the beam as neatly as Edward had. We locked up tight.

We passed by Old Crow Spring.

"Charles can sleep on the floor," Louis assured me as we rode. "He's young and vigorous."

"Hell," I said, "I'll get a room at Wesley's."

"Don't be foolish, Brant," he insisted. The rest of the trip was solemn.

It was eight o'clock when I parked by Louis's house. We clambered up the bank and went in. "It'll do you good to sleep in an Indian shack one time," he said.

How rarely I'd set foot here! It astonished me to look it over: debris in every corner—yellowed catalogs from outfitters, bits of board and tar paper, snowshoes, toggle chains, unmatched gloves, rusty plates, broken decks of cards, empty jugs, a clothless umbrella, a milking stool, an earless plaster rabbit, a terra-cotta geranium pot. On and on. "At least I have screens on the windows," Louis chuckled. "Not much glass," he conceded, "but screens anyway."

How little I know him after all, I thought. I had a hell of a nerve to bitch about getting through my winters in Boston. How did Louis do it here? There was no window with more than a single pane, nothing against the elements but those corroded screens, tacked right into the window frames. Did I understand anything of his real life?

Smoky grease coated the wall behind his cookstove. Generations of fried things had expired their residue onto the boards.

I had to find something to say. "Where do you suppose the boy is?" I was wondering how Charles, so neat and prudent, put up with all this.

"Probably out tomcatting," Louis answered. "We'll see him before too long."

"Well, you can't beat Blanche," I said.

"Right enough." Louis smiled, turning from me, picking at a sliver in the crude table. "I'm just jealous, is all," he muttered, turning back with a wan smile.

"I expect so."

"And not much time before he's left the country."

"You'll miss him," I suggested.

"No two ways about it." He loved the boy, in his fashion. I patted him on the shoulder. A gesture I'd made before, it always bewildered us both. He slumped out from under my touch.

Just past midnight, Louis's preoccupation turned into something else. He was at once a casual father and, in strange ways, a protective one. We'd fought about this. Charles had earned enough the summer before to buy a car; he could have driven it all year long to the Pinkham high school. But no: his father insisted on the early bus, though this meant Charles needed an hour for the walk to the stop at McLean Road Junction, another for the trip to school, and the same route home. It meant that he had to give up most of his after-school chores in town. Looking around the shack, I guessed it meant he didn't have time to get any but his own corner tidied up; or maybe his father's attitude toward housekeeping was another rule here.

"As long as that bus is running, he'll be on it," Louis had told me. He didn't like a motor, was uneasy even with his outboard kicker, and would use any instance to reach for the paddle. I liked that in him, but it had another side.

"He's not a little boy anymore, Louis," I had prodded.

"Never mind," he replied, always. There were times when it was hard to distinguish Louis's concern from his perversity, his damned superstition.

As in the forestry camp, as in my own on so many wet days, as no doubt in this hovel of his on days even more countless, there he sat for brief spells, whistling, drumming. Then he'd walk out and peer into the night. I saw his silhouette against the Tannery rapids, the constellations above him, and my mind reeled back an unspecific memory—Louis against water after dark. Radway Pond, maybe; not quick water like the Tannery's, but big water. He was minute. Why this melancholy vision, and why tonight? Surely Charles was simply courting his girl, the old men, as he thought, well out of the way.

"Relax," I'd urge each time Louis came back in, but of course he wouldn't.

We played gin, and I beat him, even if I tried to throw the games. At two in the morning he slapped down his cards: "Run me to camp."

"For Christ's sake," I protested. I'd just gotten tired enough to attempt sleep. "You don't think he's working by starlight, do you?" The moon was a wispy O in the sky, beginning its slow fall downward.

"I had it this morning."

"The weather."

"Maybe," said Louis. "Let's go."

Just who was the boss here? Louis's order made me bristle. But I did what he told me.

The afternoon's humidity and the evening dew had collapsed on the river road. Toads and frogs hopped through the wet, and I gentled the Buick through their ranks, Louis stamping his feet whenever I slowed. To hell with him, I thought. A barred owl swept out of the woods and nearly brushed my hood. I remembered shooting one as a kid, and how little he was when I plucked him, dove-sized. You pay, I've come to learn, for such violations, and I must have paid for that one. Maybe I was paying for it now. A few hundred feet on, a second owl startled me, sweeping the other way.

"What do you suppose *that's* all about?" I asked, waving my hand above the dash to mimic the owls' flight.

Louis sat rigid, his tireless fingers drumming. "The Old Indian could tell you," he muttered. The Old Indian was some authority he'd refer to as others might say, carelessly, "God only knows."

My headlights bounced off the wounded dooryard oak and onto

the cabin. I rubbed my eyes. Good as new. In two days Charles had replaced the broken ridgepole and shingled the break. There'd been a brick missing from the top of my chimney, and he had replaced even that. I was stunned, and a bit heartsick: the place didn't look quite like home.

"What's *that*?" Louis's words came loudly in the dark, and I snapped to. Blanche's bicycle leaned gleaming against the stoop, a hammer poking from its basket. I cut the lights and we got out. The camp seemed to glow, too, though the moon was pallid, sinking.

"Louis," I said, my tone measured and desperate at once, like the one you use on a dog who's about to get into some trouble before you can get a hand on his collar.

"Never mind," said Louis, striding toward camp. I caught up with him. Together we looked inside at the young bodies, unblanketed in the heat: the country whiteness of their breasts, the pliancy of slender limbs, the fox-fire shine on their slumbering faces.

"Why, that little son of a bitch!"

"Louis!" I hissed, dragging him back into shadow.

"Never *mind*!"

"He's not a little *anything*, Louis."

"He's got no business . . ."

I looked hard into his eyes. "Good place to breed a woman, Louis," I said, grinning showily. He tensed, his expression enough to frighten me. Then suddenly it all went loose.

I saw Louis lower his eyes to earth. For a long moment I let him alone; then I put an arm across his shaking shoulders.

"How about you and I go way uplake tomorrow, Louis?" I said. "I haven't been uplake in a lot of years."

Part Two

12

THAT summer of the big wind passed. It passed, and I went away. From Louis. From McLean. From myself somehow—so that I paid: cause and effect, I'm sure of it. You don't murder an owl. You don't quit hunting a crippled deer (as once, chilled and bone-weary, I'd abandoned a gut-shot buck and driven home to find my Back Bay apartment robbed and wrecked). Sin exacts retribution. I believe all that.

Just so, the next summer, when I ought to have been making ready for my forty-first return to those cold waters and dense woods, I lay in bed at Massachusetts General Hospital.

If, feeling mortality's cold chisel clank on the matter of my life, I'd been impelled, that morning on the bridge the June before, to some kind of summary, how much more desperately so in this June a year later. My hip had gone bum, I lay on a bed of pain. And it was still fact, detail, particular that bombarded me. More than ever, I wanted something besides mere accrual. A shape.

How did one start?

Perhaps with childhood—whose prevailing motif for me, however, was impasse. I could remember myself walking down the street after school toward our brownstone, which spanned the alley, dead-ending the thoroughfare. There was a daunting brass griffon on the door. Just inside, on the wall that fronted me, a portrait of some stern ancestor. The reflection in its framed glass showed me myself, ridiculous in school cap and knickers. Less than nobody. Upstairs, after a powdery peck of greeting, Mother would thrust up the black boards of her botanical print portfolio. In another room I could study the starched, wrinkled expanse of Bertha's back as she tended the stove with almost military precision. And in yet another I beheld the pinstripes of Father, gazing as ever out on the gray Back Bay.

What did they all see?

But of course I couldn't think back on children of my own. No first steps or words; no mugging; no pearly finger- and toenails, no gleaming milk teeth. No replications of self. Lying in the hospital, I had Charles to recall, but he'd never been mine. I had also the memory of Anna's swelled womb, the inexact fantasy of what it boded: a baby—but grown now, I thought with a start. It was not that I hadn't considered that child before landing in sickbed. The opposite. But now I imagined an adult, and the adult appeared to me somehow as a woman. Not mine, either, Anna had said. Four decades gone, it was too late to argue. A "child" of forty: still young, but, when I half-glimpsed her in imagination—ever from behind, no face—her gestures seemed so mature and responsible. She bent over a bin of fruits or vegetables; over the abrasion on a little boy's knee, his grass-stained trouser leg rolled back; over smudged newspapers spread on a kitchen table amid the hisses and sputters of cooking. Or, the world being now what it was, over a patient, plying her scalpel.

THE night nurses passed on crepe soles in the corridor, ghostly in its low fluorescence. Around my bed the walls had turned livid too. Under the Demerol, I felt a pulse in my hip, but I could stand apart, looking down with inward eye on the neat stitches in my flank, as if from a slight elevation. I could even peer inside, where the pin neatly transfixed the honed socket. Disinterested, I admired the surgeon's craft: like an engineer's or architect's, really. Artful, this precision, on which I thought I might model my life.

This was my delirium, this backing out of my childhood's austerity, quickly through a vision of busyness, clutter, muddle, gregarious flesh, then into austerity again: the night-silent ward where I lay, where the stainless-steel rivet and the smoothed cup of bone were objects of my distanced meditation.

Drugged and trussed, I forgot for that spell the heaped path of my recent arrival here, its own clutter and muddle: the sloppy washes of pain in my lower back in last summer's cold McLean; the wind that almost took my cabin; the sudden, silly impulse (to hell with this fishing business!) to visit Europe for the winter and spring—Costa Brava a month too early, Italian lakes a month too late, Venice already thronged, littered with dog waste. And finally Chartres, going all wrong for any season, the old quarter shrinking within a hideous suburb. The great church still loomed as I approached from the north, but inside, graffiti everywhere, on every monument. Scrawled. Gouged. And there I was, who had chosen to take The Last Trip.

FOR all of this, I had spent my first afternoon at Chartres, hours of it, in the cathedral, waiting out the slant of early evening light through the celebrated windows. It was no high-minded notion of culture that kept me there, nor a religious urge. Or perhaps my notions of culture and religion ran together into a feeling that gradually took me over.

The sorriest tradesman and peasant in the community had had something to do with this church, even the windows that now admitted a gleam at once palpable and bodiless. A community, acting on shared beliefs. The obscene graffiti signaled an end to those days—but I was just an old man grumbling, as they will do. And despite myself, these little gnats of disillusion fluttered away. My breath began to come in longer drafts, the way a fit young person's will do so soon after the race. The jabs of pain in my body—not acute but pervasive, especially in my time-weary lower parts—seemed also to fly off. I inhaled the buoyant stone- and flesh-dust of centuries, and it seemed, with every exhalation, I might travel out of the vessel that would so soon betray me.

I can't guess how long I sat in the cathedral before those breaths began to whiten in air. They looked so like ghosts hovering then that they startled me from my reverie. I felt myself return to the physical; it was darkening, cold. Or had I been brought back by the custodian's step, reverberant, tendentious in such solitude? I rose very slowly, my legs and hips, for a time forgotten, protesting.

In the Hotel Grand Monarque next morning, the hip crumbled. I envisioned the great stones of the church, their imperceptible erosions suddenly accelerated: a tumble to earth, then a high column of dust, like chalk billowing from a schoolmaster's clapped eraser.

It had begun at the first turn of the hotel's stair, as I descended for coffee and baguette: a weakness more than actual pain. I tried to ignore it and came on, but after the meal, I simply couldn't get up. There'd been no trauma—just that vision of collapse and chalky cloud. It seemed the bone had quietly resigned itself to its own dust.

The waiter, a slight Arab, laid a sympathetic hand on my shoulder, and for that instant I ached with gratitude to this stranger. My tragedy might simply have been his nuisance. Lifting my eyes to his face and its confusion of unshaven whiskers, I made to thank him, but he slid away.

The desk clerk must have called the doctor, a brisk young woman with strong hands, who palpated the hip right in the breakfast room, the other guests studiously averting their eyes.

"*Vous avez quelqu'un qui peut vous rapporter à Paris?*" the doctor asked.

"*Personne,*" I responded.

"*Et alors à Boston lorsque vous arriverez?*" Someone to meet me in Boston? I thought of Louis—impossible. I imagined him standing at Logan Airport, having gotten there God knew how, the world around him teeming with traffic, noise, refuse, despair, and dust. Dust everywhere.

The Arab came back with a peevish chef, who moaned *oo la la* every few feet, pausing showily to wipe his forehead. But together they managed to lift me, chair and all, into the lobby. I sat there sweating—picturing the McLean trout that would rise in less than a month's time—until my call got through to the States. I knew I'd scarcely recognize my broker's face in the airport throng, but who else was obliged to me?

The French doctor returned after the phone call, bearing a medical release of some kind. Once more she examined me, this time taking both my blood pressure and my pulse. I dreamily signed her papers.

"*Votre santé est excellente.*" She smiled. "*Autrement.*"

Well, perhaps. Perhaps I *was* in good shape. Otherwise.

I was back in Boston in thirty hours, with the help of Air France and Calvados.

AT two in the morning in my hospital bed, I woke from a dream—all right angles and brilliant, efficient design. The operation was now three days old, the dream but a few minutes: gleaming steel, buttresses in the Gothic manner, but metal, their warty griffons and gargoyles buffed away. I pushed the button, and a nurse arrived. Not pain, but panic; it was as if I'd seen signs. I took the injection and toppled back into sleep, into something pure white, but a dream still.

When I woke again the pale sun of morning bossed its way through the venetian blinds, casting bars on the walls by my bed. My cocked leg's shadow lay across them, like a fish arched in a net. A dark orderly was thrusting a telephone at me. I couldn't place the voice on the wire. Not at first.

"Hullo, Doc. I have a message for you," it said.

"There's a mistake," I muttered. "I'm a patient. My name is—"

"Doc. Edward here. I have a message. Are you sitting down?"

"Edward."

"Edward."

"Hello, Edward."

"I have a message from up home, Doc. But you better sit down."

"Is this a joke, Edward?"

"Wish it was. You sitting?"

"Done," I answered, a little sullen.

"Charles was killed."

"Charles," I said, vacantly.

"Louis's boy."

Oh God in heaven, I thought, it *was* a joke. You know the way. But Edward went on: Louis was pretty bad; could I come up? I couldn't. Would Edward speak to Louis and see if he'd come *down*? Tell him I'll arrange for everything, Edward. I'll send a chauffeur,

I'll get him a hotel right handy to me, I'll have meals brought in, he won't have to do a thing, I'll do whatever I can do in my goddamn pathetic condition—because, Edward, as I'm not telling you, I love Louis McLean and therefore I must be able to save him. Isn't that right?

It doesn't rain but it pours. It's an ill wind that blows no good. Black cloud over my head. Crowded by every morose cliché in the language, I arranged things. My arrangements! A joke all right, a bad one.

13

MASS. General's public-address system, with its eerie mono-tone messages, and the general clickety-clack in the ward's corridor—these reached me only intermittently. In those moments I'd think, How easy to become an addict. It wasn't so much that the Demerol eased my physical pain as that the chemicals softened the edges of my consciousness. I seemed able to swim at will to where and when I wanted. I was almost *there*, in that preceding August, chugging out past Mason Island in Louis's square-stern canoe, the vision of Charles and Blanche in a moonlit bed still fresh in mind. Sweet, unsettling.

I could feel that morning again, how I'd kept my eyes on the distant headland, avoiding the rows of new camps on either shore near the town landing. I'd rigged a seat against a thwart and poked my legs into the bow cavity, dry and comfortable. I sighted north-westward along the splash deck at Little Porcupine Mountain.

"Well," Louis asked, "now what?" We'd pulled abreast of Togue Stream Landing, after a speechless ride uplake. He had still been in a dark mood over Charles and Blanche. I almost wished for another high wind to blow off the listlessness settled on him like the day's own calm. Something to brace me out of my torpor. I had lain all night on Charles's bed in the crude shack, wide-eyed, un-speaking, even though I could tell from Louis's mutterings and sighs that he was awake too.

Louis was no puritan. Down in my campyard, I'd at first been confused by his reaction—part rage, part sorrow—to Charles and

Blanche. He was, as I say, a protective father, but only when he remembered to be. There'd been something else: he'd seen a sign on the other side of my cabin window, where the kids lay oblivious, beautiful. A sign that insulted a different instinct.

I'm guessing that when a child happens on his parents in love, he gets angry and sad at once. Already he sensed it, but now he knows: even in the near world there are corners that don't include him. And, while Louis coughed and rolled on his cot, I guessed the reverse was also true. The truth flew home to Louis when he saw his son in a woman's bed—Charles had gone to a further place. He was growing up, and away.

Yet he'd been in a far place right along. This was surely part of Louis's pain when we found Charles in my camp with his lover. I've spoken of a certain evasive quality in the boy, which I'd only broken into on those long-gone days on the sealed winter lakes. But hadn't we been evasive, too, Louis and I, in a friendship that so rarely made room for him? Charles's virtues, the fabled Yankee self-reliance above all, were products of necessity. At least partly. Louis bragged of the boy's independence: at a distance, in my company. I echoed the bragging, scarcely conscious that my love of that company called self-reliance into question, that neither Charles's father nor his godfather really wanted it for himself.

Charles wasn't a little boy anymore, I'd said to Louis. And the truth of my platitude shocked me, surprised me into the nightlong wakefulness in Louis's wretched shack. I'd been overwhelmed a few hours earlier by the simple beauty of two young healthy beings. But as I peered into the cobwebbed gloom of the shack, my mind went elsewhere. It would be vain to say I shared Louis's torment, but not quite right to say otherwise.

Charles was making ready for college, surely a notion as mystical to his father as the cryptic signs he got from his spirits. Maybe more so. Maybe even beyond *their* ken. Charles was rushing to stranger and stranger worlds, would likely soon leap out of reach forever. Both Louis and I had believed, whatever the distance we'd kept from him, and he from us, we could narrow that gap at will.

In the silent dark, only the occasional thump of a june bug on the screen or the shuffle in junk of a rodent to upset it, I had smiled, if uneasily, at how ridiculous we are. We don't want to trouble our own blood, so we spend half our lives concealing thought or deed from parents, the other half from children. "Not here," we say, "my mother or father might catch us." Then: "Not here, my son or daughter might see." The silliness of it all! That, and the sadness, the tenderness, so often too late in showing itself.

"Well," Louis repeated, as we drifted in the mouth of Togue Stream, "*now* what?"

"I don't know," I said as lightly as I could. "Let's just poke around." I hadn't had a plan the night before; I'd merely meant to get Louis away from his son and Blanche. But by God this morning *was* after all a good one, whatever the weather inside us. A fine day for poking around: the closeness of yesterday's air had lifted, but the sunny warmth stayed on. A crowd of young loons cackled offshore, staying on too. The older birds—fooled, I supposed, by the recent cold snap—had abandoned the lake. 1961, I mused: Year of the Loons Leaving Early. Year of Big Winds.

"You want to troll or something?" Louis asked, resigned and bitter at once.

"Just to say we did it," I answered. "We could fish back downlake awhile." I flopped a tandem Gray Ghost over the side and carelessly played out my fly line. I suspected that, for all the cool, it was too early to do much on the top water; the fish would still be deep. But I didn't care a lick about trolling in any case.

"I can't get over that damned kid," said Louis.

"Not a good, God-fearing one like we were," I chided.

"That don't mean it's right for him to take a job, and then—"

"And do it quick," I interrupted, "so he can be with his girl for a while?"

"*Be* with her!" Louis cried. "Humped up in the Boss's camp—"

Again I interrupted: "What if the Boss doesn't give a fiddler's damn?" My blitheness was only a posture, and I hurried on: "What if the Boss is maybe a little jealous, that's all?"

I glanced back at Louis over my shoulder; he was quietly studying the shoreline.

"You?" I coaxed.

First he looked at me hard; then he breathed. "Well, I guess that may be."

* * *

BLANCHE was three years older than Louis's boy. Her father had been a Québécois logger and had flown the coop early; her mother was a delicate, pale McLean Lake woman who had moved away when the logger fled. I don't know the story exactly. McLean people referred to the father as Crazy Pierre, but if you asked them why, they shrugged and shook their heads and sighed. In time Blanche had somehow made her way back to McLean, had lived in at Wesley's Sporting Lodge from the age of eleven. Tall and slim, she was late to develop, and the hot young boys of the county ignored her for the busty girls whose charm peaked at about sixteen—girls of twenty or so now, with three-year-old children and unpredictable husbands. They had special tiny rooms where they holed up against the household mess and their men's dazing swings of temper. I felt a real sadness there in Louis's canoe, imagining such retreats, small caverns of tidiness in the chaos. The truth of their lives had come down to this. Never mind all the sweet stupid dreams they'd brought to their weddings. The women crammed these special rooms with the useless remnant keepsakes from their hope chests, trousseaux, showers, whatever: sexy nighties, silver-plate picture frames, ceramic statuettes, costume jewelry. The white dress hung in a narrow closet, prettier than anything else they'd ever owned or would.

Girls with big veins, stretch marks, frog flesh under the Dacron; red hands and doughy skin, swollen ankles and tobacco hacks, crackling snowy televisions, views from their house trailers onto the rusty wrecks in their mud yards. You've seen these places everywhere: a wormy hound, tail flat to his stomach, barks listlessly at the end of his tether out front. It wasn't supposed to be like this.

But Blanche at twenty-two was all grace—shy, understated, elegant. She spoke almost in a whisper, which suited her, though it was a mark of embarrassment at her cleft palate. Once or twice a month for several years, she'd come in summer to clean my camp. I would watch her, obliquely, for as long as I could—she was so easily flustered. If I asked a question, she stammered, blushing to the roots of her pale hair. I was in her way, so I'd go outside to walk the river's bank, a hum of longing, not quite amorous, in my old frame.

Like a curse, never touching the men, the cleft palate had passed through three generations of women in Blanche's family. Her grandmother, the first to be struck, had been a Prince Edward Islander from a prominent farm family. When the bottom dropped out in the new years of the century, she abandoned the place to the hardhack and steeplebush. Somehow she landed in McLean, and for fifteen years—despite her pupils' mockery—struggled as a schoolteacher. Edward remembered her; they'd shared a birthday. On her thirty-fifth, she abruptly died, leaving her child adrift in adolescence. Whose father that child was, no one ever knew. Some rumormongers claimed it was Edward, the same ones who'd always cackled about his infertility with his wives.

"If you think Blanche is shooey," Louis said suddenly, halfheartedly plying his paddle, "you'd ought to seen the mother."

"Was she as beautiful?" I asked.

He didn't answer for several moments. Then he said, "Blanche would look plain beside her."

The soft flood started. Louis trained his gaze on the ash rib at his feet, looking up only to correct the canoe's drift. He spoke for half an hour.

I reeled in. The hazy robin's egg of a sky fused itself to the lake's blue. The heavy freight canoe floated like a shed feather. Dream stuff, story and setting. I closed my eyes and listened as Louis whispered on: how Mary, Blanche's mother, would comb out her yellow hair and, as if that were a narrative ritual, tell ornate tales of Prince Edward Island. She had never seen it, but its name evoked knights and cream-skinned ladies, a world napped by wildflowers and emerald. Everywhere, ogres and tyrants. But in the end hero and heroine always fell together.

"Regular fairy tales!" Louis exclaimed at one point, breaking out of his subdued account. "But they all came out of her head!"

I was amused: here was a storyteller in his own right who wondered at the existence of such tales in the world. And I was touched too.

At last he stopped. I opened my eyes, made ready to ask something, then closed them again in silence. Louis's inflection told all, and his sigh: "It was like religion or something."

"Oh," I breathed. There'd been another thing to keep Louis McLean awake and restless the night before, one I hadn't known of till now.

He bit his lip and looked over his shoulder, astern. One of the young loons, briefly cut off from the flock, babbled for a moment. Then he sang—long, lonely, mournful. Calling the wind, they say.

"How in hell did you let her get away?" I asked.

"You know how kids are. I was a wild thing like any of them." He paused and looked back to me. "And next thing you know, I'm married up to June, and Mary's gone off to work in Trafton, and then I hear she's dead."

"*Dead?*" I coughed. It was a wrenching turn in a sentimental movie that had sucked me in.

Louis balanced the paddle on his lap and ran the tip of a rough finger across his wrist.

I wasn't angry this time, the way I'd been to learn of Louis's affair with Velma Morse. Maybe I'd learned something else by now. Louis had withheld nothing; rather, the time had needed to be right, candor to have its moment.

A person can have a friend, I was thinking, and take two lifetimes for all the moments to be right. The Death of Mary—Chapter 100. How many chapters *were* there? The Wife at the Old Trafton House. Velma and the Ghost of Middle Lake. The Graveyard Haunt. The Naked Slobs of Jake's Island. The Day the Roof Blew In. Faerie Mary. There would always be more on Louis's mind than a friend could figure, or than he could say.

I sat in the bow of the aimless canoe, the glum one now. I couldn't find the words for apology, and I didn't know what, exactly, I was sorry for.

Louis brought me around. "They tell a story about the old schoolteacher, Blanche's granny," he began.

I loved Louis—it was never clearer—for the way he strung his pain upon these stories of his. There in the stern I beheld a man who might just now be mad with his own emotions, if he hadn't been able to stretch their occasions and memories behind him on the delicate thread of his telling. I turned my seat to face him, prouder than ever to be his listener, his almost exclusive listener as these late years piled onto one another. I didn't know him, did I? Yet I followed that thread farther back now than anyone, and I was at least familiar, if certainly not with all, then with many of its loops and tangles. It was in his valiant, persistent efforts at form that Louis rose to what I've named elegance. There he was, and I stared at him in the wonder of it all: this small, cable-muscled man of few teeth and filthy clothes. Elegant man.

"The schoolteacher didn't talk plain. In fact, she talked exactly like Robbie Ross, but she didn't have the split lip. None of the women had that lip some people have when they don't talk plain. Like Robbie had—you'd hear him inside the store, all locked up in there, and him drunk. You could hear him singing 'The Old Oaken Bucket.' Only, the way he was, it come out 'The *oh oh*-en *buh*-et.' "

I chuckled, and laid my rod along the thwarts.

"One day," Louis went on, animated now, "Eleanor comes into the store. That's her, Blanche's grandmother. Maybe it was because they talked the same, but Robbie always thought the world of her. There was a gang of people inside, it was just before Thanksgiving, and that Mrs. Spencer that Robbie lived with—she always made up these little packets of seasoning for the turkey."

"The clock thrower," I said.

"That's the one," said Louis. "But whatever she did, this seasoning was good. Everyone wanted it. And they're all in there, because Robbie's selling it, and it's close to Thanksgiving."

I could imagine the tiny store full of people, edging aside to make room as the bell over the door tinkled, a new arrival entering, stamping feet against the late autumn cold. All along the road outside, the upended bucks are hung.

"Eleanor walks to the counter and asks for some of the seasoning for dressing. But the way she talked, it came out *teednin for dettin*.

" '*Oh* yes!' says Robbie, and he turns around and goes to the shelf. Then he looks at her and says, 'What was it?' And the schoolteacher says it again—*teednin for dettin*.

" '*Oh* yes!' says Robbie, and he turns around again. He doesn't know what in the devil he's after, but he doesn't want to embarrass her. So then he takes a pencil and a paper sack and slips them to her. He tells her, write it down. So she writes it, and Robbie throws up his arms and yells, 'Well, Dee-zus Chrize, you want some *teednin for dettin*!' "

I steadied the boat. Louis's imitation of Robbie had almost upset us. I hadn't heard this one.

"Said it just the same as she did!" Louis laughed. Then, suddenly distant, sober, he added: "All those girls talked like that."

14

THE creaks of the hallway gurneys, the faint moans of discomfort in neighboring rooms, the sirens outside, the frightful late-night steps on sidewalks, the screaming of tires—these, I dreamed, had their hidden pathways and mixed significances, let alone the welter of more inward articulations, half-thoughts, nonce words, shivers. No plot could move merely forward. The world was an unfathomable tide.

My poor mind babbled, throwing up banality against the mysteries, its own and others: sea surrounds us.

SEA. Why had Charles wanted to go there? It had been hard for Louis to imagine. Until our boat trip to Scotland, he had never seen the salt water himself, though it lay only forty miles or so south and east of his town, and the salmon came up from it and returned there. In Charles's final McLean summer, the bright fish long gone, Louis had come to conceive of ocean as a realm of destruction, depravity. I could guess, again, what this was: the pain of seeing a child leave the fold, of saying good-bye to something he hadn't yet rightly greeted.

I had done what I could for my last three weeks in McLean to keep Louis off his son's back. Louis's desperation showed itself as nitpicking and sulking in the boy's presence. I made sure we spent a lot of time out on the lakes: with the shorebirds bobbing on the pebbles, eagles screaming high, the clean water rolling, my friend's volubility returned. For those hours he seemed to forget what he foresaw as the end of a story.

TOWARD dusk one late August afternoon, I came across Charles outside Edward's. I still hadn't paid him for his work, and I used this as an excuse to invite him down for a chat. His father was off on a day job, Charles was a busy kid, I'd never had the opportunity to discuss his decision about the Maritime Academy with him alone. I was curious, about that and more. And I wanted to say something, felt somehow that I should.

As we walked down the road to my place, though, everything came up small talk. I was deep in thought, but what I remember now is his easy, manly stride. It was cool again: I recall also the shocks of the flickers' white rumps when they flushed before us, nervous, the temperature dropping another few degrees each night; the restless little bunches of evening grosbeaks gritting in the roadbed; cedar waxwings among the scarlet berries of Edward's mountain ashes; a red squirrel racing across our path with a spruce cone bigger than himself. Already, too, the orange-edged leaves of soft maple now and then tumbled through shafts of light ahead of us. Fall comes early to McLean.

We went inside, and I wrote a check to Charles for fixing the wind's damage. I gave him a check for Blanche too; I wouldn't see her again—not that summer. I was bound for home before Labor Day; I couldn't face the lakes when they were crowded with motorboats.

As I handed payment to Charles I smiled and congratulated him on the speed and quality of the repair.

"It was a pleasure," he said, solemnly; then he broke into a smile too. I knew what my own grin represented, but guessed at his: did he recall the satisfaction of the job or, as he thought, of putting one over on the old folks? I didn't begrudge him either way. I told him truthfully that I admired his industry, and I wondered aloud if he regretted not having more time for the outdoors. "I think it would kill your father," I added.

His grimace was so quick I scarcely noticed. "Well," he said, "there are times when I miss it. But I figure I have to keep a lookout for the future."

I remembered that ball of vitality on the ice-locked lakes of winter and made ready to speak. But it was years too late for the counsel I'd pledged at his distant christening, and what might I say in any case? What did I know? Only what I was feeling just then, looking at this handsome, erect young man, shocked that that's what he was. You don't ever pay attention, do you? I told myself. Children perpetually lean toward the life to come. And like their parents, they let the life at hand slip by, whatever we say. The habit of preparation becomes the habit of existence, and our aspirations suddenly show up far astern.

Charles lounged against the upstream window. The light from behind him transformed the dead moths, millers, and stone flies on the glass to incidental gems. The white chop of the rapids moved ceaselessly in the background. He planted his broad hands, the fingernails cut square, on the sill.

Yes, I had meant to say something, but what?

"Anything rising?" I asked. He turned back to me.

"Nothing doing," he answered. He knew what I meant.

Would this boy's eye brighten if he could see the red-spotted, pink-fleshed native Adirondack brookies before the water went bad with sour rain? Before I knew a goddamn thing *except* those fish, if I knew a goddamn thing now? However heedless those summers seemed, it was always a matter of a chase, of pursuing something more, something beyond.

I had agreed, unknown to him, to pay Charles's tuition at the Academy. In making the arrangement with Louis, I felt the same old twinge I'd felt each January as I covered June's stay at her hotel. And what were my motives this time? Oh yes: to help a fine young man toward useful employment, and to keep a fine old one away from it—his father, my friend. As Charles and I talked in the kitchen, I looked for reassurance. My apple tree ticked against the west window, its burden of fruit now smeared with scarlet. The rapids mumbled out by my ledge. I offered him a drink, the first time. He accepted, and pulled down Old Bluey.

"Daddy's cup." Charles grinned, no slouch.

I poured him a couple of inches.

"Why the Merchant Marine?" I asked.

"The future. Naval engineering."

How to argue with the choice? Charles was as handy with machinery as Louis was inept. It must have come down to him on June's side: her grandfather had been the boat mechanic back in the days when the train stopped at Vaughanboro, and the sportsmen came up Lower Lake in a steam scow.

"You like the ocean?" I asked.

"Well, I'm curious, you know," said Charles, "but it's mostly other things."

He meant money. Why not? He'd met a man from Pinkham who was head mechanic for a fleet of tugs in Baltimore Harbor, and who worked an alternative monthly shift: four weeks on the job, four up home. The pay would in no time make Charles a rich man by McLean standards, would be a lot more than I could afford to pay his father; and even if Charles had *wanted* to find one of his own, old hunting and fishing bums like me were relics nowadays.

Still, I kept thinking of Louis's stories about his stretch in Massachusetts, where he'd been trained to turn a metal lathe. "I'd see some godawful piece of foolishness come off that line and it'd look like a duck to me." I remembered. "A duck, maybe a deer. Whatever. I had to get home. That's all I could think of—getting home."

I was being sentimental as usual; Louis and Charles had been lifted from different molds. But I had a vision now of the young man in an oil-spattered overall, wrenches in its belt, Charles on his hands and knees in a stinking engine room one liquid Baltimore summer. I could almost hear the flotsam in the greasy water outside—orange rinds and cheap wine jugs and scraps of oyster crate—tapping at the squat tug's hull, the gulls in their vortex above, squabbling over garbage.

"If I can get the schedule right," Charles was saying, "that's the main thing." As if a soul could be scheduled. "I'll have the whole deer season if I'm lucky," he added, but he was talking for my benefit, hoping maybe I'd relay his intentions to Louis. Louis, who in his bewilderment had become something close to a nemesis for Charles.

What the hell? I thought, coaxing myself a bit. It takes all kinds. I raised my cup in a toast, and we knocked down the rest of our drinks in quiet.

THAT first, last drink: the instant bore down on me as I waited in a hospital bed for Louis McLean. I vowed to keep that instant. I'd keep it, along with the winters long before in our bob-house, collapsed now into one: perch fillets in the pan, so fresh they curled head to tail as I dropped them into the grease, and I flattened them back with a spatula. My hands made the gesture now. Even back then, something was looming. I recalled the night in my cabin, the picture of Charles against all the ice and snow, so small.

And yet, sitting there on my sill, big hands wrapped around his father's ghostly cup, his confident baritone conjuring life ahead, Charles was and is in my own conjuring a type of the young hero, a prospective artist, whose task it would be to leap like a dolphin from the sea of platitude that surrounds us.

"Oh, Bulkington!" I suddenly cried.

"Beg pardon?" asked a nurse, unclipping my chart and frowning at it nearsightedly.

15

I GRUNTED myself to a semi-sitting position and offered a weak hand. Louis's was limp, and at length, not wanting to, I dropped it. He collapsed, a small bent man in an oversized chair in the corner of a high-ceilinged room.

Edward had said something about an explosion, but he hadn't offered any details. Now, cautiously, I sought to coax them from Louis—the old response to disaster—as if by knowing every minute part in the dark narrative we might rewrite the coda, make it bright. But Louis gave me the story tersely: Charles had been one of the few freshmen with significant responsibility on the shool ship's training cruise: Philadelphia, Norfolk, Savannah, Miami, San Juan, and finally Kingston, where the sailors would be given four days' shore leave.

"Blanche didn't like that. Jealous," said Louis, flicking a smile and swallowing it.

Charles was of course assigned to mechanic's duty, or whatever they called it. It was when the boat was pulling into Savannah that one of its antique engines blew. The body was being shipped north to school; the state demanded an autopsy. Louis didn't know when the corpse would finally reach McLean, though it didn't matter; he'd have the rest burned, too, out of his sight.

Not that there was anything unceremonious in Louis's character. Not at all. I made a grotesque mental allusion to the cooking of game, in which his fondness for ritual so often revealed itself, as if to treat the kill with such respect and to feast on its flesh were retribution for taking a life. Louis wouldn't cook a grouse, for instance, till he'd cut away a small bag of those red mushrooms that grow on oak, and which the grouse themselves love to browse; and when the bird was broiled he'd place a circle of the mushroom slivers around it on the platter before he'd carve. Yet he hadn't gone to June's funeral, and he wouldn't have a funeral for his son. *That* kind of ceremony meant as little to him, it seemed, as comfort in the woods or in his hovel. Maybe for some reason he thought that a person could be used up, as the saying went, in a way that a wild thing could not.

He broke into my thoughts, the voice dispirited. "I got a good piece of writing here." He handed me a mussed sheet of paper, an official condolence from the Academy's commander. Its language was formal, but there was a handwritten note beneath the signature, the script ungainly: "Charles was the most promising sailor we've had here in my time. Everyone mourns this tragedy." An inscription no less hollow than the formal notice, but the awkwardness of the lettering itself overwhelmed me. There was a momentary hot feeling in the back of my throat. A white boat against the deadly plumes of smoke from Savannah's paper mills; now a violent jet of blacker smoke shooting up among those off-white plumes behind the levee . . . and that is that for the promise. I was weeping.

"Do you mind the time we went to drop him off?" Louis's voice surprised me with its steadiness.

"Oh, Jesus!" I choked, glad for my own wet smile.

CHARLES had been due to register at the Academy on September 1, and I agreed to run him down on my way to Boston. It would make a big detour for me, but the urge against all odds somehow to catch up with him at last made the inconvenience seem worthwhile. I'd treat myself to a night at oceanside. I had a craving for fresh seafood among other things, and you couldn't find such fare anywhere near McLean. And there remained eight empty weeks for me to kill before I took my plane to Europe.

I was looking forward, but the prospect was ambiguous. Maybe it was a sign of getting older myself, I supposed, this impulse to step back into the older cultures. I admit there was some warm feeling in me at the thought of cities in which people through long practice had learned to accommodate one another. An old man could still walk out into the Paris night without much worry about being smacked on the head and robbed. It was crazy at my age to think of romance, but maybe there was something of that in my scheme too. It's hard to find that mood, that fantasy, when you're forever looking over your shoulder as I'd begun to do in Boston—catching my breath on approaching an alley, letting it out in a huff after safely getting by.

Paris. Chartres. Barcelona. Venice. Who knew where I might go? Smooth, pebbled paths and orderly gardens beckoned. I admit, too, that I was a little unnerved by my own eagerness. This self of mine was supposed to be a woodsy thing, but there in mind stood another Brant Healey, the one who spoke classical French and who had longed for the woman with a rangy "European" mind. I had tried for so many years to drown whatever little of that other person there was, to wash him away in cold northern water, rub him off in the dense thickets around McLean, dissolve him in conversation and whiskey. What would I do if I encountered that ghost as he stood at his ease by a splashing fountain, while the piping jackdaws swooped, spire to spire, above?

There were times when I almost considered chucking the trip, running Charles down and returning, staying on at McLean till I felt secure again. Till it froze hard. There'd be leisure to read. There'd be hours to watch autumn come to the shores upstream, the spray hardening to crystal on Mink Rock, the young loons calling up the migrating breeze they needed so that they might cross the flat-topped moon of November. Once again my Atlantic wood stove would glow and the teapot chatter and the puddle ice crack up underfoot as I walked out at morning.

And yet, I had to remind myself, the fall always rings loss. More so even than spring, which at least gives the illusion of abundance and plentiful time, daylight stretching in that northland from dawn till almost ten o'clock. After the afternoons shortened and finally went away entirely, I'd be shut in on myself, cornered into rehearsal of the grim old mathematics of my life. No, I'd better go.

Louis would go too. Partway. He had finally insisted on traveling with Charles and me to school. He'd get back somehow, he said.

"Would you look at *that*?" Louis had exclaimed as we pulled into the lot. The Academy's main building was long, and four stories high. It glared in the late afternoon, each window returning the sun's red, the flag on its roof blown taut by an onshore wind. It would rain by nightfall.

Charles left us at the car. Off he strode in his white shirt and blue pants, one of those people whose clothes seem never to wrinkle or muss. There was a new, a practiced stiffness to his gait, and his arms hung rigid at his sides. I noticed how he held his chin tight to the chest, as if he were on parade, hundreds watching, though as far as I could tell there wasn't a soul around. Indeed, the building and the grounds had the eerie feel of an abandoned stage set, or a fortress with its inhabitants sequestered out of sight.

There was something in me that rankled at the boy's affectation, and something that was touched. How important it was to appear collected. I recalled my own strenuous efforts, walking into the brick schoolyard as a child, praying that none of the older boys, who, I believed, really *were* serene and self-confident, or the girls, whose beauty made them invulnerable, would shout an insult or even a friendly tease to undo me.

Louis and I lounged against the warm hood of the Buick, gazing out on the bay. I wondered what Louis had "had" that morning. He kicked at the gravel and tires now and then, cleared his throat as if to speak, but didn't. Already it seemed that Charles had been gone so long.

A big black bird sheared off the water and pumped over us. "What's that?" Louis asked.

"A cormorant, Louis. Shags, they call them. Fish eater, like a loon; can't walk on land. You see them on the piers and jetties. They sit on their tails."

"Big as a loon, anyhow," Louis acknowledged. And that's all he said till we saw Charles coming back, a canvas duffel in one hand. He had the same walk, but even more pronounced now. A man in whites strode along next to him. He had the walk too.

The wind turned off, suddenly. A boy was hauling in the flag, which slithered slackly down the pole, its stars collapsed in a weak heap. Hundreds of shags lifted along the near shore and headed for open water. All was plain. Charles and the uniformed man came on, their pace authoritative, but the coming seemed slow.

Louis's son had assumed a grave expression, though his struggle to do so was evident: his eyes sparkled, his chest heaved, and he held the corners of his mouth firm against a proud grin. And Charles's father wouldn't embarrass anyone.

The officer introduced himself, shook our hands. He was surely the most relaxed of us all, full of smiles and chat: how had the ride been? what was the weather like up north? what did we think of the campus?

It was over quickly enough. Charles marched away beside the officer, and Louis got into the Buick. I stood on the asphalt alone, watching the retreat. The two went more rapidly than they'd come. Lights began to flicker on in the barracks, and—just as they reached it—a floodlamp on a pole burst into brightness. Charles walked briskly across its yellow circle on the ground. At the doorway, barely visible, he turned and threw a smart salute. I don't know if Louis saw it.

THE silence was thick as I pulled away, veering north along the bay and crossing the low bridge that would drop us into a village, one of those former fishing towns that was now a summer haven, a gin-and-tonic town, a town of tasseled moccasins and madras. I'd been raised to that nonsense, but I felt as much out of my element as Louis must be feeling, if he was thinking about elements at all. Probably he wasn't—at least not of these.

We were three or four miles down from my parents' old summer place, and I thought of the brief weeks I'd spent there as a boy. Mother coming from Boston for the season, as it was called; Father training down for the weekends, and then for the full month of August. I'd arrive from the Adirondacks at New Bedford, where I was met by a driver and taken prisoner for the last two weeks that Father was there. Family obligation, though I'd much rather have stayed in the mountains. My parents' awkwardness and displeasure at my presence were palpable even to me. Those two weeks every summer seemed to pass more slowly than my two preceding months on the trout brooks. There was nothing for me there, and what Mother and Father took for sullenness was rather helplessness: I couldn't learn the code, merely lapsed into tongue-tied silence at their cocktail gatherings and fancy picnics.

Directness is hard to come by, wherever you are, and certainly there amid the tinkle of ice in expensive tumblers, the *tock* of croquet balls, the dirge of the groaners offshore. To this day the sight of neat white yachts at their moorings calls up in me a mix of bitterness, anger, and inadequacy.

But I do remember one summer, when my parents hired a Portuguese yardman whom they called Al. He moonlighted by pulling a few pots in the harbor, and I went with him one morning. My parents, sleeping in, didn't know that, and never would. I was always up with the sun, however hard I tried to sleep late, knowing that a long, empty day stretched ahead. I was riding a spidery bicycle around the village when I saw the gardener. He was on a bicycle too. I recognized him from behind, less by his appearance than by the scent of his cigar: it trailed its exhaust as he pedaled, and I pumped through it, oddly eager, like a hound on scent. You can smell that cigar even now amid the stalls of the North End markets, and whenever I do I recall that short, dreamy chase down the seaside street, the rolling *r*'s of Joao's speech, the hollow coughs from his inboard engine before it caught. The sun was a dazzle just over the bay's horizon; it changed the gasoline slicks around the tiny pier where I waited, nibbling sweet bread on a bench. Joao spoke in his language, mild and melancholic, with three other olive-skinned sailors. His was the small boat *Astrud*. Then we cast off. On the next wharf a boy about my age pulled up a yellowish fish on a handline; it flipped two or three times, then puffed itself up like a toy balloon. The boy was so sure of himself: he knocked the fish across the snout with a short baton and it deflated.

Joao's first trap was empty. He dropped a fish head into it, mumbling what was probably a curse, but so soft that the words sounded soothing. There was a shedder in the second pot, and he slipped it overboard, repeating the oath. In the third there were two substantial lobsters. "Santa Maria!" Joao shouted, and the utterance of glee, oddly, was the harsh one. Joao lifted the shellfish out and put them in a huge bucket of brine. I could hear them click at its sides. He rebaited the trap.

There were only three more pots, one empty and two with a lobster apiece. The business took less than an hour, and we chugged back to the pier. I helped him lug the bucket onto the musty wharf. The only lobsters I'd seen had been on a plate, steaming, scarlet, motionless. These had the hues of old terra cotta, like brick with a green, mottled overlay. I heard them crawling, then rushing from one side to the other of the pail. But when I looked it was only the crawl I saw.

"How does a lobster move quickly when he wants to?" I asked.

"He fly with his tail," said Joao, with a stunning white smile. The words were not much, but there on the wharf, somehow they coruscated in brain and body like a passage of thrilling music. I liked Joao, and more. The summer's stay would seem less bad.

These few days, though, would be the only ones I'd spend with him. He wouldn't be back next summer. My parents would replace him with Walter Adams, who limped behind his mower like a convict, and had nothing to say to me.

"What happened to Joao?" I asked my mother a year later.

"To whom?"

"Al."

"We let him go," she said. "He wasn't our sort. You know how they are." I didn't precisely know who "they" were, but it was clear that Joao *wasn't* my parents' sort, not even as a menial, and I wasn't surprised.

Joao. Was he *my* sort? How can I answer? I never knew him, someone might justly say. How weak my claim, that it was a kind of knowing, that shiver at the aptness of his language in that factual surround, the one he loved. The lobster flies with his tail— even metaphor need not entirely shy from fact.

WAS Louis my sort? As I crept along the bay in my car, he remained quiet beside me. My mind tangled. The boats in their slips were vanished in darkness, but for a light here and there in their cabins. A haze had settled on the water, small ribbons of it blowing across the road. Soon it would drizzle; soon you wouldn't know east from west, north from south. Out on a pile, a lighthouse flashed, disappeared, flashed again. I could briefly see Louis's profile; it was stone, and he said not a word.

Directness is hard to come by. I liked things. I liked to talk about things. The loon calls the wind. The spawning cock salmon puts on a fighting face. The rutting grouse drums and bursts into crazy-flight. Things leap, things fly, into figuration, and you can't help it if you will. Your boots get "friendly" after a season. The metaphors, the figures, stand clear on the horizontal, but to what do they point on the vertical? There is something up there. There is a big, encoded story we want to tell, not merely act out. Joao, Louis, Brant.

THE fog had rolled over the road, and I made my way at fifteen miles an hour. From the mist itself Louis spoke up, startling me. "We've made a lot of tracks together," he said.

"We have," I agreed. We were together to be sure. And had been, for a long time, making tracks. I could almost smell the cold mud with the paired bootprints in it. They wandered on for leagues, but I could follow them, whatever the switchbacks and crossings—around a knoll here, a rock there, across a shallows or a shaded sidehill.

I bought a couple of rooms at a guesthouse, and we dropped our bags before driving out again. A drink or two and a good batch of seafood might set us up. We were blue, but blue together, and that mood wasn't all unpleasant. I'd given Louis one of my old tweed jackets to wear. The rest of him would be under the table, and who gave a damn anyway?

The smile of the maître d' stiffened at our entry. I could see him labor to hold it. He led us to a table at the rear of the room, by the kitchen door. I puffed myself up a bit, my hand on the back of my chair, preparing to make a speech of objection. There were certain skills I'd acquired as an upper-class boy, and I could turn them on when I needed to. I could see the host puff up as well; it might be a good fight. But Louis had already sat, all unconscious, and I contented myself with a significant scowl. The hell with it.

I ordered a dozen littlenecks on the half shell. Louis watched in awe as I ate them. I couldn't urge a lobster on him, either. I asked for one, and, after a good deal of mumbling over the menu, got him a Chateaubriand. The cut was for two, but there was nothing else he would try. "I want something that moves on legs," he said, "not some damn thing that crawls along like a bug." I chuckled. Fine. I got a bottle of Muscadet, and Louis drank two double bourbons.

When the waiter returned with the beef, Louis moved his china plate and hefted the whole pewter serving platter into his place. Before I got my food the same waiter handed me one of those paper bibs with the red effigy of a lobster on it. I sneered, laying it on the table, looking around for the huffy maître d'. Some class establishment! But Louis pointed the tip of his jackknife at the bib. "You ain't using that?"

"All yours." I smiled.

He put it on, and made two rolls in the jacket's cuffs. His thick wrists poked out several inches. The buzz in the dining room had slackened; now it picked up again, lower than before, sprinkled with inhibited laughter. I stared down three tables. Louis plowed on. He held the knife in his fist, point down, drawing it toward him.

I made quick work of my meal compared to him, and sat back to watch him carve great chunks of Chateaubriand, the juice running down the paper bib. He took a break midway to order a third whiskey. "Got to clear the pipes," he explained. I returned his grin, inwardly congratulating myself, though, for leaving half the wine. It would be a twisty ride back to the guesthouse through the fog.

Now, less than a year later, Louis sat in my hospital room. When he went for a pee I hunted in my bedside drawer and found a five-dollar bill. The hired driver was leaning by my door, peering into his black cap as if he had lost something in it. I tried to imagine him pulling up to Edward's store in the limousine, jingling the bell when he stepped across the threshold in his uniform, silent old men on the pine bench pausing at their cribbage to inspect a stranger. I called him in.

"Set my friend up at the hotel across the street, will you? He's not used to the city." I handed the driver the five, which he folded and stuck in his breast pocket.

"Yeah," he said, "it must be something for him. I felt like Daniel *Boone* up there, I can tell you!"

Louis came out of the john and meekly surrendered his suitcase, a bizarre affair made of shiny metal. Where in hell had it come from?

In a quarter of an hour the driver returned with a key and a paper, Louis's room number written in large ciphers upon it. I gave the man another five, thanked him, and let him go. After Louis and I had eaten, or rather beheld, the gelid supper brought up from the cafeteria, we sat quiet and still: one of the few stretches, I thought, in which he did not drum his fingers, did not whistle, did not stand and sit by rapid turns.

At seven o'clock I caught a housekeeper going off shift. "Maeve!" I called. She was a brassy Irishwoman, all heart. We'd been carrying on a mock flirtation.

"Now what do *you* want, you rascal?" she asked. "I've got a man to get home to."

"You don't know what that is," I teased.

"Don't let himself hear you say that," she warned, blushing. "Not till you're up on your feet, anyway."

I rummaged around in the drawer again and found a ten. "Go out and buy us all a drink, won't ye, love?" I tried to mimic her rollicking brogue, a flop.

"That awful bourbon, I suppose." She said *boorbon*.

"I'll teach you to drink good whiskey yet," I chided. "Get a fifth of Old Crow."

On her return, I poured us all an inch or two. We toasted each other, though Louis barely sipped. I made to refill Maeve's paper cup, but she held it away. "Now don't be trying to ruin a good honest girl."

"Where could I find one?" I answered.

"Devil have ye, you black rascal, you."

"You can't mean that, sweetheart." I made a hurt face. She rose from her chair to pat me on the head.

"Of course not, lovie. I'll ask you both a blessing tonight from Our Lady."

"What lady?" Louis asked as she walked out the door, but he didn't seem to care about the answer.

MIDDLE Lake. The Black Pool. A beaver crossing upstream from my ledge. The deadhead popple that rent my roof. The red chimney over that roof. The wood-burning Atlantic. In my torpor, after the night nurse left me my bedtime pill, my mind grasped at these specifics and others by way of staying wakeful. The trick worked better than I might have guessed, yet when I'd come to for a spell, I wanted to move on. With Louis sitting so silent and mournful by my bed, it was as if *I* were on the point of death, had been told—as the saying goes—to get my affairs in order.

Philosophy is the art of learning how to die, said the Frenchman. And so, I thought, maturity must be the high road to death. Yet what was it really but a knack for arrangement? Certain ambitions you sweep up and throw out—they don't belong, and get in the way of more important ones. I wouldn't, I thought, ever get around to trying the bonefish down in the Keys. I wouldn't see the Andes. How does a steelhead fight? Is a snow goose easier to fool than a Canada? What are those glass fly rods like?

Perhaps I'd make new acquaintances, but like the old I'd range them in their proper categories: this one for talk of the theater; that one for old-timing about the thirties; this one for lamenting the state of the world; that one because he really knows painting. So on.

What after all was Louis?

In the hallways, interns twitted and flirted with the nurses. An orderly's radio rattled Latin percussion. Life was about to go on without my witness, and Louis's listlessness deepened my own. I was helpless, literally tied to a bed, and it was impossible to dispatch him anywhere in the city. Even if it had not been, where might I send him? I began to feel I was under siege, that Louis was waiting me out for some reason. He was still numb from catastrophe, and I was a tired old man, and sick. Now and then I would try to render the scenes I called to mind, to summon objects, to touch on situations in which I believed we had felt like brothers. I found myself now and then in the stupid position of telling him his own stories and jokes. He sat on, ruminative.

At length, made tactless by my own pain and exhaustion, I broached a subject he hadn't referred to. Had he not been warned? "Did you have it that something was up? I mean, when Charles—"

He cut me off. "Yep."

I waited, but that was all. God forgive me! I'd grown self-pitying, and I was angered now by his incommunication. I told him I was sleepy, and sent him to his room across the street. He gave a single head nod, rose, and shambled to the hallway, more stooped than I remembered, slower; the shoulders of his plaid wool jacket hung down his arms. His salt-and-pepper hair was a wilderness on the back of his head, and his neck was deeply grooved—I thought of a remark he'd made about Leo, tribal governor on the Indian point: "Each of those wrinkles would hold a week of rain." I might have called him back, but sleep was on me. I fell into it with a hope that he'd make it safely across the road downstairs, dangerous with traffic even this late.

THE bartender kept pleading with us to let him close. He could lose his license; *we* could get into trouble. But we shouted him down. To hell with it anyway!

Louis leapt over the bar and drew a dozen mugs of beer himself. He sang "Nine Inch Will Please a Lady" and the crowd roared. He sang it again, and the barman relented. He stooped down, brought up an immense bottle of Old Crow. There were beads of water on it. I touched one that fell on the counter; it broke apart, shining like mercury, and it was ice cold.

Now the bartender drew a pitcher of some clearer liquid. "Spring water!" he cried.

Mixed clientele: Indians, whites, dark and fair Europeans, woodsmen in their clashing plaids, blacks. They all fell on the free fare.

A beautiful young waitress, skin like snow, brought in a tray of smoked salmon slivers, wafer thin, the color of good oak. We put on our paper bibs and fell on it too. No one had ever tasted better, and the bartender said there was a limitless supply. We couldn't believe our good fortune.

A very fat man had drunk too much. He took off his clothes, poured the pitcher of water over himself and shivered, jogging his great white belly, wetness trickling through its folds. The waitress blushed to the roots of her hair and stammered. Louis fought to get back over the bar: "You ignorant son of a bitch!" I could hear him shouting, but the fat man had disappeared.

It had been windy when we came in, but now, through the venetian blinds, you could see how still it had become. A flag hung limply in the night square outside. We couldn't decide whether to open the windows or not. A man with a scar on his cheek announced that there were bugs, frantic to enter. We looked, and there they were, bits of scarlet tinsel on the panes, backlit by the sinking sun. We left the windows shut.

Louis tried to lift the sudden gloom. He jumped on top of a table, started to sing again, and to dance an odd, stiff-legged jig. Then I noticed that his song was soundless; he was mouthing the words of "The Shores of Gaspereau." So the barman reached under again and came up with a bagpipe in the shape of a large black bird.

He had just begun a lively reel when he stopped, the instrument's bellows collapsing with a whinnying sigh. We were all quiet again. The bugs were coming in through a hole in the roof. Dust rained into the pub. "Look out for your drinks!" the bartender yelled. I covered the top of my glass, but it was too late: the whiskey had turned to paste, and I set it down. I lifted a panel of the venetian blind and saw that the shore patrol was approaching the door. The waitress put her tray down beside me and wept. The salmon was gone. The platter was full of little yellow blowfish, smothering in the dust clouds. I coughed.

There were two police, each armed with a short, lead-filled pool cue. No point in resisting.

Why did they single us out, Louis and me? They tied a bell around his neck and wrapped me with a thick rope. They let everyone else go. The bartender began to say an Ave Maria, but paused long enough to call after me, "Tight lines!" It seemed cruel.

We were hustled outside, then down to a river and aboard a vast, double-prowed boat. The crew weighed anchor. The violent wind had sprung up again, and we were scuttled toward a small island in the middle of the salt bay. Far to the south, across the water, another boat was flaming, foundering. Louis buried his face in his hands for a moment, then looked up at me and held a bloody knife to the underside of a wrist. *No, no! Don't go!* I screamed. The high wind carried my words away from him, back to the shore, where a tall woman raised her head to hear them, but she turned on her heel and strode with a peculiar gait to a bicycle. I tried to rush astern to cry out to her, but I was in leg irons now. I could feel them cut into my upper thigh. Was it bleeding? I couldn't stop the pain.

The ship ran far up on a sandy beach. A curious island. Otter paths marked its muddy scarps, pure vertical slides. I thought the otters must knock their brains out on the black rocks below, and they'd soon be extinct if something weren't done. What could I do, shackled?

There was a wide stream dividing the island, flowing briskly to sea down the sharp pitch. It was glutted with fish, a shower of astonishing color, even in the twilight that was passing to darkness. All these fish tumbled toward the bay, where the fiery white boat had now gone under.

Salmon!

Louis was shaking me by the shoulders. "There's the camp!" he yelled. "There, on the island." I saw nothing. "We have to stay there the rest of our lives," he shouted, and I didn't know what to feel. Would the fish come back or were they gone forever? Louis wouldn't answer. He just kept up his rough shaking, now saying only my name, again and again. I tried to rise, but the leg irons held me fast.

"Brant! Brant! Brant!"

THE hospital room had its ghostly look again. Evening. I smelled the whiskey on Louis's breath, and smiled, but he was sobbing.

"Louis?"

"I'd better be headed, Brant."

"Sleepy?" I asked, forgetting that he'd gone to the hotel much earlier.

"Hell, I can't sleep. I mean McLean."

"No, no, don't go," I said.

"This isn't any place for me," he countered.

I sighed, rubbing the slumber from my eyes. "Of course," I said. "I'll set it up tonight if I can." I reached for the phone.

"You can't call anyone now," Louis whispered.

"What time is it?" I asked.

"You humpback son of a bitch." He smiled, ever so faintly, and turned the bedside clock to face me. Four A.M.

IT was a slow morning. The limousine service had promised a driver by eleven, but it was already noon. Louis sat hunched at the foot of my bed, shivering despite his eternal plaid mackinaw, picking at threads in its wool. I combed my mind for something to say;

for us to part so wordless would be a death. I was struggling, as a miler who has trained for months might do; all that work and purpose can't come to nothing in this last stretch.

But I wasn't getting anywhere. It was Louis who would save us. "I had it that morning, Brant." At last. "I mean, I had about *all* of it." His face was set; there was none of his animation now, none of that odd look between pain and eagerness, which, for all my scoffing, had always accompanied this prologue. His eyes were empty; or perhaps they were so full of something that they had the appearance of vacancy. A matter of boggling scale in either case.

He had suppressed it during these long Boston hours, as they must have seemed to him—the fact that he'd gotten his message differently this time. It had not come as a hint, a whisper, a trembling of the veil, but full of specificity.

As he spoke I saw that his demons, his portents were, with the dying of his son, tropes of dread alone; that happy omens now would be irrelevant; that he didn't know if he was anymore man enough to deal with the graphic bad ones; that he mourned not only the death of Charles but perhaps, also, of his own resilience.

Louis had "got" not only that it would be bad, but also that the evil involved fire, explosion, water. Though the images were general, they were images still, not suprasensory rustlings. Fire. Explosion. Water. He went first—God bless him!—to my camp. Propane? Freak lightning? Arson? Some weird, fiery flood from the river? I could picture him hurtling around the last bend in my drive, leaning into the turn, almost losing his footing on the rutted gravel, his face slacking as he found my little camp intact. Catching his breath, he rushed on to Blanche's room at Wesley's, for his spirits had never mentioned anything about the world outside his own small circle of affection. He wasn't a diviner. He couldn't have told you that Truman would upset Dewey, that the Cubans would erect missile sites, that a war would start or end. Blanche's room was fine, and Blanche as well: she scrambled out onto the porch of the big lodge, a dish towel in her hands, and shouted to Louis, who by now was already tearing cross-lots to look at his locker, where he stored his gasoline, outboard motor, canoe. But all was tranquil there too.

"I figured the bad thing that was going to happen just hadn't happened yet," he explained to me. "So I went back up to my place and got set to wait it out, whatever it was."

Then it came to him. Charles's world had been so distant from his, more distant even than my own in the Back Bay. It took time for Louis to think of his boy. But when at last he did, he walked, already resigned, to Edward's and asked the old storekeeper to call the Academy. The secretary must have been bewildered; they had just received the dreadful word themselves. She didn't even yet have names of the injured or dead. Could Edward leave a number? But I can see it clearly: Edward, turning, begins to speak, is cut off by the slap of the screen door behind the ruined father.

I LAY in my bed, the throbbing leg jacked on three pillows, so that the pile half hid Louis from me. What I could see of his face was as vacant as it had been all along. I felt that old guilt descend on me like a fog, I, who had financed the disintegration of my friend's tiny family. I tried to call up the joyless face of his wife, but found I'd forgotten it. I wondered if Louis himself could remember, so long had she lived apart in the hotel room I'd paid for. And Charles's face—I convulsed at the image of it, melting to nothing in the ship's sudden fury of heat.

Louis seemed to read me. "Never mind. It was a bad day. I had it, Brant. It was coming, and never mind."

But it had come, and I did mind. The going away had come.

The pain throbbed in my pillowed bone, but I'd get over it if my luck held. Some pain, I knew, you didn't get over; it sank into your character. I knew that from my own experience, which seemed puny, almost pastoral, by the standards before me. Yet when the driver picked up the silly lunch-box suitcase and walked from the room, I hugged Louis hard. As if I were hugging myself.

Part Three

16

My letters that autumn were full of exaggerated encourage-
ments and well-wishing, and of course they went unan-
swered. Writing came hard to Louis. Once I'd asked him to
transcribe a poem of his that slung mud at the downcountry crew
who'd been sent by the PWA to build the McLean schoolhouse.
Louis set about it at three o'clock on a September afternoon. For
hours he sat gloomily by my upriver window. As the outdoor light
dropped off, I could see his reflection in the big pane: he lolled his
tongue, gripping the pencil like a stirring spoon. Finally he rose
and walked out, wordless, homeward. I never made such a request
again. He composed in his head, and that was that. Somewhere I
still have the beginning fragment of the schoolhouse piece:

> They built a school in McLean Lake Stream
> For seventeen thousand dollars.
> I don't know why they'd build a barn
> For educating scholars.

I wish I had the whole by heart.

To check on my friend, I was forced to call Edward. Om-
nicompetent Edward! Well into his nineties now, he seemed to go
on forever, but something in me was checking on him too. Mad
with the Boston summer, with thumping around my flat in a
wheelchair, with the company of my practical nurse, who seemed
for some reason to blame the world's bad order on the Beatles, I

sensed Edward as a monument in my life. We'd never become friends in the way I might have hoped: he was so industrious, there was little leisure, and the years ripped by. But I admired him and wanted to communicate as much, to say at the simplest that I liked him. I'm not sure I succeeded, ever, but he had meant so much to me, for things he likely didn't remember. On the telephone one morning, he told me of some geese that were spending that summer—the one of crumbled hip and deadly boredom—on the beaver pond near the sugar orchard. How did he notice these things? Wasn't he always there, behind the counter? He said the hen had three eccentric white feathers on her back. Three, he said. So specific.

But did Edward remember, from twenty years before, when fall geese were common in the right weather, when he'd been the best caller in the county, using voice alone, scornful of any store-bought reed? I couldn't do it that way, yet he was large enough to let me honk my call on every other pass. One evening a single drake had appeared out of the dusk's low clouds; I blew for what I was worth as he sat silent, but all I could get the goose to do was to circle out of range, and then go on. Time was against us. Still, he said I must try the next bird, too, should he arrive. And he advised me, "Cut back on the call; it's toward evening." I'd never thought of it, how the night goose merely clucks— not calling anyone in to feed, not calling to anyone already feeding. The darkness is growing, he wants to know what's going on, but the night will be big and he feels small. Cluck. Chirp. Cluck-cluck.

The next one came in like a dream, so close we let him hover over the decoys, then spooked him deliberately. Edward's scar lifted in his version of a smile. Wisdom is toward evening, famously.

Edward taught me a lot: that call; the double-haul cast for the brisk wind or the distant rise; and something, I hope, about endurance, though like *affection* or *admiration* that was a concept so disembodied he'd never speak of it directly. There are rules. Perhaps it wasn't a failure of skill on my part that prevented me from moving the talk that summer, or ever, off fish and game and weather:

Louis looks a little used up, but he's getting along, and that vet who's moved to Pinkham took a hell of a brown on a nymph last week, and he's a good one, he don't kill many of them, even fishes a barbless hook, not a bad egg when you get to know him, Louis is guiding a bit, and Blanche is looking after him some, a good girl, she seems a little used up herself, and I'll be damned if Bill Ware didn't catch a squaretail in Middle Lake, I thought the bass had eat them all up, Louis told me to tell you he was fine if you called, and the camp's okay, and I got a girl boarding at the house now, Doc, and when I saw what she could do with a needle and thread I taught her to tie flies, and she's about the best you'll ever see, selling her stuff right here in the store and people calling for it from all over, and I'll tell Louis you phoned, and I bet you miss the river, and you can give them the devil *next* summer, Doc.

Edward rarely spoke more than a sentence at a time. I've run the summer's conversation together. All of it. And most of the next two summers' too; it would take me that long to get back home. The hip healed slowly.

I'D like to say that I spent twenty-seven months—from June of '62 till September '64—away from my cabin and river because no part of McLean had ever been for me a part of sickness, death. But this would be false on all counts. Truth is, I was too infirm. Let me pass, then, as abruptly as I may to August of 1964. A bright young leader had died violently meanwhile, yes. Things happened. But of me there is nothing to report. Nothing, at any rate, that I *want* to report from that purgatorial interlude in Boston. This is exact, not evasion. The dull terror of my life was that, in my circumstances, every day a nothing would come again, a nothing stay.

It was sweltering hell. I had broken down and gotten a small air conditioner. There had been another operation, corrective of the first. And for all that its seasons ran together, McLean became more than ever a needful place. If I had a prayer of recovering, I required home ground. Ground on which prayer might be valid.

I had the place in mind, and do.

Suddenly I determined to throw down my canes, to rid myself of Susan the nurse, demon from the realm of Despair, sent to wheel me toward inanition. I recognized her tricks at last, and knew I must counter them. She told me that I had needed the follow-up surgery because I'd tried to rally myself too quickly. I should stay in my wheelchair, she warned. I came to see her as a beautiful seductress, with the heart of a crone. Her church beads click in memory like the ratchety bearings of the chair itself. I forced myself to keep the tumbling cold rapids of my northern river in mind, lest my bones sink back into that chair, lest I sit unspeaking beside Susan as by a poisoned, lifeless pond.

It was a struggle: I huffed and puffed in my tiny hallway. Susan would prevail if I couldn't bring that cool and moving water right up close. I had to imagine my stiff back relenting. In mind, I dropped to a game knee, drinking till I was alive again. Drinking till the nurse's prophecies of destruction were lost in the tumble of Big Falls.

How ludicrous, to support this fantasy of regeneration by means of a machine! The air conditioner hummed, and I dreamed of the surge in the Black Pool. We live our compromises, and I haven't gotten this far without saying so. But it was bad enough to force those laps back and forth in my hall; I didn't have to *sweat* through the calisthenics too. I pictured myself walking, sound and bold, out of the thrumming mechanical world. If I did so with the help of a mechanism, so be it.

Susan knitted. She told her beads. But mostly she clucked in front of the TV. The world was doomed. She could see it in the brashness and popularity of the Big Texan, as she called him. Breathless in my corridor, I'd pause and spy on her, and those intervals all stream together in my recall with black-and-white images on a screen: her execrable Beatles almost innocently whipping up the frenzy of girl-children on *The Ed Sullivan Show*, one of their microphones dead but no matter, and Ed himself expressionless, uncertain whether he approves or despises what's going on; a line of blacks on the road to Ole Miss, hatred and panic exploding from hecklers' faces; the President smiling like a crocodile as he holds up his little beagle by the ears.

It was this last clip that drove Susan almost to distraction. But Johnson had a way of turning things aside. He repeated the act for reporters, who hurried back and wrote that the dog seemed to like it. I remember feeling good that someone with a little country in him was living at the White House, somebody with a hound, someone whose figures of speech conjured barnyard and grain field. I liked the Texan manner. There was a handful of Quakers and malcontents, as I thought, who were after him for the police action in the old French colonies in Indochina. They, too, showed up on the endless television parade, quiet, earnest, inscrutable. They saw a world out there that you and I could not. But no one appeared to pay them much mind, least of all Lyndon. Who'd have imagined it? We'd gone from Harvard to the Pedernales in a wink. There was some change afoot, and I didn't mind a bit. The Big Texan was in for a big win in November. I'd vote for him myself, though this would be in part a vote against Susan. That's the way my mind was working in its desperation.

My response to the rest of television fare, or what I saw of it in those winded glimpses from my hall, was boredom and impatience and contempt all rolled into one. Those, and a kind of fear. What would become of me? Sometimes I caught myself sitting at my desk, drumming fingers like Louis, even whistling through my teeth. Susan was a jailer: to converse with her was like listening to the anchorman's gloomiest headlines. No life penetrated her life—so I'd think in my rare softer moments. A baby still, well trained, handsome, intelligent. And so disapproving of everything that boiled around her as to keep out of the world as fully as she could. Soon, though, my guard would come up, the compassion turn to resentment, the resentment again to fright. I might look into the mirror and see that same grainy texture of black-and-white dots, that general gray: that flattened life, that Back Bay, that ash I was becoming.

I got her out after Labor Day, '64. I was down to a single cane, and was even moving around the city some—on her days off. One afternoon, Susan having gone to her mother's after breakfast, I taxied to Charles Street on a whim. I call it that, but now I nearly believe there was a spirit involved. My project was to hike through the Common and land in the Park Plaza. The day was good, one of those short lulls in the humidity. The grass had gotten back some green overnight, and even the wretched bums on the benches seemed languorous, Mediterranean, almost healthy, at ease: all delusion, of course, but there it was. Something in me was fighting back by whatever means, seeing differently. Different light. Different odor falling from the trees. Whir and commotion of the pigeons' wings as they burst up in their blue clusters. I imagined a spring in my step, and climbed Beacon Hill rather than walking straight across to the square. The gold roof of the State House flared with the afternoon sun; the bricks looked Florentine. I wasn't out of the woods, but I was in a clearing.

It took me an hour to reach the Gardens, but I made it. I stood on the bridge and watched the swan boats glide by. It was no place for me, but I was there, the croaking of mallards recalling wonderful old mornings in a blind. I wasn't dead. I discovered myself conning the filthy water for the impossible flash of a nymphing trout's flank. I laughed aloud—I'd survived, I would survive.

I came to rest in the hotel's oak bar.

The bartender and I fell into conversation, no one else in the room. He was tough Southie Irish, and I liked him right off. We talked about this and that over an incongruous track of Mozart. He knew some white boy, training right then outside town in Marciano's old gym, who'd show this loud colored kid a thing or two. (I've forgotten the name of the white hope; I don't think he ever made it out of that gym.)

I hadn't seen the young black, not in the ring. "At least," I said, "from what I read he's put a little excitement back in the game." I hadn't followed boxing *since* Marciano, but I'd watched the handsome champion recite his wild poems on the news shows. It was rumored that his sad-faced little trainer actually composed them, but the trainer never spoke in public; he hung in the background, pensive, unsmiling. Was it he who came up with the phrase I read in the *Globe,* as good as anything in Rimbaud? The reporter had asked Clay if he'd be willing to give such-and-such a palooka a rematch, and Clay had answered, "He'd rather run through hell in a gasoline sport coat!"

"Excitement, you call it?" The bartender was counterpunching, having fun. "I wish the Rock was around to teach him a lesson."

"Well," I said, "I gave up following it when that Swede took the title from Patterson in '59." I smiled. "You want that back, huh?"

He laughed. "Johanssen! Now wasn't *he* something? The Hammer of Thor, remember? Jesus Christ!" He poured me a shot. He didn't note it on the tab.

But where had I been since '59? I was getting out of touch. I could recall Marciano's short arms, his pumping hooks, his flat face with its soulful eyes. His tough Italian mug, as I pondered it, began to blur with another boy's. Was it Charles's? It was and wasn't. I had to start noticing things again; I had to make some accounting for where I'd been and where I was and where I meant to be going. I had something vaguely in mind.

I laid down my money, a big chunk of it tip, and made for the door. "Nice talking to you," the barman called; I looked back, caught his quizzical expression, and smiled as broadly as I could. "Likewise," I shouted, tunefully. I was already thumping across the hotel lobby. There was a travel agency near the restaurant. I had something in mind, even if I was mad. But I was done with sitting around in the city.

17

WHAT does he want, old relic propped on his cane, day-tripper? The travel agent's look was so obvious, there must, as I say, have been some not-me to give me resolve that day, or I'd have backed right out the door, mumbling excuses, as soon as I entered. And even if I hadn't retreated immediately, I'd have recognized right off that there was a kind of perversity in choosing to go south, where I hadn't been for four decades and more, and not the other way. To McLean.

I propped my elbows on the counter and waited as the agent feigned business at his desk, shuffled his glossy brochures. Eventually he heard me out, impatiently. It wouldn't be easy, he warned; his outsized cuff links clicked on the airline maps—yes, there was an airport close to the old campus now, but I'd have to change at Pittsburgh (*click!*), lay over two hours, change again (*click!*) at Raleigh, then bus the long road to town.

When I sighed I could tell he thought that he had me. He folded his papers, stepped back two or three paces, and ran his white fingertips up and down his lapels. I felt a cold draft at my heart, but the higher power wouldn't let me quit.

"Where can I rent a car?" I asked.

"There's a Hertz at Charlotte," he all but chuckled.

"Give me a map!" I barked.

He strolled back to his desk, so casually I wanted to beat him with my walking stick. He smelled of cologne and cigarettes, and his paunch swelled the glossy synthetic of his shirt. One of the new men, mass-produced.

Two hundred miles, I judged. He slouched, arms folded, against a file cabinet as I flattened the road map between my thumbs. He didn't know what their trembling meant.

"Rent me a Buick," I ordered.

He stepped back to the counter: "Manual or automatic?" He leaned far over to eye my bum leg, cocked like a tired horse's.

"Manual," I said, staring by God till I stared him down.

WE ran into rough weather just ten minutes south of Logan, and for the rest of the trip the airplane shuddered, lurched, fell through pockets and whacked against their bottoms till the sweat stood on my cheekbones. The pin seemed ready to burst from my hip socket. I couldn't even buy a drink. I got behind the wheel in fear. What was I doing, and why? Something in me half knew by now, but I cursed the old demon of ego: the winding, rough road to the college would be bad enough in any circumstances; now I'd be pumping the clutch with every incline and stop, the pedal pushing back at me like coiled steel.

I must have been mad but something was also becoming clearer with every mile. It was curiosity that gripped me, though how deeply that curiosity ran I wouldn't know for some time. Anna had insisted that her child would be a boy, and that it wasn't mine. But how could she know? A gulf separated me from that frenzied final moment when I'd hit her, yet my thoughts kept vaulting over it. Maybe she'd been wrong. I caught myself wheeling along the snaky roads at suicidal speed. For all I knew, she had been all bluff.

Toward dusk I felt myself cross some line. Catfish parlors with their billboards of smiling bullheads. Barbecue shacks. Car lots draped with light-bulb strings, the automobiles twinkling—good enough to eat, to love, to sail in over the miles of American highway, as I was doing. My stomach lost its knot, my jaw unclenched, I inhaled the piney air, floating—suddenly, smoothly—past the sign for city limits.

City Limits!

I blinked, slowing. The little town had fixed itself in time for me, but now a hideous concrete stadium loomed where girls' horses had whickered in the evenings. There were restaurants whose signs substituted *K* for *C,* discount stores, warehouses. Rows of bungalows with keyhole driveways.

Coeducation now, not the conventual life I'd witnessed. Football, not fox hunting. But what could I care? I had put it all behind me, this village and sleepy quad. The place could mean nothing to me, if it ever had, and it wasn't a place I sought in any case. Not here. I couldn't even find a room at the Holiday Inn, which glittered green by the Student Center.

Student Center?

"First game of the season, sir," the desk clerk explained. He seemed incredulous at my naiveté. "There are motels out by the lake. You may find something there."

I had driven and walked that lake road one year. I'd found something then. My one worry now—almost a panic at moments—was the difficulty I'd have in finding the child among such a crowd. If, that is, she hadn't moved on, married or not, to some far city. She.

Out past the limits again, I pulled into the Water Lily Inne, booked a room, and collapsed on the immense double bed. I slept like an invalid till next midday.

My leg propped on a coffee table, I carefully sipped whiskey till late afternoon. I'd let the weekend throng disperse. In the hall, a machine hummed, then rattled as it dumped ice cubes into a bin. I didn't use it. I sat, outwardly still as a rock. But in my unrootedness, how easy it seemed to fall back into a torpor I'd lately swum out of. How easy to push the remote control of the television, lean against the headboard, be lost. No Peeping Tom could have guessed my vision: an old man's corpse, crumpled like a carton, discovered by strangers, cursed by them, a nuisance. By four o'-clock I knew I had to be moving.

I drove in slowly, gawking at the flood of traffic headed the other way. Alumni, returning home.

I went to the Arts Building for bearings. It seemed an island of old inertia, its whitewashed brick an understatement, almost lost against the Floridian hues of the newer college structures. The reports of my heels against its stone floor, though uneven, sounded familiar.

Drafts flitted into the corners of the lobby. Limestone cubes had been mortared into the hearth. The ugly easy chairs of my day were gone.

The library was locked. I looked in through the fire-door windows: free-standing bookshelves in the back of the room, steel desks catching the red flicker of an EXIT sign, travel posters on the walls. Where did they have their tea now, if at all? I was simply curious, I said to myself. No reason to sentimentalize anything.

I struggled upstairs to the first landing. Anna's husband's painting—the awful *After Claude*—was vanished from its place. I marveled at the ill will I had bestowed on it. Something in me filled with pity too: where was the picture now? What illusion of achievement did the painter cling to, if he still lived, and was it surer than my own? And what was my own?

I stumbled along the second-story hall, my shadow gigantic behind me, and found my office. Locked too. I walked back till I found the classroom with its bay window onto the quadrangle. I sat on the sill and tried to recall the scents of young women and leather, the whirs of locusts and mowing machinery, far snorts of horses. Nothing came. The redbud tree was gone.

I limped over to the metal desk and sat on it. There'd been no desk in my time: I couldn't have imagined it, couldn't have dreamed the vanishing of the redbud from all but my mind. Through slight branches, Anna's stern face, with its mess of hair and its prominent teeth, still stared upward. I could see as well her stiff salute, watch her bicycle roll around the corner of the building, out of sight for the only moment.

It arrived and went: a gust, that's all, of an old feeling. Before it came to be reflected on. Before I dragged it all the long miles and years that rubbed their mystery all over it. Here and gone. No holding it: but I couldn't in that minute catch my breath for it.

I found myself with an old man's uncertain erection.

Downstairs, on the outside wall of the library, was a plaque that bore the name of the building, some Latin nonsense, and the date of construction. 1859. I chuckled—what a sense of timing! Next to the plaque was a black panel with a list, in removable false-ivory letters, of faculty in the arts. I inspected the names in my old department, now grown to twenty-five. Everyone, of course, was gone. Even Fratti, the single face that still came clear to me, thanks to Anna's imitation. The other countenances had puddled together and evaporated long before. Anna had made Fratti out the buffoon he surely was, and yet I found myself hoping he was happily retired somewhere. Were there old folks' hotels in Italy like those hulks in Brighton and Bournemouth, where the guests scramble from their suppers into the foyer, hoping for a chair by the electric log? I imagined harmless Fratti, a bud in his lapel, rolling his *r*'s, his courtly flirting with the cynical widows.

"CAN I help you?"

"Help me?" I turned to find a youthful face, its pitiable blond feelers passing for a mustache. They gave him the appearance of a high school kid at the end of summer.

"Are you looking for something?" He bridled, as if he'd seen into my reverie.

"No," I said flatly, studying him head to toe. Gangly, sandy-browed, he stepped closer, and I noticed the crosshatch of wrinkles on his forehead. Older than I'd thought.

"I'm afraid I shall have to ask you to leave," he said, stiffly, his accent a blend of highbrow and Deep South. I'd heard it somewhere else.

"I'm sorry?" I responded, absentmindedly.

"You see," he added, seemingly eager to repair any impoliteness, "I merely came in to pick up some materials from my office. We lock the building at five on Sundays."

That much I remembered. How often had I called campus security, scatterbrain that I was? In my eagerness to find the quail, or more often Anna, I'd have fled the office after the long week, abandoning my papers inside, and my keys. There I'd stand at dusk, sheepish in briar pants and hunting vest, as the cop opened the outside door and then the office door. Now I muttered, *"Plus ça change, plus c'est la même chose."*

"Comment?" he rejoined, falling in step along the corridor. A French teacher, then, though his accent was wretched.

"They always did," I explained. "I used to teach here."

He nodded skeptically, his hand on the knob of his office door.

In the dim light I read his name on a paper pinned at eye level. *William Graves.* His father's son. I coughed.

"Yes," I went on, "I was a professor here—a little before you were born, I'd say, son." I walked down the front steps as surely as I could, not glancing back.

In my room that evening, I chewed at a take-out order of greasy chicken and downed most of a bourbon fifth, my mind floating to inscrutable Charles. A connection that, in my rush, I hadn't imagined till now. And I drifted into self-castigation. The trip had been a waste. The prospect of a hangover was perversely satisfying, what I deserved—fumes in my nostrils, churning in my gut, skips in my heart. It was almost a pleasure to mock my reflection when I staggered to the bathroom, my bladder too old for this excess. I sneered into the mirror, hung vulgarly over the toilet.

Yet I woke early, with a clear head. Gauzy curtains billowed with autumnal air. I gathered the bedspread around me, drew up my knees, breathed the weather in. It felt for all the world like McLean when the fall northwesterlies foam up the lake. Plovers bob nervously along the beaches; duck broods break up; brown trout move to quick water. In the old days the male salmon would be torpedo-slender, his hooked lower jaw gouging a groove in his nose. Dense summer was honed, and soon the crisp leaves would scale down, all but the sailcloth beech and umber oak. After early October's hysterics, things got sharper, more elegant. Cock grouse drummed, tails spread to show the sable band, dark ruffs raised. Come the harvest moon, woodcock started to flutter down in the alder runs.

That season, before the ice and snow set in—I should never have missed it. I should always have been there, bad legs, bad eyesight, broken body and heart or no. I wouldn't miss it again this side of the grave. If this crazy trip southward had proved anything, I knew I was fit for travel. Not to some Water Lily Inne, but where I belonged. I'd call Edward right from the motel. Louis would ready the cabin, lay in a cord of wood, drag some brush up the chimney to clear it. In mind, the cabin shone.

As I listened to the telephone's purr and crackle, I was already there, the goldeneyes flighty in the pool by my ledge, the east shore yellow and rust, the west one's evergreens blacker in the autumn light. Tonight the first loons and mergansers would pass, their cries sitting me upright in bed, full of an ancient longing. Poor loons and ducks, though; poor long-vanished salmon: figures of freedom for us, but so constrained—get out of the lake, says the season, and out they go. I could stay by the lake, by river and woods, for who knew how long? Long as I damned well was able. I might try a cast or two from the bank, smoke from the Atlantic rising behind me, straight with the coolness.

"Edward? Brant."

"Hullo, Doc." The same.

"What's the news up there, Edward?"

"I got someone here who can tell you."

"Hullo?" The dear old voice.

"Well, god-*damn*! *Louis*!"

I HUNG up on McLean at 7:30 that morning. It was two hours to Charlotte, and my flight was at 3:30. I needed something to get through those yawning hours. Okay, I thought, the deliberate man: first, breakfast—an hour if I'm careful. Then maybe a little drive around the countryside: where did I step over that crushed blacksnake as the bitterns boomed in the wet grasses, the far hounds wailed? My mad walk on that distant evening was a blur at the time, but became clearer and clearer in memory. Dim moon, pungent air, a sense of being watched. Dogs' voices a descant over my own rushed thoughts and the chirrings of insects. All might so easily have been the signs of a much different story from the one I'd lived. It might have been a good one at that, but never mind. There was nothing for me here. The old signs meant nothing, or meant something so deep by now in my soul I'd never root it out. This wasn't my country, ever. That fantasy train trip to Paradise: it was meant to be taken on a roadbed held up by cedar ties, not cypress. The cypresses might still stand, dark and moss-hung in the far field by Anna's lake, but they would always be as dark and far. It wasn't a matter of going to find them; they were right at hand and hopelessly remote. The scuffings of my hurrying feet and hers on the red lane to the cottage—wiped out if indelible.

I'd have my share of driving in a few more days, the ghost train for the rest of my life. No need to court anything. It would all come on its own. I'd soon be passing into weather even brisker than this, into a landscape where fact was familiar: basswood, soft maple, hemlock, hardhack, ironwood, white hare, fallen wall, clean cold water, the browns' spawning ring in spangled shallows.

Call that home, I told myself.

I simply sat in the Water Lily Inne till eleven o'clock. I meant to find a restaurant that would serve an early lunch; then I'd leave for Charlotte with plenty of time to get rid of the car, check my bag, get on board. Wasn't I the soul of discipline? To my surprise, I was still feeling pretty high on Brant Healey. I had emptied the vessel, and could fill it again.

I went to the hotel in town, the one that Anna and I had not dared risk. I'd never set foot inside it. This wasn't my country, had never been, I repeated.

The dining room was one you can see as well in Boston as in San Francisco, anywhere for that matter: ferns, exposed woods, local photographs on exhibit and sale, brick wherever possible. The waiters and waitresses are students, the owners alumni whose lives climaxed in a town like this when they were young and life simple, who can't bear to get too far away ever after. But I checked my scorn. Hadn't I kept my flat in the same Back Bay it had always been my dream to flee?

And wouldn't this one be my forty-fourth year on the McLean? But that was different.

I ordered a Bloody Mary and eggs Benedict. After two bites of the eggs, though, I thought of the long ride home and put down my fork. "Get me another Bloody Mary!" I shouted, to no one in particular, and the drink arrived from somewhere. Crusty old bastard.

A girl in a T-shirt dragged a barstool and a guitar onto a platform at the far end of the room. My ears weren't sharp anymore. I couldn't pick up the lyrics against the buzz in the room; all that came through was the same chord progression she strummed behind each song. Give me the Cotyville road twenty years back, clear dawn reception from distant cities, Benny or Louie or Hamp or Teddy filling the car with energy. Like mine and Louis's and

Minnie's. Give me Minnie's squeals in the back seat as we leave pavement and she feels the washboard bumps and knows we're on our way to the best grouse cover in the state, all ours.

I looked at my watch. Nearly noon. I ordered coffee, closed my eyes, staying with McLean. The hangover I'd escaped seemed to threaten now, after the two vodkas. I'd better keep my mind up there.

I had not and would not seek out Anna, who was gone, or dead. Gone for certain. And I hadn't found the child. Not the right one. I'd fought free. I'd been right—the shape to sustain me, if anything might, lay more than a thousand miles to northward, had lain there from eternity. I had to get there.

I had always had to get there.

In the lobby, a midday crowd milled. I blew on my coffee to cool it. My gruff manner at breakfast had been out of character; I've always had a strange solicitousness for serving people, even back in boyhood days when I'd sat alone in the dining room of a big Adirondack hotel. I didn't want to be a nuisance in other lives. Anna and I had quarreled over this. She called me neurotic, guilt-ridden, and maybe she was right, but there it is. The place would soon be in short supply of tables, and I had to leave anyway. I scalded my tongue.

Then I noticed that the crowd in the lobby was moving up the stairs at its far end. I jerked my head in that direction. "What's going on?" I asked a waitress, sneaking a smoke in a corner near me.

"A lunch or something for the big shots," she said, nervously peering through an immense fern.

"Big shots?"

"Yeah. They picked a new president. Finally."

"Good choice?"

She was flustered: "To tell you the truth, this is awful, but I don't even know his name or anything. I just know he's taking over after fall term."

We watched from our separate places as well-dressed guests kept thronging the marble staircase.

"There goes the old—" The waitress blushed. "I mean, there goes the former president, or whatever he is. . . ."

A gangly man was mounting the stairs with obvious difficulty, his back stooped. Her hand reaching to steady him, a tall woman with thin white hair walked behind him. She was bent, too, but managed the steps well. Even climbing, her stride was a kind of lope.

My waitress giggled. "That's the Bicycle."

"Bicycle?"

She blushed again. "Mrs. President. Or whatever you want to call her."

18

I WALKED in as surely as the hip allowed.

"Hullo, Doc. Welcome home."

Forty years flew in on his words. And more: wings, water, cook fires, mayflies, dogs, tents, and the eternal rest. Even my good leg buckled. Edward's greeting, after my longest absence ever, was so exactly the same. Did that signal indifference or the opposite? Some things I'd never know. I blinked and shook his hand.

"How're things, Edward?"

"Not too bad, considering the competition." Nothing had changed; he was still cock of the walk, proud of being so, and I smiled at his gently arrogant joke.

But it wasn't a joke: "New store in town, Doc," he said. I could just discern the disapproval. I'd heard the inflection before, if rarely. Ten years or so back, for instance, a young bird dog had crashed through the screen door and dragged some meat out of Edward's case. I came on him as he was disposing of a mauled ham. "Harry Clacey's new pointer," he'd said. Same tone.

"You'll see it on your way to camp," Edward added, and now I thought I noticed some difference after all. Not in him but in the place, a spareness I couldn't identify. Had he cut back his inventory? I looked around, as if casually. The hand-tied flies still under glass by the register, canned stuff on the back row of shelves, ammunition at eye level behind where Edward stood in his scuff marks. Beside the clock, the Utility Club calendar. In their rack by the wall phone, this fall's paddles, gleaming with varnish. I couldn't say what was missing, yet I sensed anyhow that the store had lost some of its dear clutter.

Or was it some demon of diminishment that had ridden with me ever since the new patch of interstate highway? I'd been glad for the time I was saving, but mournful, too, for old route 172 around Thousand Acre Heath.

The interstate now ran over that wetland on a causeway, thanks to the state's work during my two years of absence. Eerie, the way my Buick floated at sixty miles an hour through country that used to slow me to twenty on the secondary. The new highway had been empty on a weekday morning after Labor Day, but this stretch of pavement meant that more and more people would make their way to my dark woods and drinkable lakes. I hadn't seen a heron. Not even a coot dabbling in the marsh.

The state had already begun to post signs with messages that stressed the word *historic*. As if history were an honorific that simply attached itself to days long gone, self-evidently glamorous. The region would transform itself into a museum. The fat guy and his cronies in the station wagon at the landing, the young woman at Middle Lake Dam with her men and her briefcase-sized radio, the urban refugees who would establish outlets for Authentic Local Crafts—they'd be arriving in their numbers, each thinking to walk ground that had hallowed itself merely by excluding them till now. The interstate, boring northward, would bore into that ground's weathered soul.

As if history were any old story.

I wasn't sure if the welter of stuff in Edward's store had been cut back, and I didn't have the heart to probe. I supposed that even a few old-timers had leapt at the opportunity to shop elsewhere, after Edward's years of monopoly and good luck. I cursed the small-town spite and envy. I changed the subject: "How's Louis?"

Edward leveled his gaze at me before responding. Maybe he had wanted me to lament the new competition; or he may have been curious to see how I took the news of it.

"Oh, Louis drops by about every morning and evening," he finally said. "Done well, I judge."

"Been in today?"

"Early. He's all right. Blanche is helping him out, and he's been guiding steady. Over to Scraggly today." Edward took in my sigh. "I'll tell him you're here; he'll be down."

"Thank you, Edward."

"Sure thing," the old man said as I turned to the door. He stopped me as I crossed the sill. "You doing some hunting?"

"I really can't say," I answered, surprising myself.

T HE Tradin' Post, for the love of God!

I saw a rank of vans by the gas pumps. Out-of-state number plates, NRA stickers, glass canoes on roof racks. A sign for Schaeffer beer blinking on and off in the window of the squat aluminum building; below it, another sign, handwritten. I touched the brake: "Native Indian Moccasins." There they hung on a string, soleless shoes with buckskin fringes and welts of red, white, and blue plastic. I stopped dead, squinting: on a varnished plaque a large walleye pike arched, a metal lure in its mouth. There wasn't a walleye within two hundred miles of this watershed!

I was trembling, the way I recall Louis trembling once, when he heard of Wesley's plans for bungalows on Middle Lake. Wesley had already gotten the lease from the paper company and printed up rate cards for the bass fishermen. The prefab houses would go up just after mud season; the contractors had already hauled the materials.

"Wood burns," Louis had announced to loud applause at town meeting that spring. Everyone knew what he meant. Wesley decided to back off.

"Wood burns," I repeated aloud. What does aluminum do? I wondered, eyeing the Quonset in my rearview.

T HE evening turned cool, and I lit the Atlantic. Gazing out in this September, I might have been seeing the same old place, smelling the same succession of smokes in the firebox—birch paper, cedar kindling, rock maple, and oak. It might have been 1925. At sunset hen ducks gathered in the camp pool. I remembered scaring them off with gunshot, back when I assumed they were hard on the fishery, the mergansers and grebes. Now I muttered, "Live and let live." But I was thinking, too, of the Tradin' Post, watching it in the mind's eye as kerosene huffed with the match I'd dreamed about throwing at its block foundations.

It was good to have my stove going, and I had an urge to *use* it. I lifted the coffeepot from its nail in the corner. The smudge of its soot on the wall pleased me—it had been there so long. I walked out to the ledge for water, breathing deeply of the chilly, smoke-sweetened air. I carried the pot back, then opened the plywood box under my table. There was a tiny hole in one of its walls where the mice had gnawed their way in. They'd gnawed through the plastic lid of the coffee can, too, leaving a turd or two inside.

"Spiteful little bastards!" I said out loud, but I had a smile on my face. Autumn mice were part of the return.

Edward glanced over his shoulder as I came into the store again. "Looks like he has him a pretty nice trout," he said, nodding downhill at the Tannery Pool. I walked over, puzzled. Through the back window I saw a man kneeling near the ruined riverside chimney. He laid a metal tape along a fish, took it away, laid it on again. The shadows were merging with night.

"For Christ's sake, man, he's short! I can see it from here!" Edward's voice was sharper than I'd ever heard it.

"And out of season too!" I yelped, the words cracking over two registers.

Edward struggled to lift the window, painted shut. By now the fisherman had released the brown, and even I could see, despite the dusk, how the upturned belly gleamed whitely, floating downriver.

"But the river's closed!" I squealed again.

A look like pain flashed into and out of Edward's countenance as he turned to me. "Smart boys extended the season, Doc. License revenues and all that." The sharpness was gone from his speech. "And you'll notice the equipment." I must have blanched to see the sidearm snap of the fisherman's wrist in the gloom. "Bait fishing now, or anything else. The first three miles."

I remembered going straight down to Trafton when the salmon petered out after the second war. I'd spent half a day in the Fish and Game commissioner's office, and at last persuaded him that the salmon would never be back, that brown trout should be the replacement.

It had taken some real doing to get the fish, and to keep the

McLean a fly-fishers' stream with a one-trout limit. I recall the commissioner looking out his window, where a stream of sulfury smoke jetted from a pulp mill. "Well," he finally breathed, "all right. One-fish limit it is—but just till they get themselves established." I'd made my case.

They got themselves established, all right. I had that much to be proud of in my life. The McLean became a better trout fishery than it had been a salmon. The spawning salmon had ignored the may- and stone-flies and caddises, on which the browns prospered. Their wariness also kept the meat fishermen off the river. So had the tight limit, which Fish and Game had forgotten ever to alter. So had the fly-only rule. It was a nice, quiet stretch of water, its few anglers the genuine article. To cast for German trout in a stream where native salmon had run since the melting of the icecap: it rubbed off some of the wild feeling. But I wasn't so wild myself anymore.

Back in camp, I sat staring at my blank stationery for half an hour, having penned only "Dear Sirs." I wanted to pull all stops, to summon authority, seniority, and sympathy all at once. I thought of my ancient labor over the poems about Anna, and how my language ended by covering their urgency, not revealing it. I couldn't render the associations that had moved me. I wondered how anyone could.

> It was I who in the late forties successfully petitioned your department to replace salmon in the McLean River with brown trout, and I take pride in the stream as a haven for true anglers today. So it's with *deepest concern* that—after a hospital stay and a long recuperation—I discover harmful changes to the river I've fished for over forty years. Its greater portion by far lies in the unwadable stretch below St. Pierre Dam, open to all methods of angling, so that if your aim is to counter discrimination against certain kinds of fishing, I suggest that you have rather increased it . . . against flycasters. If revenue is your aim, I also suggest that you are being shortsighted. You have wisely held the limit here to one trout per day, but survival rates of released fish will greatly diminish if spinning and bait equipment are permitted on our stream. Moreover, the extension of the season into the browns' spawning period

promises a further depletion of the fishery, and will result either in the abandonment of the McLean by *all* anglers or in your costly future obligation to provide annual stocking, speaking of which, I'll end with a personal note. I should hate to see "put and take" hatchery trout in a river I've loved so much for so long.

My hip might have had a knife in it for all the time I'd put into this miserable draft. Argument sound, writing literate—you could follow it as neatly as any schoolmaster might wish. But it was so stiff. It stood in relation to all I'd known as "Sailor Takes Long Trip" might stand in relation to the *Odyssey*.

I drank an inch of bourbon. Then I came back and added a note, that I was—as I wasn't—confident in the department's attention, signing my name at last over a McLean address. How I longed to speak as a native. I gazed out my window at my Buick, dozing like a benign monster, its Massachusetts license plate winking back at the moon. I always got the car out of sight in my grouse-hunting days. Not just to keep my favorite covers a secret, but to hide some part of my identity, one that had nothing to do with my true heart.

I stepped out onto the porch, headed for the woodshed. Same old river upstream, from the look of it. Yet I stood there imagining six-inch rainbows, gray of flesh, dumped from a tank truck, "fishermen" trailing it from hole to hole. You couldn't get what I was thinking into a letter, couldn't waste the bureaucrats' time with meditations on the trout that had spawned in the river, my very river, itself. Only a crank would go on about how slowly the region had come to accept the browns as natives, how catastrophic sudden change would be, how a charge shot through him when an exhausted trophy brown, held patiently into the current, tensed with the life come back to him, then finned his way out of reach. The umber and red spots, haloed, flaring in the last of the light. Only a crank would dream this was the same fish he'd been catching for years and letting go, a permanence, something to link up and shape all the loves and losses in his life.

My writer's trance had been pitiable, but this after-trance had held me on my little square porch for I don't know how long. Back inside the kitchen, I was reminded by the cold that I'd left to fetch wood. I marched to the woodpile and came back, a load balanced on one arm; then I cocked the draft on the Atlantic and dropped some kindling on a last live coal. Finally I put on a stick of rock maple with two pin knots on either side. Three years old now, this stick. There are always one or two you remember splitting, and they speak to you as you burn them: you put them on the fire with a kind of gratitude, put them to bed like old friends come unexpectedly to visit.

It seemed impossible to stay out of such reverie, but all at once, past midnight, recalling the glint of his blade above the pile of wood we were working, I felt it. Like the stroke of an ax itself—no Louis!

I poured myself another small drink. It was a night to struggle for clarity: first, the letter; now, the fight through this panic. I made myself think. Louis had likely tied up with some bassers who'd paid him to stay till dark. Too anxious to waste time in Boston arranging my meager affairs, I'd simply come ahead, and he hadn't expected me. Maybe he'd gotten back to town too late for Edward to give him my message. He'd get it in the morning.

At nine next morning I jumped to my feet. My hip ached, white spots rambled through my vision. He hadn't come by. He'd have left a sign at least. Maybe fired the stove, but the stove was cold. Old Bluey sat on its shelf, no bluer than you or I. Old Bluey.

There was a waviness in my legs that had nothing to do with the hip. I wasn't as young as I used to be, but who was? Not Louis, I thought: I imagined him taking on something bigger than he could handle. I remembered the blood seeping from his mouth and nose and ears outside Biscuit's Place, and I pictured some raw boy on Jake's Island in Scraggly, breathing hard, standing over Louis with a smirk, like Johnny Morse. There Louis lay. Here I had lain, in bed, my own mouth oozing its boozy fumes into the good air. I should have been with him.

Or something in the night, and I should have been there: something that woke but pinned him, all alone, in his shack. No one to call the doctor, no one to run him in.

I dressed and drove to the store.

"Well, yes," mused Edward. "He *was* in this morning. Looking for Blanche."

"Wasn't she at Wesley's?"

"You don't know?" Edward asked.

"Know what?"

"Blanche moved down to Louis's. Hell, almost a year now."

"Oh." I couldn't tell what I thought yet.

"You didn't know?"

"You bastards don't tell me anything."

"Funny. I'd have sworn I said something."

"Not to me," I answered.

"She's keeping house for him."

Edward wiped some invisible dust from his fly case, frowning a little. "It's made for a lot of foolishness around here, I can tell you." Again I noticed the tiny edge in his voice. He kept looking into my eyes: I wasn't going to fall in with the town gossips, was I? When things got dull, especially in winter, there were always villagers to talk about Edward's young boarders. Each time one married, he'd replace her with another. It didn't occur to the rumorers that a childless old man might have better motives than the ones they suspected. None of the latest girl's famous flies were among those still crowding Edward's display case.

Edward broke the silence: "You wouldn't recognize Louis's house."

"Did you tell him I was looking for him?" I asked.

"I did. But he was worked up about something."

"Why?"

"Couldn't ask. He was out of here on the clean jump."

I got behind the wheel of the Buick and drove back at a crawl. Then I flopped on my bunk fully dressed, asleep in the instant, not to wake till noon.

Still no Louis when I came to. A greasy egg. Too much coffee. Two o'clock. Still none.

The sun south and west, I could take a hike downstream past the Big Eddy, where a long stretch of sand lay under shallow water, where the light would be right. A quarter mile through the woods from the town road, it was too far for the casual trouters who fished the stretches they could see from a car. I'd be alone, but not so lonely as here in camp, where the bedroom clock clucked slowly on.

The coffee hadn't helped. Nerves. I seemed to hear the little squeaks of my hip with each stride, small yelps like a mouse's in a trap. Twice I made to turn back, but I kept on. I stepped over a mound of apple-loaded bear puke, steaming on the path. It seemed early to me for bears to be in the apples. But it was cool, all right, cool as November. If I came on too much bear sign with my old pointer bitch, Minnie, she'd tuck her tail between her legs and scurry back to heel. I don't know why, unless one day she had seen something in her ranging that I hadn't.

I could see the trout, right enough, platooned above the sandbar. Hiding in the puckerbrush, I spied down on them. Shapes, that's all. I couldn't make out the details, just the slick shapes—fish after fish in restless rows. Now and then one would drop from the order, hold an instant, flick its tail, and shoot back. It wasn't till I came out of my crouch that I remembered my hip.

And remembered again: no Louis.

H E was sitting on the upriver stoop when I returned, his back to me. Measure for measure, I thought: I'd creep up on *him* for a change, my approach from this angle unexpected, the rapids covering the sound of my feet.

"Hello, Louis!" I shouted, loud enough to shake him. It would have shaken me. But he only revolved his head, like an owl. He lifted his hand behind him, and I reached to shake it. Two long years! Then I felt the scrap of paper that fluttered in his fingers.

Good-bye Grampy. I feel like I must leave here. This is NOT because I didn't love you, you are the best person but Charles and Richard I ever knew. I thank you and always love you!! Please don't worry over me, I am alright, and I will always love you and remember you.

BLANCHE

P.S. I dont mean Charles or Richard was better.

P.S. There is milk and can salmon.

It was getting like a sad old song's refrain for me and Louis McLean, but mostly for him: Good-bye, Good-bye, Good-bye.

And I was getting to feel, more than ever, like the touch of death.

19

I HAD the spare bunk, winter was coming, two could live as well as one in my camp.

It was a job to haul Louis's stuff down over the bank to my car, but he didn't have much. After three trips he told me to sit in the chair by his stove while he finished up.

Edward had been right about the change in the shack. It wasn't the same one Louis and I, run off Middle Lake Dam, had spent the night in. The night we discovered Blanche and Charles in my bed. Two steel ammunition cases stood in the kitchen corner, their tops removed, one filled with kindling splits, the other with newspapers and brown bags. Both were painted white. The shelves, empty now, were pink, and the checkered curtains matched the table's oilcloth, on which—crusty with candle wax—squatted a cheap Chianti bottle. My chair was bright yellow. A scent of pine disinfectant everywhere; glass in the windows; a door on the wood oven. Over the stove hung a plaque: NO MATTER WHERE I SERVE MY GUESTS, IT SEEMS THEY LIKE MY KITCHEN BEST. By Charles's old bed hung another: MY HEART BELONGS TO DADDY—I pretended not to see Louis slip it into his tattered mackinaw.

Neither of us had an appetite after we'd unloaded the grip. I'd decided, after the past evening, to limit the booze even further this fall, so I stayed pretty clearheaded while Louis went back and back to the jug. I took it cold turkey.

Of course he'd had signs.

"I guess it's better than I doped it out," he said.

"How's that?" I asked.

"Well, I signed on to fish late with that party," he explained, "and I could see Blanche was nervous when I got in. I didn't give it too much thought, figured she'd been worrying about me. I didn't come back till around half-past nine."

He'd gone to bed. At midnight he woke up, terrified. What were the signs when Charles died? Water, fire, explosion. This time it was Blanche's face, clear as a photograph. A stream of automobile exhaust. A hill that wouldn't quite be made out.

"You'd guess I was uneasy. Those women always had it in them. Nobody knows about the old schoolteacher, but it was strange. So quick, and her in perfect health, everybody thought. And there was Blanche's mother . . ." He got up for more bourbon.

"Mary," I began. As before, uplake, he ran a fingernail across his wrist, sloshing whiskey over Old Bluey's brim. I winced.

"I lay right still till I heard her get up in the morning. We ate a lunch." Louis called every meal but the evening one lunch. "Ate a lunch," he repeated, as if that somehow deepened the mystery. "I thought she didn't look so nervy now. I prayed to God for once in a man's life that I had it wrong. When I came back from the toilet she wasn't there, and I headed over town."

"On the clean jump," I said, stealing from Edward. Louis nodded.

"All I could think of was her smothering herself. I've heard tell of that, automobile smoke."

He began to lose control, and I got out of my chair to comfort him. He waved me back down, almost savagely: "There's so goddamn many cars in this town nowadays!" he growled.

I pictured him, a tough little man but out of his prime, scurrying from house to house all over the village, leaning a big ear to shed doors and garages, listening for a motor, wondering about the hill.

There's nothing in it, I thought. Damn it all to hell! A man doesn't dream such things. What was Louis talking about? What had he been talking about since I'd known him? Was he lying or hallucinating, or what? I'd sort this out one day if it killed me. It would all come clear. This something between us, this bar: it would fall right down some time.

"I ran back here to see if she'd come home. I could see that smoke flying out both sides of his car. They was just flying over the knoll, Cotyville way."

In my mind I stood on the road by his house, Louis panting beside me, the twin streams of exhaust from the overpowered car fading into air as it bounced south over the hump. At our feet were two long scars of burned rubber. She had known he'd be guiding all day, had sneaked back, left her note, and fled from right under his nose. Why the cruelty? I hated Blanche for a moment or two. But maybe she'd had to fulfill Louis's vision.

What in hell was I thinking? I felt blood rise to my face. I wouldn't let the nonsense suck me in! But Louis spoke now, softly: "God love her," he breathed, "at least she ain't dead yet."

Just a couple of kids. They might have gone anywhere, without leaving a clue. But in the morning, as Louis was reloading the Atlantic, I offered to hire someone to track Blanche down.

"No," he said, kneeling, tossing logs into the stove like darts. "Once I have it, I have it." I argued for a moment, but the spirit had gone out of me. Off Louis went—he'd signed on to guide for Wesley, and he'd stick by the deal. He hadn't expected me, of course. He'd expected worse, and maybe got it. I ran him to the landing at six-thirty, but I couldn't make myself wait as his sportsmen slid their boat from its long metal trailer into the clear water.

DRIVING back campward, I got to thinking again that my urge to salvation was tied to destruction. A small town can do that to you—everything so known, so visible. Coincidence, if that's what it is, slaps you in the face. One year, I recall, poor old Teague Williams died. Nothing strange about that; she'd been fighting cancer for longer than anyone should have to. But within forty-eight hours of her death, three other people tipped over, two under fifty, both of heart attacks. The third had hooked a pickerel on one of the chain lakes, and the fish, flopping his last next to the canoe, had lodged a hook in the fisherman's thumb. He was a man famous for fear of the sight of blood: he keeled over into the lily pads, and that was that. The eerie part was that all four victims had lived on the same dirt road by the landing: side by side, in a row. Something like it could happen in a Boston apartment building and no one would notice. That's what I'm saying.

My presence seemed a bad portent, but I wanted to *be* present where it mattered. I kept fretting over these visions that Louis had. Surely he fancied them after the fact; surely whatever he picked up, as if from the atmosphere, were human signals, humanly given. Still, something was spooky. I had to admit it, despite myself. Almost hourly things seemed to bear down on my friend, and I wondered how *I'd* fare day by day in a world so freighted with omens.

Or did I live in that world after all? The Tradin' Post with its hanging walleye; the boat-trailer tracks in McLean Lake sand; the gathering miles of asphalt turnpike; sea minnows heaved into my river on an angler's hook; the vanished salmon. These showed the future as eloquently as Louis's visions, foretold its deaths, even if I brought to them no supernatural interpretation.

"No, no, no!" I shouted, alone in the car. Those signs were there in the light of day. *Anyone* could read them if he looked clearly. And they pointed to the deaths, the disappearances of places, not people. Yet how might I of all people sustain the distinction? McLean. Louis. Louis McLean. There he was just now, surrounded by predictable talk in a Chris-Craft. Broads, booze, sports, whatever. There he was on the lake that bore his name, gasoline making a brilliant slick in the wake. Lovely, really, if you put other considerations aside. I remembered the *Astrud,* the sheen around its hull. The cough of its engine, loud in the scene—as an ax is loud when there's no breeze between you and the old boy chopping onshore, laying in wood for the cold weather coming. Who might that old boy be? His orange suspenders flare in the morning against his union suit. Now Louis unbuttons and throws open that tired old green-and-black mackinaw in the sportsmen's boat. His suspenders flash the same.

So I thought, There's some cause and effect in his *character.* But that explained nothing, since the catastrophes in his life were so bound to his auguries that I couldn't separate them out from his being. His superstition *was* so much of his character, his wounds inside him now for good. Time would not heal them; they had merely sunk inward, his view of things strengthened by each, as scar will strengthen a physical hurt.

Of Richard, the young buck who had scooped up Blanche, I came only to gather generalities. I sought information even from the town's most incorrigible gossips, right down to Bev, the post-mistress, whose account diverged from less sensational ones only in rhetorical degree. She said what everyone said about the boy: a logger from Pinkham, working for Rawson paper; good hand with a chain saw; given to whiskey brawls at the dances. Bev herself had to admit that he wasn't much different from most of his kind.

"Just another lumberjack," she sighed. "Chopping and drinking and the girls."

"Just another lumberjack," I repeated.

"That's all. I guess he's a good deer hunter. They say he played some instrument, too, and made up songs. Maybe that's why Louis didn't care for him. Too much alike, him and your friend."

Her smile was loaded with insult. I turned and walked out of the post office. What it all came down to, though, I agreed, was that Richard and Louis were cut from the same material.

"What was Richard like?" I asked Louis once.

"Didn't see much of him," he answered. "Wouldn't have him here." That was all I ever got from my friend on the subject. If I brought Richard's name up, Louis would lift an eyebrow, or scowl, or make some apparently random allusion to a logger who mis-treated his wife. I loved Louis, but he had it in him to use Bev's tricks. Maybe we all do. I wondered how June's parents had felt when they saw her go off with a woodsman and hunter and drinker and storyteller; I wondered if one said to the other, "She ain't dead. Not yet." We're all possessive of the things we treasure, and the people. Maybe the world needs us to feel their departure as death. Otherwise the world would blow away, even more quickly.

Surely Blanche had been Louis's treasure, a token for one thing of his son's scorched promise. What else did she represent? Ro-mance, as Bev had meant to imply? All I know is that Louis was a good man, and would stay that way if it drove him crazy.

And it could very well drive a man crazy. I knew what it was to be lonely. It had been years since I'd nestled in the arms of someone I could say I loved, and in my later years the other kind seemed even less satisfying than the insistent dreams of the former kind. The former one, imaginary One.

And I knew about the moment when your yearning for the firm young person comes to be seen by her as a joke, or an insult. You can be fatherly or you can be a Dirty Old Man—your options now. In mind, you're stuck at twenty-five or thirty. It surprises you when you slide down rather than leaping from that rock by the river, when you walk around a deadfall rather than vaulting it or stooping under. It's a shock when you see the disgust or amusement, or both, in the girl's eyes. You meant nothing offensive; you're too well mannered to act on it, but you'd hoped some romantic flash would find a counterflash in those eyes. Your own are a little bleary now, and your teeth ground shorter. Your hair keeps clotting the shower drain. But the drives are still young. How could she have imagined they were not?

But you imagined the same thing once, when you were going to live forever.

Blanche was gone, pearl of great price. And here I was, reeling back memories from almost fifty years past, sitting on my doorstep, fuming about incursions on a *river*!

Still, it did seem that everything was getting used up.

I BEGAN to keep his hours. There was no sleeping when he was awake, and I found myself actually prizing the rustles and snaps in the kitchen outside my little bedroom. I'd even smile, lying under the quilts, at those callused fingers drumming the tabletop, at the tuneless whistling. I was living the way we're meant to live, give or take a daily inch of John Barleycorn. Up when it gets light, down at dark.

The frost came early. At daylight of a late September morning I saw it, halfway up the hardhack whips on the outhouse path. Though my bladder was talking to me sternly, I gazed at the pale woods for several minutes. In the earlier times that pallor was Louis's cue to get in touch. Edward would make the call, and I'd race out of Boston, where I'd gone taut and nervous after only a month or so. My city-fevered bitch rushed from window to window in the back of the Buick, stumbling over gear I'd flung onto the seat in my hurry. Time to scout the bird covers.

We'd leave camp the morning after I got to McLean, scraping ice from the windshield, headed west out of the softwood. Back then, the traffic almost nonexistent, I'd let the dog run ahead for miles before we got out ourselves. We'd all work into shape together, Minnie coursing like a greyhound on the dirt lanes, then bustling through the thickets and up the knolls, Louis and I puffing after. I liked a fast dog.

I nodded and smiled at Louis as I hurried out. He was fussing with an ax we'd stored in the outhouse. The porcupines had nibbled for salt in its haft. It made me think again of Minnie, my good dog. She couldn't resist the first porcupine, never learned a lesson. She'd take one on at the start of each season. Then we had to catch her and wrestle her into the car. We'd crank the window up till we had her head in the stocks. Louis would hold up her hind feet while I plucked quills with pliers. Give her a little traction and she'd break the window. When I pulled the last barb she'd calm, waiting for Louis to reach over and let down the window. She'd hit the ground with a puppy growl, collapsing her front end and waggling her butt, a doggy grin on her face and a mustache of scarlet blood-beads.

"Let's go look the bird covers over!" I all but shouted to Louis when I came back, shivering. The air had smelled good; it had had that heft.

Louis eyed my hip. "Scouting cover, eh?" I was coming along, no doubt about it, but I still needed an hour in the morning to limber up. The hip was pulsing now from my dash outside.

"Just a couple of pasture covers," I assured him. "We can cruise in the car for the rest."

"What the hell? Why not?" He smiled one of his few recent smiles. "It'll do us good to get out of here." I hadn't thought about it until the frost came, spelling an end to an interim season: I was restless. I had all the wood I needed, the camp was in good shape, there was nothing but pickerel to fish for. I wouldn't hassle a spawning trout; let the flailers take care of that. Maybe this cold snap would drive even them from the stream. I hoped so, hoped the fish would get a week's break.

But Edward was looking through his window onto the Tannery Pool when we stopped for sandwich fixings. "Sons of whores are merciless, ain't they?" he said, indicating two men who were thumping the water below the store.

"We ought to lift the gate," said Louis, jerking his thumb toward the dam upstream.

"Good for local commerce, though." Edward smiled, jerking his own thumb the other way, toward the Tradin' Post. "Lot of change since I took over," he added.

"All bad," said Louis. "Ain't been a soul to sing 'The Old Oaken Bucket.'"

"You say so. You never had to *hear* the old bastard." Edward poked a finger in either ear.

A HALF hour west of McLean Lake the country changes as abruptly as someone might change his mind. The roads climb fast, hardwoods take over from cedar and hemlock, puckerbrush clots the dead pastures, native bamboo leans in and out of abandoned houses and barns.

We passed a dead farm and I remembered shooting a double on grouse as the birds sailed under the cross timbers of its unroofed hayloft. There were more grouse in this land's brush, in the thickety little apple stands and alder runs, than there had ever been when the farms were alive. They were alive in another way now. I was all through with thrashing those tangles for birds, so why should I care?

Because of the boy. I didn't know him, the one who'd fight through this mess, wild as his young dog, swearing as the grouse flushed wild and he shot two quick holes in air. I wished I could be there—that day or the next or the year after or years after—when, having persisted in his pride, he finally got it right: the point, the flush, the shot, the retrieve. The country whose long miles he had cursed would suddenly look so lovely, so compact.

I was happy for the birds too. For the foxes who prowled after them. For the pale hares who stood up, manlike, to crop the sucker buds. For the bears groaning with their glut of wormy apples, drunk with plenty, growing fat for the white winter dream.

In the old myth an apple causes the trouble, and part of it is that you can love a ruined orchard. Your pleasures tax your moralities: the best cover here or anywhere was ruined ground, orchard or pasture, and I could look at it and treasure all that hard labor, now undone. Buildings falling or fallen; stones spilling out of sheep fences, so heroically gathered and built, the oxen plodding ahead of the stone boat, patient men after. They had stopped and lifted and piled and disappeared, and what had I ever done?

Soil gone thin and bad. They thought they'd put all the rocks in their walls, but the boulders kept rising from earth, an annual spring crop. And their sheep made useless by people far enough away they might have come down from the moon—Australians and New Zealanders with their free-range herds. It must have been like a hurricane or a July freeze: you're doing your same bone-wearying business, and something rushes in from nowhere and knocks it all apart.

And then along come two old men, and they look at your place, and they picture the game parading over your very headstones. Invigorated, despite their years, they applaud your heartbreak.

We rounded a bend and started down Tarbox Drumlin. I saw Louis return the laconic salute of a solitary walker as we coasted by.

"Wildcat Willie," he breathed.

"Where the hell's *he* from?" I asked.

"Right here."

"Never saw him."

"Generally don't in the daytime."

He had worn a huge overcoat, like the stars in old-fashioned spy films, but this one was shredded, held together with baling cord. I'd noticed the brimless baseball cap, the wild hair and beard. A smudge on the jumbled landscape. Unadorned. Only himself.

To think that I've grumbled and mourned at how little my ego extends into the world: no children or wife, few friends, no reputation beyond the bounds of a hamlet of eighty souls. It must be why I once tolerated the publication, however obscure, of the Anna poems. The ambition failed, or I failed the ambition. Whichever, I fell back on other scenes in which my presence might be central.

I was that dream boy in the brush, of course, the world coming round for me: round as the chambers of my shotgun; round as the perfect swirl of a trout who sips my dry fly; round as a ring of men by a fire, the circuit of the hare, of the hound who harries him.

The human universe is so full of people whose pathetic hungry selves extend into the world not an inch. Willie was a second's impression in the eyes of a speeding stranger. I let out my own sigh now.

"Why Wildcat Willie?"

"Cat hunter. Good one," Louis answered.

"That's all?"

"Just about."

"Hard way to get by."

"Yes," said Louis. "First they lifted the bounty, and that shut him down. Then the fur dropped, bad. So he chased them to eat."

"Bobcat?"

"It's what he does," Louis replied. "What he always did. It's not bad. You know, the wild flavor. It's about all he does that's halfway legal, anyhow. But he went right on after them when they closed those two seasons a few years back. Everybody knew it, wardens too."

Louis had been with him once on a hunt. If a cat wasn't too big, he said, Willie would climb the tree and shake him down for the dog. He didn't like to waste a shell. "And hand him a cigarette," Louis chuckled, "he'd grind it up and put it in his pipe. Everything had to go through that pipe."

Hunting on snow, Willie had worn a pair of old basketball sneakers. "There was a hole in the heels and a hole in the toes," said Louis, feigning a shiver. "He stuffed them up with paper. Every now and then he had to stop and fix the stuffing."

"Jesus," I whispered.

"Always had a good dog, though." Louis glanced at me. "Both ways."

I nodded. We rode down the west side of Tarbox. Birdier and birdier. We flushed a grouse picking gravel at road's edge, and Louis slapped the dashboard. But I had to go back and ask it. "Good dogs? Both ways?"

"Trail and table," Louis answered.

"No."

"Well, I can't swear to it. But Charles told me he needed a piece for one of Wesley's machines, way down in winter. He came out to take it off some wreck in Willie's dooryard. You know, get him a little cash."

"Good boy," I said.

"Yes," Louis whispered, looking out the window. "Anyway, he saw Willie's hound wasn't hitched out front, and he asked about him. 'Had to put him down,' Willie said. Then when Charles went to torch off that piece, he passed by the school bus Willie keeps for a shed. He said he couldn't swear to it, but there was something inside the bus—not a deer, not a cat, nothing he knew, and he knew what was what. . . ."

"No."

"Well, it was dressed out very neat." We drove a little space before Louis said, "I guess I been lucky in a way."

I gentled the Buick through the tall grass and over a knoll. I still had that furtive urge: don't let them see where you're hunting. I was pleased I still felt it. A half dozen steps and we were wet to the waist. The wild asters, goldenrod, and steeplebush were heavy with molten frost. It was just nine o'clock, still cold, but this might do harm to body, I thought, not soul. Maybe I could walk the edges of this deep stuff come hunting season, after the frost had thinned it. Not like shooting over a point, not like the old days, but better than sitting over dominoes in a Boston club.

"Good chance for a shot here, Louis." The words were poised in my throat when four partridge busted out at my feet. It had been almost seven years since I'd fired a gun in anger, as they say, but my finger squeezed the first round out and slid by the lead trigger to touch off the second barrel. The phantom gun dropped the two hind grouse. I heard their papery crash on the sparkled earth.

"By God, we ought to come back here next week!" Louis shouted, red in the cheeks. The broods hadn't broken up yet, and maybe they'd still be intact. Soon the male birds would lurch into crazy-flight, crashing into windows and wires, even tree trunks and the sides of buildings. But for now the grouse were still roosting together.

"Always a good cover after frost," I said, stating the obvious. A nice open sidehill with south exposure, full of feed—raspberry vine, ivory plum, mayhaw. I envisioned the parade of wary grouse, creeping from the evergreen thicket west to this sun-drenched bank.

We weren't dead yet, though my hip was a little cobbly and Louis complained of stomach pains during the ride home. "*I'll* do the cooking tonight," he joked. Then we drove on, each in his own quiet reverie.

I was playing back a lot of seasons. Luck, I was thinking, is a relative thing.

20

"So, you goin' deer huntin'?" The dentist leaned over me, and I smelled his cologne.

"Gnnngh," I replied.

Of all the fragile gifts God gave me, my teeth had always been the soundest. I'd shot my ears half away, my eyes were never much, and my legs were gone. But now, far back in my mouth, a molar had throbbed since dawn. Maybe it *was* a sign. My first toothache, and then the reply from Fish and Game to my letter, almost six weeks after I sent it. The address read "Mr. Healey Brant," and I knew some machine had swallowed my plea, half-digested it, and spit up a categorical response.

Dear Mr. *Brant:*

Thank you for your inquiry regarding *McLean River.* Our office is grateful for public input. Attached please find information pertinent to your question(s). Our correspondence is extensive, and we regret the use of this form. If you have further questions, please use the number listed below.

Good *fishing*!

Just a matter of filling in the blanks. The attachment cited the revised statutes on public hearings. Over his or her initials someone had scrawled a message: "Thanks again for input."

I could convene a hearing by petition. I drew up a simple request for a department official to come and discuss the McLean's status.

Then I wrote a kind of editorial paragraph, expressing the same apprehensions as in my original letter to Fish and Game. I patiently made three copies of each document. On my way out of town I posted a set at both stores and taped one to the wall outside the post office. I didn't want to go in; I wanted to get to Pinkham and have this goddamned fire in my jaw put out.

I was glad enough to be on the Pinkham road, concentrating on its potholes and dips, my mind off the pain. The highway was a hazardous, looping tunnel through the black swamps on the lake's east shore. It was a little before eight o'clock, and a ground fog slowed me. At the turn by the abandoned sawmill I saw a young moose cuffing a steamy pile of sawdust. He lifted his head to watch me pass. The prospect was at once elegiac and eerie: the short-horned bull, peering unconcerned at me through ribbons of fog; the looming sawdust chimney; the shimmer of moldering chips; the rotten husks at the far edge of the swamp—abandoned stores, forgotten shanties of long-gone Indians, their doghouses scattered in the sumac; fireweed bursting upward through orange railroad tracks.

For all this mystic eloquence, I was reminded in Pinkham that it was a day for forms. The receptionist, strange vision in rhinestone eyeglasses, handed me a pile of papers directing me to fill them in as thoroughly as I could. Age, occupation, address, allergies, and finally, ominously, *Church of your choice.* I wrote down "Chartres Cathedral." I wonder if she ever saw it.

The receptionist slid a small yellow card into her typewriter, clicked away for a moment, and, without looking, stretched an arm behind her toward her files. Her hand wavered in the air as she asked me again if I'd ever seen Dr. Prale "prior to this visit."

"I didn't even know," I said, "there was a dentist's office here." I'd had to look the office up in Edward's phone book.

"Oh, we're on the move in Pinkham," she answered cheerily, pulling the "New" file. I stared out the window at a Shop-N-Sav mall.

"I'm takin' the whole season off myself," Dr. Prale informed me. "Ngoh?"

"Yeah. Me and my buddies have a beautiful camp out on Middle Lake." He said *beauty-full.* "You know where that is?"

I tried to nod.

"Little wider now. Yeah. Built it from a kit. Three days, it's up. Beauty-full. You want to rinse that out?"

"Whereabouts on Middle Lake?" I asked, my stomach tight.

"Finnegan's Point, they call it. Way the *hell* and gone!"

So much, I thought, for the otters. He didn't look like he'd do the *deer* much harm. His thighs billowed on the stool.

He giggled. "Get away from the old lady, know what I mean?" He shot me a wink. I grunted around his suction tube and his milk-white fingers. He passed a flirtatious look at the red-haired technician holding his tools. She swallowed a yawn.

"Does her good, too, you know? You live around here?" He asked the questions in quick succession, then glanced at my chart. "Oh yeah. Up at McLean. Come on out sometime. You can go with us. We bring in a few cases. You know, play a little cards, that kind of thing. What the hell?" It was his Regular Joe act, I could see. "Hell, come on out. You know where it is?"

God preserve me! Did I know where it *was*, he'd asked. I bit down on the tube and growled.

"I work it with the wife. A month for me in the fall, then something with her when the mud comes. You go nuts around here that time of year, am I right?"

"Unngh."

"Went to Las Vegas last March," he chuckled, shaking his head. "Lost Wages—that's what I call it." He paused for me to smile, but I didn't. He nodded at his attendant, and she took out the suction tube. "Lost Wages, am I right?" I spat in the basin while he waited. "Well," he sighed, "that's about it. Not a bad job, if I say so. But you got good teeth for . . . You retired now?"

"Yes."

"Nice. Me, I can take off when I want. It's nice to work for yourself, but let me tell you, it can be a headache too. So come on out sometime. A pleasure to meet you. And I ought to see you again one of these days. It was a pleasure, honest. Take care."

By the time I got to McLean the Novocain had worn off. My posters were already down at the post office and at Edward's, nothing left of them but their little corner dog-ears. The one at the Tradin' Post was still up, but someone had scrawled across it, in large block letters, FUCK YOU.

21

WE left the birds alone after all.

I did drive out to Tarbox one morning, on my own. We'd gotten four hard frosts in a row, so I had to go easy along the switchbacks. The soft maple leaves sheeted the gravel, slippery as ice. It was a splendid October forenoon, the light a miracle through the leaf showers. You could find yourself in trouble watching those cascades—it's like watching snowflakes fall, big and slow, over a highway: your mind goes off the driving and the traffic.

Easing the Buick out of sight, I flushed two grouse by the gravel pit where Louis and I had parked three weeks before. They skimmed the brown stalks of steeple, lifted slightly, set their wings, and dropped by a clump of gray birch. I marked them well.

I could have kicked the birds up again, dog or no dog. My hip wasn't bad today. Instead, I sat a long while in the warm car, thinking. There was still a blanket of mist on the cover. The wet puckerbrush blinked at me in the pale sun: soggy in there, though it looked warm and starry. I had a vague need to move my bowels. A hike would make it more urgent, and I shivered in my seat. A man feels absurd, vulnerable, squatting in the dew next to a jumble of woods. I fought with myself, there in my car, then slipped the Buick into reverse, ashamed. The mighty hunter.

I had never shut off the engine. I was doing the right thing, no? There *was* a little pinch in the hip after all. Probably from the drive. I'd save what I had left of me for a deer hunt or two. Provided I could bring Louis back up to snuff.

His stomach had gone on troubling him after that scouting trip in late September, and he was losing weight. Like all the old-timers, though, he was shy of doctors.

He was in the store when I stopped at Edward's. "Well, that was a quick hunt." He smiled, a bit ruefully.

"I'll admit it. I was a little nervous to try it alone, with the hip and all."

Edward broke in, speaking to Louis. "You'd let the old boy go by himself? Some friend!"

"Feeling a little used up myself," Louis muttered. He had a hangdog look, and he held a wide hand against his abdomen.

"Still bad, huh?" I stared hard into his eyes. He knew what was coming.

"Don't start in," he begged.

"I can't get him to the doctor, Edward."

"Christ, he's *living* with a doctor!" Edward answered, winking at Louis, half-grinning, his scar twisting like a worm. He wasn't much help.

I kept at it all morning and afternoon. Yes, I needed company out there, whatever I was going to do. But I was more concerned for him. The fog had turned to a kind of hovering rain. You couldn't see a hundred yards upriver. Louis drummed and whistled, and I harangued. "I don't know," he repeated, over and over, till I could have thrashed him. I wouldn't give up, though.

"Well," Louis sighed at last. "I'll see Swett if he's still in business." He wouldn't hear of the new Pinkham clinic, but Clyde Swett was an old-timer, and would treat a McLean in any case. He'd been one of Louis's father's few friends, had, in fact, delivered Louis, back when he had had a summer office on the lake. He was nearly as old as Edward. I'd been to see him once myself, years earlier, having run the hook of a streamer fly through my nose in a high wind. I'd used my nippers to cut the leader and arrived at Dr. Swett's camp looking like some Papuan tribesman with an amulet of red-and-white feathers draped from my face: Parmachene Belle. I remembered the small room he called his surgery, the vials of amber fluid, like the ones they used to display in pharmacy windows; the narrow examining table, complete with obstetrical stirrups; the white deal cabinets, their array of tools; the coal-oil hot plate for sterilization. But I could barely picture Swett himself.

"I always called him Satan," said Louis, reminding me, on the drive down to Cotyville. "Little chin whiskers. Couple of bumps on his forehead, just like horns."

I waited in Swett's parlor, the round Oak wood stove roaring and a big Victrola too—the Pastoral Symphony. Finally, he and Louis came out. The doctor spoke directly to me. "His pressure's a little high. I think he's wrought up. A bad few months, you understand." Here he looked over and nudged his patient with a bony elbow. Louis grinned sheepishly at the condescension. Swett turned my way again, the band of his speculum riding across one of his horns, the mirror glinting dully. He raised his voice above the Beethoven, so that his counsel sounded even more avuncular, simplified. "Probably the pressure and the nerves go together, don't they?" I nodded, briskly. "I gave him something to help," Swett went on. "He's all right. Keep him away from the salt, and give him half a phenobarb—but only if it's bad."

"Only if *which* is bad?" I asked.

"The nerves or the pressure."

"How do I tell about the pressure?"

"Count on it if the nerves are bad." He winked. "And," he added, looking over his shoulder again at my friend, "we don't drink if we've eaten one of these pills. Understand?" Louis smiled.

"And," I added, falling into the same diction, "I suppose we don't eat one of these pills if we've been drinking."

"There you are," said the doctor.

Louis appeared reassured, even happy. The doctor had given him a shot. Well, I thought, whatever does the trick. I guessed that Swett had meant no harm, but Louis was a grown man, and I was his friend, not his daddy.

Yet I did take a kind of fatherly pleasure that evening to see him go after the chicken legs I'd broiled. And I hid the salt shaker in my closet.

22

I WAS soon enough grateful to old Dr. Swett—Louis had a new lease on life. His symptoms more or less disappeared in the weeks after our visit. He hadn't taken a single one of Satan's pills by the first of November. I was delighted, though a little nettled to think of the anxiety we'd have saved if Louis had only seen a doctor sooner. I kept daydreaming of those two grouse booming out of the gravel pit. We'd have gone to the mark, surrounded that gray birch patch, and one of us would have gotten an open shot. You don't often have that advantage with partridge. On the other hand, my irritation reassured me: we'd gang up on those birds *next* October!

In the persistent overcast days, the country had gone spare, all the loud colors tumbled to mulch. A time of year when most people grumble over the death of summer, but I've always loved it: the hard outlines of the ridges, the even line of ice on the shore's every dent and swell, the darkened evergreens—the mind coming clear, breaking through the clutter of more indolent seasons.

"DOESN'T that loudmouth dentist have a camp out there now?" I asked Louis. We were talking after supper, sipping tea by the Atlantic, putting off the dishes, planning a trip to deer country to check for sign.

"Yes, I saw it," said Louis, swirling Old Bluey. "Looks like a duck blind—on Finnegan." Then he looked up at me. "I don't think he'll get too far from it, do you?" I shook my head. I was thinking of Prale's slushy thighs on the stool. He hadn't done much brush busting.

So we drove to Middle Lake.

We followed a trail that Stubby White had swamped out a generation earlier; it skirted Finnegan Point by about two hundred yards, then made up the east side of Dead Stream. Back when there were ducks, Louis and I would jump-shoot the stream from a canoe. Even now we flushed a pair of blacks as we kicked through the bent grass. A pair where there might have been a dozen then; some blame it on the hunters—not much said about the 'dozers and backhoes draining the coastal marshes, about the asphalt sealing them tight.

I watched the ducks pump over Magazine Ridge. All that energy in a duck! We passed the setback where we used to launch, and I felt it all—low moon on the stream, beavers slapping its gleam when we arrived to disturb them, the far Montreal radio station crystal-clear on the car radio as we unloaded our grip by the headlights, my retriever standing hock-deep in the shallows, moaning, ears cocked and head high, impatient for us to get on with it. We lingered, sipping coffee from a thermos lid; he smelled duck in the breeze.

It was tough going, even for Louis. The path had grown up and the hardhack whips all seemed to lean against our progress. They always do. Louis stopped occasionally to look back at me and catch his own breath, finger pressed to a nostril, snorting out chaff. The weather had gone briefly back to Indian summer, a last fling. My hip beat at the nerve ends, but it didn't have the weak feeling.

At length we sat together on a flat rock where the stream grew wide with more beaver-work. A ridge rose straight from the far side of the pond, running several miles north till it melted into the black hole of Dead Lake Swamp. My imagination followed the ridge's contours, encountering a sudden gloom as the hill collapsed, the footing spongy and the skyline erased by the heavy cedar. I came back to a nice patch of puckerbrush between ridge and stream, downhill to the east. You could spy on the scrub oak below, on the ghost of Stubby's orchard and clearing.

"You stay here if you want," said Louis, suddenly standing. "I'll go up by Stub's and poke around." He'd been traveling to the same places as I had in mind. "If I drove a buck out from the back side," he continued, "he might just head downstream, and there you'd be on your rock." He hadn't sounded so good for a long time.

The sun was full out now, and I was happy enough to linger on the warming rock. I watched Louis teeter across the beaver dam. Just before climbing into the woods, he waved an arm. I smiled and waved back, but he'd already vanished.

It was some time before he returned. I got up for moments and crept like a heron to the edge of the beaver pond. I could see brook trout sweeping their spawning beds. They didn't come into the lake anymore, so they stayed small, but they stayed beautiful too. A kingfisher startled me, whacking the surface after a little wild fish. The trout shone, twisting away, and I laughed out loud at the bird—on an alder limb, he shook his feathers, bitching loudly about the fishing. Back south, over the lake, a pair of eagles sailed an updraft; one of them screamed, twice. Gadflies, too fat and cold to be a nuisance anymore, bumbled among the cattails and duck-weed. These noises, and the riffle of wind, were part of the composition. But for them, an utter quiet.

"Well?"

"Oh, he's—in there—all right," Louis puffed, flush with excitement. "He went out—the other side—the back side. I only heard him—but what—a thrashing!—I didn't go around—too lazy—but I'll get around him—you bet—next week." He dropped onto the rock where I'd been sitting, his eyes keen.

After he got his breath, Louis told me there'd been a lot of other sign in Stubby's lot. But this buck—big enough to keep down the competition! All the other sign was doe, tiptoe tracks, not heel-heavy. The big boy's cuffings were all over the stream side of the ridge and down in the feed stand too.

"Good place to breed a woman," I joked.

"Right enough. He's hooking all through that country! He had one alder down, clean to the ground, big as *that*!" Louis held up a circle of middle fingers and thumbs. He was voluble now, and it did my heart good. Our walk out was a stroll, Louis pausing over and over, gesturing: "An old *brute*!" or, "Big as *that*!" We leaned against the trunk of the car for ten or fifteen minutes. A wind kicked up and dried our sweat. We were lazy; it was down-right warm now. You could feel the sun in your bones when the breeze lulled, and I relished it. But Louis frowned back up-stream. "Now we want the cool weather. Something to move him around a little."

We drove as far as Old Crow Spring. "Think a fella can buy a drink here?" I asked.

"A small one," Louis cautioned. But he was smiling again.

That night I cooked a mess of pickerel over the fire. I can do a pickerel so there's not a bone in him—you cut out the rib cage and then score him up and down his flanks, about every inch. Then you drop him in grease that's hot as you can get it, so the little free-floating Y-bones shrivel up. Hot grease was off our regimen, but we both felt up to it. It had been a good day, and an outdoor fire means something.

THE season opened on a Wednesday. November 14, I remember. But the wind howled for a week before and after, and it blew the woods tinder-dry and noisy. We could imagine it. Wind means something too. One day we drove as far as the Mason Brook turn-off but decided to come back and wait out conditions. We were all right. It seemed good to have spent so much of my time where wind did mean something. North—cold. South—rain. When it blew west I used to swear I could *smell* fish in the air, and ducks in the sloughs when it blew east. As I turned the car campward I suddenly thought that wind must have meant something to Charles, as well, but I didn't say anything about it: it likely had meant a thing neither of us would understand.

We came back because high wind also means jumpy game. Sitting by the Atlantic, I went on imagining: the alders on Tarbox were leaning in my direction, thirty miles distant; the cattails on Dead Stream, bent over too, going the way of the moving air. I thought of whitecaps at the head of McLean Lake, up to Porcupine Landing; they'd be in town in half an hour, coming the route Louis and I had so often come by canoe.

The gale finally let up the next Tuesday. But as it swung off south and feeble, rain fell in buckets through the weekend, and I had to put up with Louis's deepening mood. His resources weren't as rich as I'd begun to hope. I kept waiting for him to speak of his gift, of signs from his source. But he just stayed gloomy, quiet.

I think we both felt a little old to be soaking our bones in that
stuff, anyway. There was a time when we could break brush all
day, wet to the marrow, clothes like a ton of bricks, and still be on
for a party at night. We were better off to sit it out now. Besides,
I reasoned, there was a lot left of the season, the going would be
quieter, the sign easier to read, and the timing right for Thanksgiving. We might even have a heart and liver to dress our turkey. We
didn't speak a word about all this, but I think we knew a week of
deering was probably enough, at least for the old man. That rock
would get hard and cold in the early hours.

Sunday—eleven full days into the season—was a closed day. A
pity, because it was perfect: cool, with just a mist in the air, and
the wind gone a little more west now. Louis could have crossed the
ridge, circled behind Stubby's campyard, and come up on the feed
lot from downwind. After the days and nights of storm, the buck
and his harem would likely be in there, and I on my rock seat.

A closed day, and long.

We rejoiced when Monday looked to be a copy. We piled into
the Buick. Our headlights bobbed with the rain gullies on the way
out. I love to be traveling before dawn. We swung around the bend
by Old Crow and jacked a doe in her tracks. I cut the lights and
leaned on the horn, then threw them on again. She was gone.

The first swatch of amber was clearing Magazine Ridge when
we reached the rock. I took down my pack and rifle, wrapped a
blanket around my legs, unscrewed my thermos. Louis took a slug
of coffee and moved away. I listened to him slosh across the beaver
dam, always in a rush. He cursed once as he stepped in over his
boot. I chuckled. After he reached the other side, I didn't hear a
sound.

I used to like these last minutes of near darkness in a duck blind;
sometimes you'd hear the *whuh whuh whuh* of invisible wings above
you. No ducks to speak of here anymore. I remembered sitting on
the edge of a slough when a flight of woodcock showed up just at
daylight, tumbling like so many dark snowflakes. Edward was
with us that time. Now, it was ravens that came pouring out of the
woods. There were hundreds, but their squawks sounded lonely,
the first noises to break the seamless calm. A snowshoe hare, his
legs gone white to the shoulder, hopped down the trail and sniffed
the ground by my feet, back-to. I touched the Remington's barrel

to his hind end. He swung his head sideways, saw me with the one eye, took a stutter step, and leapt four feet off the trail. Again I chuckled, softly.

Ka-WHOOMP!

Louis's .303, I was sure. That was quick. Upstream, I figured, less than a mile. The report echoed twice, once off Magazine, once off Slewgundy. I kept my eye out. If Louis had had a good shot, *that* deer wouldn't be down through. But I kept ready anyway. You never know.

Then I heard our signal: three shots, a minute apart. I left my pack on the rock and headed up the brook.

"He had a set of balls on him anyway, treading around here." Louis was wiping his knife blade on a trouser leg as I came up. The neat pile of entrails lay steaming, a yard downhill from the spikehorn. The ravens had already gathered in the woods nearby.

"I figured I'd do him a kindness and kill him before he met that other fella." Louis grinned. "*You* ought to shoot the big boy anyhow."

My smile was full of gratitude, and he read it: "Oh, hell, you old sap!" he growled. "I just don't want to lug him out from way back here!" He was smiling too. A pink bloodstain shone on one of his cheeks.

Even the little buck was a job to drag out. We sat panting on my rock, resting against the last leg of the carry. We'd lashed our spikehorn upside down to a weathered peavey handle Louis found in the weeds near Stubby's fallen cabin. That's how small the deer was. I was reaching over to reknot my end when I heard the noise.

"What the hell's that?" I asked.

"Beats the hell out of me," said Louis, the crow's-feet gathering at the bridge of his nose.

It came from over Finnegan Point way, angry, whining.

"Not a saw," I said.

"Wouldn't think so," Louis replied, hefting the carrying pole onto his shoulder. "But maybe. Been a while since my logging days." He grunted with the first step. "God knows what foolishness they've come up with," he added, and we grunted together the rest of the way.

The spikehorn was tiny and still loose enough to fit in my trunk. "A fella ought to be ashamed," said Louis as we closed him in.

"Poor little guy. Suitcase special." It was another of his coinings, like "sandwich size" for a trout.

"He'll eat," I said.

I LOOKED upstream just at dawn next morning. I could see clear up to the bend by the Tannery. That time of year it worked the other way: a crisp day coming meant the fog would hang on the river at daylight. Today might be a little mean.

"Maybe he's home now," Louis said, but I could hear the pain in those first words. He didn't want breakfast. He was probably already feeling the wet of the woods, like me, but I found myself a touch angry. Was he losing heart or nerving up again, just when it had begun to feel like old times, at least a little? In a way, I couldn't blame him. After our workout of the day before, today's prospects chilled: the temperature was this side of frost by a good deal, but not exactly warm. And if one of us shot that big buck, how on earth would we ever get him out of there?

Still, damn it, *I* was the duffer, and I was ready to go. "You want to stay home, Louis?" I asked.

He heard the edge in my voice. "Hell, let's get after him," he said, his tone falsely hearty.

"You want me to drive him?" I couldn't keep that edge off.

"Why, you old gimp! We'd be out there all day." He could sharpen up, too, if that's what I wanted.

God forgive me now. I walked to the cupboard and lifted down the bottle of phenobarb. Louis waved it away with a chop. "I want to be all there today, *Doc!*" Louis McLean wasn't a fool. But at least I'd gotten him up and out.

The rain came in one immense wave as we drove over the Tannery Bridge out of town. I had to stop for a few minutes. I'd have turned back then if Louis and I hadn't fallen into the I-dare-you routine. But the rain went as quickly as it had arrived, and eased almost to nothing just before true daylight. So did the tension in the car: Louis didn't shed his grim countenance, but his instincts were taking over. He was all strategy by the time we reached Old Crow Spring. "I'll drop a little farther back into the swamp this morning," he said. "Not too far, because you can't see anything back there anyhow. But I might drive him out."

"You think he'd bed in that low country?"

"Well, you wouldn't think so. But I didn't jump him on the ridge, so it's worth a try." Maybe, he went on, I ought to get up a little farther on the crest, just in case the buck had overnighted in the swamp and took a high route out. I'd still be able to look down on the stream, but I could look on the other side as well. I said it didn't seem probable the deer would go that way—not much space between the ridge and the lake, and most of it cranberry bog, pretty open.

"On the other hand," Louis reminded me, "he didn't get to *be* a big fella by acting likely, did he?"

We filled a canteen. There was a buck track at the spring's edge, not bad. We saw a line of orange spots where he'd dribbled with his rut. The stains were new since the downpour. But Louis turned to the car. "Ours is a lot better," he said, smiling for the first time that morning.

Out by Stubby's trail, the wind came from all directions, confusing, confused. It blew on me and cooled the sweat from my climb. I felt all right; I'd stuck with Louis till we hit the top. When he kept moving along the spine northward, I settled on a hemlock stub, satisfied I could cover any path the buck might take if he came my way. An hour passed. Once, I got the jolt in my ears and sinuses. First, a rustle on the stream side; then the maddening wind began again. I couldn't hear. In a luff, I heard the rustle again, but I thought there was something too random and quick about it. Sure enough, a red squirrel. I hadn't thought the woods would be that loud, soaked as they were. The squirrel lugged a pinecone up a beech trunk, scuttled into a hole to deposit it, came halfway out again to bark at me for a minute or so. Then he ducked back in, and I settled again. All for nothing, but it interested me to remember that acrid odor, thick in my nostrils when I think I hear deer.

There was an ache in the muscles around my ears, too, as if I'd actually been pricking them into the nuisance breezes. And I had a tight spot at the base of my skull. All familiar again.

Crack.

"*That* weren't no friggin' squirrel!" Some random old phrase of Louis's sprang, unsummoned, to mind.

Chuff. Brushing something.

My eyes burned to locate him, bring him out against the buff woods. I could hear a faint ringing inside as I strained to sort out the direction of the noise from the gusts in the treetops.

Then he gave a tentative snort. Behind me!

Ever so slowly, I turned my head, feeling for the push safety of the .30. A momentary panic: had I jacked a shell into the action? Yes. I remembered the green and yellow of the cartridge box against the stumpwood as I loaded.

Another small snort, more like the release of a man's held breath. There he stood, on the bog side after all, thirty yards below me, too good to be true. He was looking back over his shoulder in Louis's direction, ears cocked, the wind confusing him too.

I leveled the barrel. From his forward shoulder back, he was covered by pole-sized alders. The .30 was a heavy slug, but not enough that one of those trunks wouldn't turn it. And I hate a wounded animal. If he didn't step out soon, I'd go for a head shot, clicking my tongue just before squeezing. I waited. He began to snort again, more loudly now, waggling antlers, shuffling. But he wouldn't come out.

Click. My mouth was dry. *Click.*

His nostrils flared as he looked my way, sniffing the air, but the air was moving back and forth, one gust canceling another. I'd take him in the throat. If I shot high, the way you can do downhill, I'd either brain him or miss clean. I was still as the stump I sat on, but for my forefinger, just now feeling the trigger's resistance. Breathe out; wipe the mirror clean; wait for the lull between heartbeats.

The big buck was a portrait in my sights. He had one crippled tine, dropped over his brow like a caribou's. Nine points, asymmetric—four on the left, five on the right, including the droopy one; 220 pounds, I reckoned, dressed.

Gently, slowly, I lowered the rifle into my lap. Things came unfocused for a moment, and I squinted to clear them up. There he was again, still confused. Something was in the neighborhood, but where? Better not dash off just anyhow. He swung his head almost imperceptibly side to side, sniffing, weak eyes laboring.

Good-bye. I raised my hand. His ears shot up. I waved again, more vigorous now. "One old-timer to another," I said. "Good-bye."

He stood a moment longer. Then he made one hop in place like a barnyard goat, farting explosively, and bounded around the ridge.

AFTER twenty minutes Louis came along in the buck's tracks. I watched him drop to one knee where the buck had loitered, following his escape with his eyes. He hurried up toward me: "Well?" he gasped, breathing hard.

"Caught me napping," I lied.

"Oh—for the want—of the breath—of life!" Louis dropped seat-first on the dark earth. He fiddled for a while with the strap on his rifle, shaking his head. Then he snapped his eyes up and looked at me hard, his face in a lopsided smile. "Well," he said, "we got all the camp meat we needed. Yesterday."

I smiled back at him, blushing.

WHANG!

It sounded sharp, the dampness lifted. The sun had yellowed. The whole woods got still and silent.

WHANGWHANGWHANG!

We sat fixed on ground and stub for several minutes, not talking. We heard that weird sawlike noise, moving west to east, somewhere near the gravel pit where we'd left the Buick. Damned if we knew what it was. We rose together, without a word.

In fifteen minutes—the sound ever stronger, bursting into loud snarls—we came out. As Louis and I rounded the bend by the old canoe launch, we stopped short. A rig was parked almost against the back bumper of our car. On its driver's door panel, a large calligraphic script: BAJA BRONCO. A porky fellow, charcoal smeared on his cheekbones, sat in camouflage clothes on the hood, camera raised, a tall can of beer sweating on the sheet metal next to him. He grinned at his partner, who'd heard the shot and come to drag out the buck with his contraption. A two-stroke engine, a sound like a saw. I'd heard tell of the goddamn things. It looked like a kids' express wagon, red, with four balloon tires.

The buck's crippled horn was digging a groove in the wet dust. A chain wrapped tight around his neck, his tongue jutted from the mouth. It had blackened with grit and soil.

The driver noticed us first as we hustled toward the Buick: Dr. Prale, wearing only a scarlet union suit and knee-high rubber boots. There was a spot of shaving lather on one cheek. Over the wail of his engine, he yelled, "Beauty-full, am I right?"

Oh, to be forty and fit! I stumped up to the man with the camera. "You move this fucking thing so we can get out!" He slid down off the Bronco's hood, knocking his beer to earth, where it fizzed and dribbled.

"How 'bout one more picture? You know, bringin' him in?"

"Move it, mister!" Louis was red, almost purple, in the face. His hands were balled. I kept myself between him and the guy in camouflage. Prale had cut his motor. I stared at him, and he slumped in his round seat, plump breasts hanging forward. Silence.

Then the other fat man jumped into the car and spun gravel furiously, backing away. He crushed the tall Budweiser with a front wheel.

"You pick that goddam thing *up*!" Louis screamed. They didn't hear him over the Bronco's roar.

"Hey, you guys sore or somethin'? What the hell?" Prale looked bewildered, hurt, like a left-out schoolchild. "You wanna have a brew or somethin'?"

I showed them how to throw gravel.

23

"Sons of whores! Nosing in on our hunt!" Louis was fuming as I drove the rain-rutted road from the lake, heedless, reckless. I skidded up on a sloppy shoulder as an eighteen-wheel log hauler shot around a bend. I sat a moment, quivering: too close. When the big trucks came they gave no quarter. These were their roads. The paper companies were hauling twenty-four hours a day now; there wasn't any quiet time anymore.

"They'll have it all by and by," Louis breathed, meaning either the Prales or the companies or both. His words stood out in the silence of our near miss.

"Who in hell was the fatso in camouflage, Louis?" I asked eventually.

"Christ! I don't know *nobody* anymore!"

I hate the city-billies who buy up all the beautiful land and then post it, their signs shooing you off the ground you've hunted all those years. You could tell them things about that land, could hide from them forever in it, and sometimes you go and do what you do and you do hide. Goddamn! It's yours and the next man's. They won't find you. They're saving the wildlife they wouldn't recognize if they saw it, as they never will. They love the game, they say, but what love is that? They don't mind the ski resorts that kill more wildlife than all the hunters in five states.

But I hate even more the people who make their case for them, the Prales and others even worse. I know I should be genteel, liberal, Christian, but *hatred* is the word.

We talked about it that night, Louis McLean and I. Maybe we were more smug than two men should be, but we agreed that a person could have followed us over every mile of woods and water for the last twenty years and found precious little that was cruel or exploitative in what we did. We thought of the huge buck I'd released that day, though neither of us had yet mentioned my actual decision. We just knew. And we spoke of how the Prales of this world seemed bent on undoing what we were bound to do, on doing what we willfully refrained from doing.

We got around to one incident especially. Back in the early sixties Fish and Game had opened a bow season on black bear. The result was largely frustration for the archers: that's what most of them were, not hunters. Otherwise, it was suffering for bears that took arrows and galloped off to bleed themselves dead. There's no *impact* in an arrow, nothing to knock a deer down, let alone a bear.

"Do you mind that gang of dump hunters from downcountry in Chet's camp?"

"Sons of bitches!" I spat.

"At least," said Louis, forcing a mean laugh, "they ain't been back." He'd seen to that. In those days, when the dump was still open and you could go in any time, people would drive out at night to watch the bears scavenge. There might be as many as nine or ten animals at a time, tame and fat, pawing through the rubbish.

Old drunken Murray took to showing off in front of the spectators. He'd bring a bag of marshmallows and stagger out to the garbage piles. The bears would shy at first, and he'd simply toss the marshmallows in their direction. By and by, though, one would come up close, and Murray would hand the treat to him. By late in the summer he had a 350-pounder who'd let him scratch his ears and pat him, even kiss him on the stinking mouth.

I recall an evening when I happened on this show. I'd meant to come and go, dumping my trash and leaving. Sitting at the edge of a dump in summer and watching the best animal in the woods disgrace himself isn't my idea of pleasure. But I got caught up in Murray's performance.

There he was, wavery and thin as a reed, his vanilla bottle sticking out of a back pocket and catching the glare of headlights, his mouth stretched in a series of nonsense raves.

Murray wouldn't feed his bear unless it stood up on its hind legs.

Like the circus. He'd doled out half his marshmallows when the bear went down on all fours and poked his muzzle into the bag, deftly lifting out a single candy. I heard Murray squawk, "Come back here and take that right!" He slapped the animal on top of the head.

In the headlamps you could see each bristle stiffen on that bear's neck. But Murray had turned to mug for the audience. The bear walked up behind him with a stiff-leg, human stride, one immense arm drawn back and sideways. Like Tony Galento, he let the roundhouse fly. But it was as if he meant merely to give one warning, a good one. He broke the air about five inches above Murray's hat, which lifted and settled in the big breeze of the swing. We could hear the rush of wind from our cars.

Now it was Murray who went down and crawled, all angles and elbows, back our way. The smile was gone.

The crew that took Chet's camp that fall had come for the new archery season. It was just before Labor Day, still hot as July. I guess they'd sweated and tramped around the back orchards and seen nothing but bear shit and puke. They ended up taking stands by the dump. Not after dark; there were too many onlookers then. Probably they showed up just at daylight. No one seemed to know anything about it until they shot a second-year cub, maybe ninety pounds, one of the regulars at the evening show. She'd been a favorite with the kids, because they recognized her so easily by the strange white spot on either ear. If it hadn't been for those marks, Bill Ware, headed out for a bait run early one morning, might just have shook his head and spat in disgust. But he saw this special cub lashed to the archers' fender as they pulled into their campyard. He stopped and stared. Then he drove on to the Amazon turnoff, brought his truck around, and drove casually back to the village.

The word was out within the hour, and Louis heard it. By the time he got to Chet's camp, he was breathing fire, but the hunters had gone to Pinkham for breakfast. Louis found the cub hung up, guts and all, already bloated and fly-blown in the heat. The boys had left their gear in the locked camp—cameras and bow, quivers, clothes, liquor.

"I guess when they got back none of that stuff was any good to them," Louis had told me, laconically. He didn't smile about it. He also broke into Chet's work shed and found a full box of galvanized roofing nails, with the big heads. He made sure plenty of them stood business-end-up in the driveway.

The bear hunters had quite a job to get out of town. No one threatened them, no one said a word to them, not even Edward, who actually ripped the wires from his wall before they showed up. There wasn't another telephone in town, for all they could discover. They left the store and made the long walk to Pinkham. "When they came back they needed more than tires," Louis explained. It turned out to have been Murray, of all people, who finished the job that Louis had begun on that big Dodge, but none of us knew that until a good month after the archers left town.

The selectmen chain-linked the dump and posted hours. It was something of a nuisance, but I never heard a complaint.

THOUGH we went to bed early, we were tired next morning, Thanksgiving. It had been a broody night in both rooms. Now the fog was back, and drizzle pocked the surface of the McLean. The scene was spectral, down to the blue heron Louis was watching when I came into the kitchen. I stood wordless, watching the bird too. It hid under a hemlock at the far bank. Not fishing—enduring. Ready to go whenever the sky cleared, for, whatever the day's signs, the ice would soon be coming. It was the quietest I'd ever seen Louis in such weather conditions, and I worried, for a lot of reasons, that he'd had one of his own signs in the night.

"Something on your mind?" I asked after the quarter hour.

"Not yours?" he asked back. He had me. There wasn't any need to *hunt* for omens, was there?

I left him there by the river window and went back to my room. I was working on another letter to Fish and Game, but I felt listless and scattered at once. I threw the draft into the basket and propped a pillow against my headboard. I lay back on it and looked out the bedroom panes. I will not resign, I vowed, thinking of the letter, but I'll wait till I have a little starch back.

I knew what it was, of course. You do things that you hate to see undone. Or you undo things you should have let be. *There is no health in us,* says the line from the General Confession of my childhood. Just now my life seemed a study in that theme: I felt sick with the vision of the buck, his tongue trailing in the dark dust.

You try to save something, and it ends up more ruined than if you'd ruined it on your own.

I stared a long time through the glass. I could see my small patch of woods, where Louis's spikehorn was strung up on a two-by-four between a pair of spruces. I watched the raindrops bead on his hollow fur, parading down and dropping, at intervals, from the ebony nose. His buttons of antler saddened me; he wasn't even a spike, really. I was filled with a general pity. The brown of the eyes, even two days after he'd gone down, was vivid, troubling, deep.

I had never felt this way. I thought of my flat in the Back Bay, almost nostalgically: my cluttered study, a disgrace to the neat John Marin pen-and-ink above the desk; the clawfoot tub in the bathroom; the pocket in the ugly parlor chair I'd inherited from Father—how much I'd read in that chair, the grate beside me glowing with cannel coal; how often I had dozed there, the words of some poet merging with the ensuing dream. It wouldn't ever do to stay too long in that flat. I knew that. Still, the *idea.*

Or maybe a snug apartment, nothing grand, in some European city, where this notion of wildness was no longer even a vague motif in daily life. Some place, I thought, where all was now Civilization. The esplanade from the Arc down to the Carousel, for instance, seemed immutable, enviable. You choose the country—God's country—because you want to live with the permanent forms, but maybe you ought to seek them in town, at least in the old towns. Half conscious of this vision's inaccuracy, still in that moment I felt the urbanite's longing: some kind of order, imposed by crafty hands. Not this.

That spikehorn deer, that button buck: he should be on a canvas somewhere. I wanted to will him back, maybe to the eighteenth century, quickly, finally, forever. In a strange way he seemed unfit for this territory, hanging as he was from rough lumber in a dreary north woods, a little green privy leaning toward him. He needed another focus, not my window's. He deserved someone who might precisely render the maroon shade of the slit from breastbone to vent, the mercury globes of water that trekked down his pelt, the dark chestnut eye.

"That is no country for old men," I quoted, inwardly. Was that the mark of memory bearing down, that revulsion from the welter of life, that yearning for the wrought? Was that what had impelled Bill Ware, the bait man dead in the past winter, to behave as he had in the final months? He gave away his scores of knickknacks— clumps of bird's-eye maple; eight-foot snowshoes for powder snow, each with its yards of gut webbing in a boggling grid; the cedar root that lapped back and forth through itself like a maze in a child's book. What moved him to surrender these treasures, to grow taciturn, and not only with the tumors in his throat? Why did he sit home buffing an egg-shaped stone to smoothness? They said the cancer had reached his brain by then.

In the kitchen, Louis whittled at a piece of fir. With that patience he brought to such carving alone, he peeled away the slivers. I stood and turned my back to the swinging spikehorn outside, watching my friend from the doorway, unnoticed till he clasped the knife, brushed shavings from table and lap, and lay the stick on the chair beside him. Dive of a bird, arc of a salmon.

His face was stolid, melancholic. More than ever he seemed a man who had seen a lot, forever struggling with the pull of resignation and an opposite will—to go on, to prevail. It is no wonder, I mused, that the great performers are sad. And the clowns. Once in my life I'd seen my friend's truest tragic nerve unveiled. Not, after all, when he lived back the loss of Velma. Not the death of Mary, nor even of Charles. Not indeed in the wake of any disaster, but at the edge of a cheerful bonfire.

Louis and I had come in late from a trip up McLean Lake on the paddle for brook trout; that's how long ago it was. A circle of guides had gathered on the beach by the landing. We joined them, I the outsider. Bill Ware produced a gallon of wine from his locker. Walter and Lem were idly picking tunes from guitar and banjo, but their hearts weren't in it. They were too busy chattering with the other men. The conversation was of nothing, but we wanted to talk; there was that spirit in the air. Nobody could have planned it.

At last, when the talk dwindled, we called on Louis to entertain us. It was expected. Suddenly Lem began to pick a quick-tempo passage on his banjo, fretting far down the neck. He could play in those days! The men started to tap palms on thighs, Bill to clink his wedding ring against the jug, everyone turning to Louis, who grinned a mild protest. But he hit his entry right on beat, and we all cheered and laughed. In the intervals after the refrain, Lem would throw his head back, eyes clamped, spectacles flashing, to play a dizzying riff till we whistled and stomped in the sand. I can bring the hair up on my neck to think about it. Walter clogged on the beach.

It was one of Louis's trademarks, this fixed-form, lightning ballad, each stanza filled with some bit of satire directed at the company of the moment. Pure improvisation. That night he went on for minutes on end, since there were eleven of us at the party. I came in for a teasing about the time I spent tying flies as opposed to actually using the damned things. And the rest of the windburned men were types, in the song, of the inept and fraudulent and profiteering guide. Huck Barry, whose family had moved to McLean when Huck was three years old, was cited for a foreigner:

> *Don't hook a fish with Huck, my friend,*
> *Or you'll be bound to lose it.*
> *He ain't a hometown guide at all,*
> *But one from Massachusetts.*

Yet Louis's last quatrain made genial qualification:

> *Now please don't feel offended, gang;*
> *You're okay, every one.*
> *This little spiel I gave to you*
> *Was all made up in fun.*

Fun: in which the human spirit shows itself, makes us feel, for all the foibles and failings we embody, that life will go on forever with no harm.

I had sat across from Louis, and had risen to pee after his performance. I stepped behind the row of guides' lockers. As I returned Louis was coming away from the fire, perhaps for the same purpose. I stopped in the dark and watched him head my way. Though the coals were at his back and the moon young, I saw his face before he entered the darkness, his features relaxed into sadness so deep it seemed infinite. I witnessed then how out of that well of longing, disillusionment, and mystification had struggled the very fun which held his listeners together on that strip of sand

and rock. His summons of it was a gratifying but agonizing labor, his genius that it danced in our vision flapdoodle, as if its other, truer name were freedom.

By evening the camp felt commodious, for all the blackness of our moods in the forenoon. The daddy longlegs, genies of autumn, had come in with the woodpile and hunched in the kitchen corners; crickets darted from under the baseboards. The wood stove shimmered.

I'd dressed the turkey with minced liver and heart from Louis's deer. I'd thrown away caution and laced the stuffing with garlic, sage, cayenne. Though we scarcely made a dent in the bird, huge enough to have fed a family, we ate with zest, after a couple of bourbons.

We had pie for dessert. Then I broke out a bottle of champagne I'd brought up from the city. Louis cut his with orange juice. In high spirits, we drank combative toasts to the enemy: Prale, the Fish and Game Department, the paper companies, the Tradin' Post. Cruel and crude: scatological stuff, grammar school insults, which we followed with aggressive, loud laughter.

Then, abruptly, Louis went sentimental. "We're old men now, Brant. So let's raise the jug. To old friends, *old* times." It sounds mawkish here. It wasn't.

I drank, but—solemnity turned to silence—I thought it wrong to call them old, those unspecified shards of memory: people and dogs; rods and boots and reels; hours and guns. Even clothes, I thought, fingering the threads of my tweed jacket, so worn now as almost to have become a mere idea. Time doesn't distance them from us; it locks them in, till they become us, till they underlie what we call Now.

We sat talking around this theme without ever naming it, long enough again to see the mist that draped the McLean, to drink our way past the combativeness and Louis's sentimental interlude, to feel that delusive clearheadedness you can believe in, drunk and tired. Things were all right.

"I feel so *lucid*," I said, amazed at dawn. The last leaves floated the river as it took its easterly glow—little sailboats, so delicate.

"You feel how's-that-again?"

"So full of light," I breathed. But then we slept that light away, or most of it.

IT was getting on to evening, that next day in the dark phase of the year, when at last we rallied ourselves from bed again. Supper Friday, a bland turkey soup. I left half of mine in the bowl, and Louis, sweating, pushed his chair back after a single sip.

"A little hair of the dog?" I ventured.

He looked ready to weep. "That's no kind of medicine," he said.

"You're a good old boy, Louis." I meant it, and I meant to buck him up if I could—that ancient mission. "A good friend. *The* good friend."

"Wish I was up to it."

"Wish you knew you were."

"Damned if I feel that way," he muttered, and went right back to bed, where he stayed for the better part of Saturday too.

I was due to leave town the next day, and Louis was denned up like a January bear. I checked on him now and then, finding him more often than not asleep, though it seemed a sleep like torture: he lay all but naked on his bunk, his hands fisted and thrust between his knees, his face a map of taut wrinkle and vein, as if he were straining to lift a great weight. He had shut the door to the kitchen, where the fire burned in the Atlantic, and his room was cold. At one point I spread a blanket over his body. Without leaving his sleep, he flung it off. I left the door open so the stove's heat would enter, but a few moments later Louis came out and stared blankly at me, as if I were a stick of furniture. Then he pulled the door to behind him.

I was both worried and miffed at what he was doing, or not doing: a state of mind that had characterized a lot of my relation to him. Just like a family tie, I guessed.

I did not see him again till morning.

"You'd better give me your word," I warned. "Your word on the Bible, you'll go."

"Sworn."

"I mean it, Louis!" I snapped. I was packed for Boston, and

desperate. The phenobarb that he washed down at dawn had calmed his nerves about the pain, but it hadn't done much for the pain itself.

"That dressing was rich, that's all," he said. "And I got no business, old hick like me, drinking that goddamn sparkly wine." His evasions had never been more transparent.

"I can run you right down to the clinic now."

"To hell with that place," he answered.

"Well, over to Swett's."

"Let old Satan have a holiday in peace!" Louis forced a boyish giggle. I was afraid that once I left town, he'd go back to his own doctoring: mustard poultice, hot peppermint, egg white—folk remedies for what he called arthur-itis, but what I was beginning to feel was an ulcer at least.

"You don't get arthritis in your gut, Louis."

"Pulled something."

"Well, why doesn't it hurt all the time, then?" He didn't answer; rather, he straightened himself in his chair as if to suggest that the crisis was past. But he hunched forward again. "I've got half a mind to stay over a couple more days just to see that you *do* go," I said. I'd picked this Sunday out of a hat, the end of a deer season. I had nothing special to get back to.

"No," he said. "You go along. I'll find a ride over to see the old fella. Must be somebody left in town to do me a favor."

24

I FUSSED around the Back Bay apartment for a week. My armchair was even uglier than I'd remembered, the Marin seemed nothing extraordinary in my study, whose mess was not homey but oppressive. Sourly, I recalled the vision of urbane pleasure in camp that rainy day before I left. Why in hell hadn't I stayed up there? The winter would be long and the cabin confining, but a Boston winter was the worst of both worlds: cold blowing through you if you went out, and you felt as much penned, inside, as if you lived in a kennel.

The slush had already started along the Massachusetts coast. It would be snow up north. I could be sitting by the river window, toddy in hand, a book on my lap, the Atlantic humming, the drifts climbing my half-timbers, the yard clean and trackless. Flakes would be falling through my oak, past my ledge and into the water, its voice muted by ice on the margins, then all but silent as even the rapids froze. But an undersong always.

Here, beleaguered pedestrians hugging grimy walls to escape the grimy spray of buses shooting through grimy puddles in grimy gutters. The insane highways and avenues that followed seventeenth-century cow paths—everything askew, nothing coming full circle except the color, or lack of it: gray pigeons gargled all day on the sill outside, their feathers the livid shade of stone, roof, streets, sky.

* * *

A PLACE IN MIND

A LETTER.

It was my second Monday in the Back Bay, and the clouds had lifted, the sun full through. Wind herded whitecaps in the harbor. I could imagine them. The carrion gulls, from my distance, were graceful, fighting the air, dipping and kiting. Even in Boston, I saw, weather could speak to a mood, could speak a mood, not inevitably grim. I was a little perked up, and here, as if to signal why, a letter from Louis. An actual letter! The first in my life.

I carried it upstairs, laid it on the desk, and set about making a good cup of coffee. In a place of few pleasures, I was prolonging the anticipation. The dog-eared envelope positively glowed in my study: I kept stepping out of the pantry just to behold it on the blotter. My flat had a new resonance.

I sat at my desk, blowing on the cup. I would not scald myself, I would have it right. I would savor the letter's minimal, crucial contents, whatever they were.

Dear Brant

Swet says I have a little hart trouble but says not serious. Take it easy he says ha ha. Camp looks very good. Wether very windy, and snow. I was over to Edwards. He says hello doc, he is always the same, miserble ha ha.

Now be here in spring, this is my orders! Do not disobey these orders. Dont wory about me I am a rugged old bird. Take it easy yourself with the wommen most of all. You are a hell of a lot older than your,

friend,

Louis McLean

The note still in hand, I reached for the phone. Angry, worried again: all at once. I told Edward to get Louis in touch with me if he had to drag him to the store. Edward gave me his word. No, he hadn't heard a thing about Louis being poorly.

Months seemed to yawn before me as I waited, and behind me too: seasons, years. No shape either way.

I remembered Charles saying that he wanted to keep a lookout to the future. That shining, ordered place, which had, after all, been empty. At least, in his moment of devastation, it must still have seemed to him a chartable ground. I imagined him lying in his barracks or in the ship's berth, mentally walking that territory. This was where he'd do one month—Baltimore Harbor. And this was where he'd do the next: McLean Lake. On the near side of the property, he'd put up a small bungalow, half-timbered cedar and shingle. One day he'd knock on the walls—solid. Inspect the sills—plumb, steady. The subtle wheeze of a block chimney, drawing the way it should, for he'd build it high. There would be his wife, shy, but bright and lively. Like no one before, she'd understand him. Him: Charles McLean, former cadet at the Maritime Academy, standing fourth in his class. Coming out of the shack over there, his father—proud, difficult, a professional guide for forty years. Charles would take care of him, ease him into an older age, and an older one still. A Ripe Old Age.

I PICKED up on the first ring. "I want an answer, no shilly-shallying."

"It's a valve, I guess, some damn thing—"

"Yes," I said, "but what's the prog—what about the future?"

"He says be a little careful. And take these horse pills here."

"What kind of pills?"

"I couldn't read it if you made me."

"Well, what are they supposed to do?"

"One batch for the pressure, one for nerves."

"So you're taking two different sets?"

"Well . . . yes."

"And you know which is which?"

"Sure."

"You're sure you know how many to take, and when?" I sounded like Dr. Swett himself.

"Oh, sure."

"Louis."

"Yes, I do know all that."

"What else?"

"No real hard work for a spell, and no salt."

"All right, Louis. My order is no work on the camp. Is that clear?"

"Nothing at all."

"Nothing at all. You're on vacation, do you understand? If you see something needs doing, you hire someone to do it and send me a bill. Not you."

"I can't think of anything it would be."

"Never mind. Those are the orders. I'm the boss, right?"

"Well, yessir, boss!"

"Louis. I mean it."

"It's whatever you say."

"Good. Would you feel better to come down here? There's all kinds of room."

"Great Jesus! Now that *would* kill me!"

Off and on through the afternoon, I considered going back up. I didn't trust him a minute, the little bastard. And what on earth was I doing here anyway? I stood for long blank moments at the window. Despite the clarity and briskness of a day that had broken so auspiciously, I now couldn't imagine how to pass the winter. On the sidewalk below, angry little twisters rushed along the curbs, bearing their cinders, old ticket stubs, plastic detritus. I'd have to go somewhere, but where?

Yes.

No.

The stovewood had been almost used up when I left, and I couldn't ask Louis to get more. Not now. Maybe Edward could buy a load from one of the local chainsaw jockeys. But no: the lean-to woodshed out back had finally collapsed that past fall, and we hadn't bothered to rebuild it. So I pictured myself heaving out of bed in the middle of a sub-zero night, struggling to the rimed log pile, up to my stiff knees in snow, a rude crust cutting the blue shins to shreds. I could almost feel a blunt downriver wind, and I shuddered; it would rattle the panes in the kitchen window, and the stove would backfire. Then I cursed to consider fighting with the cold Atlantic, out of precious kindling, the embers near dead and the cabin frigid. There would go one of Louis's battered wooden chairs; I'd smash it to pieces on the floor, then choke in the downdraft as I tried to rally the coals under a log, too green, too wet, too big. And I thought of breaking through the river ice to haul water for cooking, of sitting on the frozen privy seat. I just couldn't do it.

I knew what was real up there. Or was it superstition? I wanted so to save Louis, but how often in the past that impulse had betrayed us. And in the best of circumstances, we'd drive each other crazy. I could hear the drum of fingers, the whistle, the monologue on second sight, and grew flushed. I couldn't bear the tedium. Or was it panic at that very second sight? What if he said, "I had it this morning"? I was afraid I'd freeze, as if the fire had quit. I didn't want to know any more. I was ignorant, wanted to be. But I wanted to save him. To save my poor old self.

25

I say to myself, You have put it together exactly. For once. At last.

I say that Anna collapsed on me long ago, and in that failure I thought I saw the very failure of intellect to achieve shapeliness. She once told me, with the usual terseness about her personal life, that her parents had traveled with a theater. She grew up neither here nor there nor anywhere, and had no place, and never had a place. She was a splendor of imitation, and I loved her for that, believed her enviable—so I say to myself, and say that I understand the failure, now that I have a place at long last, though do I?

Louis.

He was cheerful all winter whenever I spoke to him on Edward's phone. After the rage, the punishment, of a record December, the young year's months turned almost mild. So sudden. It stayed that way. Very little snow, said Edward. The river broke up in the January thaw, said Louis. It did not seal again, they said, even in its laziest stretches. It must have been beautiful, perfect: the glittering ice dams on shore, the rocks above the riff flashing back every sally of sun at daylight, and the surge of the coal-black water midstream. I could have stayed in camp after all, snowshoeing down from the landing road with a bag of groceries at evening. I'd have stepped out after dark to see the stars at their most chiseled, exquisite. Not much walking: small crunch of the webbing, squeaks and rattles of the corn snow. Not like the long hikes once, our beards icicles, when the big moon came and we went. Just to be out, to bivouac in a winter tent. The huge fires we would make together, no fear of the whitened brush catching, big as you liked. Once, to have kindled a blaze in the base of a giant and hollow rock maple! The core of the tree from base to crown was a flue, and the draft immense, and the very flames were at last visible out the top of the trunk, and the breath on our whiskers had frozen, so that as we looked up at that magical roaring, the firelight glittered off our faces, and perhaps a star or two, and the moon. Not that: but we would have been out in any case. I would have been there.

How much more uncomfortable could it have been than a Boston winter, which, though mild, was was so gray it seemed a state of mind? Life, I told myself daily, must come to more than the putting in of time. For more life itself.

But I'd become inured to my own torpor. It took something for me to know that, but so it had been. Even after my weekly talks with Louis, those longed-for bright spots, I dismissed the idea of simply getting into the Buick and heading up. And I could have done so. That's what I am saying. But Louis was cheerful. I'm not deluded, I think.

How does the spirit change, how cure itself? I don't know. But on the first fine day in April, I was determined to rally. It was that or turn to tallow there in my armchair. Not that I knew *what* to do, yet I had to do something, and quickly, or soon I wouldn't even perceive how I was killing myself. I was still this side of simply letting it happen, but I shudder to think by how little.

I taxied to the Gardner Museum, just to eat lunch in the cafeteria. I had no appetite, but I've always liked that spot. The place was quiet. A smart-looking young couple and I were the only patrons; it was early, barely noon. The woman was tall and dark. She wore a heavy tweed skirt, a blazer so deeply blue it was nearly black, one cornflower in the lapel. Nordic-looking, for all her dark coloring, yet she had Italianate manners—active hands and eyebrows, great leaps and falls in her diction. He was unobtrusive and mild, a fair-haired boy, a whisperer, but his fingers were square and strong, his light complexion touched, along the flat cheekbones, with winds. Or so at least I wanted to think.

We fell into conversation, idle: the weather, the food, the museum. At length she pulled out a chair from their table. "Why talk at such long distance?" she asked. I hesitated, seeking a sign from her companion. He smiled almost imperceptibly, but his face was open and guileless.

"Why indeed?" I answered, carrying my plate over.

She was a lawyer, he a curator in the Oriental Department of the Fine Arts Museum, and they were meeting for their lunch break. The world was all before them, there was no one like them, they were themselves. And I loved them there in an odd and disembodied way that takes precedence in memory over whatever we talked about. I offered to pay their check, they refused, and left.

If I could sing, I would sing my tribute, back over time, to those friends who picked me up, sent me smiling to the large central room of the Gardner with its soft Latin hues and smells, who sent me at last outside. More colors, more odors: not mine, exactly, but the sights and smells of life, of earth. I'd walk home, creaking.

The air was mild and sweet with the past evening's rain. Robins bounded in new plots of green along Huntington. Pigeons came winging, transformed from the scruffy hangers-on at my window ledges into things swift and clean.

All over America students had begun to grow restive and political in the European style, but just now they lolled, delicious, erotic, and innocent, before the sun-drenched buildings of Northeastern University across the street. I heard the clamor of the ballpark crowd at Fenway, at this distance a dreamy hum. Even the long-disappointed Red Sox fans must be hopeful with spring. Maybe I'd take in a game.

Maybe I'd get my ancient carcass and soul up north where they belonged. Why talk at such long distance?

IT hadn't seemed to me, just six months before, that my cabin floors needed work. Louis was having them refinished nonetheless. He hadn't asked my permission, and I was angry. At least, he pledged, he was doing only the painting, not the sanding—he'd hired that out. But the job was going slowly, because the damned rain wouldn't let up, and he couldn't get the paint to dry.

"Why don't you fire up the wood stove?" I asked. He mumbled something back, I don't know what. The connection was bad.

Maybe he didn't want to see me, blathering on as he did about the dreadful weather, discouraging my proposal to stay at Wesley's till the floors were done.

"Just a few more days, Brant," he insisted, "and I'll have it right for you. You don't want to stay someplace else when you can stay in your own place, do you?"

"Well, we'd get a chance to talk anyway."

"Then I'd *never* get that paint down!"

"I could help."

"Why don't you wait a couple of days?"

In an instant of clarity, I gave him his due. What if he had wanted to visit *me* as recently as the evening past? Maybe he was going through a little spell. "How are your spirits, Louis?" I asked the question with apprehension now, not anger.

"Finest kind, finest kind!" he blurted.

"You've been seeing Dr. Swett?"

"Regular member of old Satan's club." There was something fishy in the bluff humor.

"And he's been checking you out—"

"Bled me, peed me, poked and pummeled me half to death."

"And—"

"And he's tickled pink." Something nervous in his talk. Not high spirits. Something else. I was sure.

"Listen, Louis. If there's anything wrong, I want to know."

"Come on in a couple of days, Brant."

I HAVE put it together exactly. His stubbornness about the weather, his agitation. Something to keep from me, something to do. My friend. Could he not show me his character? But that's what he was doing, waiting for the blasted weather to give him a show. It was a reflection on Charles among other things, that dripping through the roof. By tidying things up, maybe Louis thought he could arrange matters so that my memory of the boy would go on, as he also thought, untarnished and flawless. And so somehow would his own.

I've put it together, all right. The rain at last relents. I can see
the final wispy cloud blow southward over the Big Eddy, seaward,
down to the salt, falling. How quickly the wind will reverse everything: the hour, just now wet and lowery, is dry and clear in that
blue of late winter and early spring, almost purple; the buds come
back to the ridges and along the McLean and in the back burns
where the hen grouse watches the silly postures of the fantailed
cock. Now, he thinks. Now, thinks Louis, or never. If he can get
the shingles done, he can see to the water stains inside, anytime.
He will blame them on something else, who knows what? So long
as no leak may be seen . . . Fool, impatient, desperate.

He goes up the ladder, two things in mind: I will mend the roof
that Charles was too hurried to make right, so beautiful was his
woman; and I will mount this ladder to show myself that a man's
still a man, mount it—mount it!—with my heart beating like a
partridge in a box, with that gassy feeling in my stomach, with the
sweat, with the small pill that nobody knows about exploding on
my tongue. I'll get up that ladder if it's the last earthly thing I do,
and I don't care what I had this morning. A hammer, maybe, and
maybe a heart. A hammering heart.

Oh Jesus, Louis.

So I have put it together. All I can.

I STOPPED first at Edward's.

"A sad day, Brant."

I saw him in his store among the handmade flies, the green
mackinaws and wool pants and the rubber pac boots with their
yellow laces; I looked up through the cold earth and saw him
lean against the antique soft-drink cooler or the candy case with
its rosettes of oak. Would he never change, never die himself, no
matter the conspiratorial evil or natural consequences gathered
to use him up? I stared from the grave. He reached into the same
woodbox for the same rock-maple split. He opened the stove's
door just so, threw in the log just so. But there was no welcome
home.

"A sad day, Edward."

"Yes." But his expression was his expression, his voice his voice.
"You made a lot of tracks together, you and Louis."

"Maybe the saddest."

"I know what you mean."

I asked it. "Do you, Edward?"

"Something like it," he said, looking down to the river.

What did Louis say, what did he do, Edward? What was there to learn, Edward? What can you tell me, Edward? Tell me *something*, Edward! Tell me, you who have been here longer than God.

"Not much to say, Brant. He was in and out of here on the clean jump."

A small wiry man, bounding. Over the threshold and up to the counter, prancing like an animal as Edward strides with his maddening deliberation to the storeroom downcellar and returns with the roofing nails, the sheaf of shingles. Then the little man bounds out the door again, a breeze shivering the sales slips on their prong. Edward walks over and pulls the door to, Louis already out of sight down the road to Brant's camp. Up and over the gentle knoll by Bill Ware's old place. (Who lives there now?) No details available: just this blur, this small man bounding, who would fly if he could—and can he? Fly over the heavy maples, standing by the ball field, still quilled with the past season's sugar taps; over the Tannery chimney, losing a level of bricks each winter, dwarf of what it was years back; over the broken mud of the Tradin' Post, where the snowmobiles leak their oil on the last patches of white; over the spated rapids in the tail of the Black Pool; over the ruins of the guides' locker row, hauled away to molder in the Forbusher Pit. From his height he can see as far as Middle Lake and farther, can see an eagle's nest on the one pine on the lake's north end where the buck rubs his forehead, catlike, with a leg, the horns just making their first progress through. He is so high now that he can look the other way, too, over past Wildcat Willie's bus with the new bluetick pup tethered to its rust-pocked bumper; over to the sidehill where the mother grouse comes, clouds having parted, to scout for forage —in a month she will draw her chicks behind her like a serpentine tail.

He has bounded like a driven little man. Higher. Longer. He is a deer! And then he spirals up like a courting woodcock, courses like a fish hawk, coasts like that eagle high over her nest, higher and higher into more and more precious air. High, like smoke.

Bright, like silvery salmon. But he is not like anyone else, anything else.

"Last thing I heard him say, Doc—'A bad day. A bad day.' Said he had it that morning. You know how he is."

"How he was, Edward."

"Whatever you like."

26

You damnable bastard!

I sat paralyzed in the car seat down in my campyard. You could not have kept me away forever. Didn't you know me? Wasn't I what I was? Was I a fool? Did you think I wouldn't see, unpacking my two duffels and my fly rod, my jug and my tying materials, my waders, wool shirts and socks, my little volumes of poetry, my net, vest, reels, and brittle old bones? Didn't you believe I'd notice the patch, like a green scar, on the roof, the patch, skewed and awkward, the patch that leaks? The stains like blood on the wall of the room where you lay, in the good times, in the bad times when you clenched your teeth and your fists and you would not wake? Would you not wake? Did you think I wouldn't wake?

Or, like the many scars, would you hope you might leave it alone, might not talk about it? Did you and I not long since get by that? Were they not common property, our selves? Damnable, lovable, taciturn, voluble Louis. If there were a poet in me, Louis, I would make a whole of you. If there were really a you in me, Louis, as I so long believed, as I must believe, there was and is and will be, I would dive into this long tunnel of grief. I'd go in the dark, I'd find the chamber where the fun lies hiding, I'd drag it up as you did. I'd let it flap and jig in the good air by the musical waters of McLean, even if I lay then panting like the beached old fish I am, expiring perhaps with the strain

of a noble effort. Or a vain and foolish one, whatever. If I were
you.

THE note lay on the kitchen table, where the roof didn't leak,
where we'd toasted old friends and memories that past autumn.
Louis had weighted the paper with my ax. The one with my sweat
in its handle, and his. I held it for a moment. Then I read the
scrawl:

Camp looks good, good place to breed a woman.

"None I'd recommend," I said aloud, smiling through it.

EDWARD and I were pallbearers, though we lifted nothing. We
marched, the casket borne between us on the shoulders of young
men enlisted by the funeral director—I ahead, Edward behind, a
big boy on the left and two smaller on the right. That's all. The
coffin was light.

He'd have preferred to be cremated, I knew. Of course he'd left
no written will, and of course he'd left not a cent. Perhaps we
should have burned him.

"But if I think of Louis, I think of the ground," said Edward.

"Me, too," I agreed. And wasn't the ritual for us?

I would not limp. I would make the rite a thing of dignity for
my part, however few there were to see: a scattering of poor old
widows, clumped together in the eastern pews of the ugly, drafty
church—gossips, rumormongers, tattlers. Bev was there, and suddenly my heart went out to her and to her entourage, their prospects so dim. I felt a surge of sympathy, too, for the furtive funeral
director, so determinedly and awkwardly professional, making
quick half-hidden signals to the burly boys bearing you toward the
altar. You. Louis. The strong lads who will take up their own
fragile lives in chain saw–wielding hands. In roundhouse fists as
the dance winds down. Their young energy churns on even now:
two in the morning, three hours till work, yet that passion will find
a way out. How formal, even delicate, they are with you, stranger,

and with these relics at front and rear of this tiny, unnoticed procession. In the middle of these black woods.

EDWARD rode with me, ramrod-straight. It wasn't far, but except for the hired helpers, the minister down from the reservation, his Indian assistants and altar boys, we were alone with the hole and the pine box when we got there. I can't say who had dug the trench. It was over quickly.

We left him there, in the plot with his parents, whom I'd never really known; with Charles, whom I'd known, if at all, in some other incarnation. There wasn't yet a stone for him. I must see to that, I thought, and to the other.

The morning had broken gray and drizzly, but the shafts of light pierced the cover, and the shabby marble orchard looked as good as ever it would. I smiled: its ghost had no more races to run. The dark leaning monuments took on a shine, and insects, suddenly hatched in the new warmth, floated in throngs over the unkempt turf, the light suffusing their wings. A Canada jay, late to head north, perched squawking on the remaining arm of a rough cedar cross.

"I will lift my eyes to the hills," the preacher began. I winked at Edward.

"To the hills," the storekeeper whispered, as if in a toast. And then: "You could run a good hound to death in this country before you found a hill." I smiled again. But there were the drumlins and ridges out by Willie's. I felt light, the way you feel after long weeping or the lifting of fever.

"Nice day for it, anyway," Edward went on. "That's *some* luck. And we put him in his home ground too."

The lightness in body and mind lingered on. I gave the old storekeeper a look.

"I could sell it for you, Brant," he said.

You cagey old bastard, I thought.

"Done," I answered.

27

I STOOD on the ledge, the eight-foot rod in hand. The water was still high, and I'd have to reach. My tippet was frail, 6x, because, despite the full flow, the pool above camp was a mirror. Each cloud in the river exactly replicated the drifting one above. The Red Quills were just starting, and the sandwich-size browns were flipping at the foot of the slick. I looked across the stream to where, so many years ago now, after the fight with Louis, after my anger had kindled at his keeping the Velma Morse affair from me, after that battle had served its function—I looked across to where a big brown had sucked in my Pheasant Tail and, after a battle also intense, had rushed free. He lived there still in memory, and I watched the spot; in many ways it was a memory of something never to be caught and held and known. The white marker stone I'd used that evening as I made ready to cast into the gathering dark: long washed away. The whip of alder that had leaned over the current above his lie: long since broken off and tumbled through the rapids oceanward. And yet there they were, those land- and river-marks. I had in fact to blink them away, so strong it is, that thing called the mind's eye. I was gratified rather than surprised, when I turned upriver, to see a large beaver towing a piece of skinned popple west to east cross-current, losing a little latitude as he swam toward the feeder brook. Full circle. He might have been, and somehow was, the same one who had performed that ritual those years ago. Each detail so sharp. But is not ritual more than detail? Perhaps, I was thinking, after all not.

Whoomp.

I felt along the streambed to get into position. He came again, in the spot. Suddenly the air was full of towering mayflies. Song-birds scampered up and down the banks, gorging, delighted. A dragonfly coursed the river in strange mechanical darts: right; left; back; hold. Hold.

Whoomp.

I made a short cast to test the drift. I was an expert fisherman; that much I could say. I drew off four loops from the reel and let them go, one by one, casting the old-fashioned silk out, drawing it back. Out and back; out and back; out and back; out—then I checked the line smartly, but not so smartly as to break the cobweb of finest leader. There.

It was the same fish. No, bigger, that other one, that one in the mind's eye. But things don't grow backward, do they? If a man reaches his fullest size and then starts to slide down the other side—but no. Water goes one way. A fish goes one way only, grows. Nothing can contain that imperial will to enlarge his domain, his presence within it. Though it be but a pocket of water, it will become his, he will enlarge it, because he will enlarge himself. Unless he loses his sustenance.

Never mind, I thought, holding the big trout upright under the surface after I'd unhooked him, allowing the quick water of the riff to run through his gills. He must be the same fish. The same spot. The same fly and rod. Maybe he has been here for the almost fifty years that I've been here. May he stay for fifty more, here, in the camp pool, above the salt, below the murderous bait crankers. There was a way to assure that he would, and I was making ready to implement it. Look homeward, angel, I thought, God help me. Look homeward.

I stared down at my feet in their awkward waders. Funny, I thought, as so often before, that a man may come to love his boots, to love things, the things in people, the things about friends. It was likely that in all these seasons the feet in these boots had stood in these same invisible tracks on stone, and so had one other man's. Exactly in these places on the ledge I had always called my ledge. Now I looked out again: upstream, toward the Black Pool where the salmon used to roll—just now one rushed over the shoal at its head, making that miraculous leap on its way to the lake. Then downstream, toward the chop above Big Falls where Great-uncle Charles tipped his hat, drunkenly, standing in the wispy canoe as the stolid citizens on shore lifted their heads from Independence Day picnics and shook them, slow and knowing, before Charles vanished seaward, the shards of his boat a bright scatter in the foam.

Before Louis was born, before fire took the Tannery.

I had had it backwards. I had wanted to be an extraordinary man in an ordinary world.

I packed with a special care, padlocked the door, then unlocked it again. I drove straight to the store without looking back. I could look back anytime, now. There was the whole of a certain story, come round, to refer to, and I could have it wherever I might live out my days. And, for that, the days seemed each an oddly wonderful prospect.